Praise for *Lord Jim at Home*

"[A] brilliant forgotten novelist . . . [a] superb book . . . a ferocious comedy of middle-class dysfunction, [it] was published to controversy in 1973 . . . Rich in grotesquerie, including several comically repulsive sex scenes, it has the unhinged realism of a fairground mirror . . . *Lord Jim at Home* is a masterpiece."

—Claire Allfree, *The Telegraph*, Best Fiction of 2023

"There is a lot of pain in *Lord Jim at Home*. And a lot of humor . . . If it weren't such a pleasure to read, I'd say that *Lord Jim at Home*—read by a novelist, like me—was an instrument of torture. It's that good . . . It is an accurate portrayal of how fucked-up people behave, artfully conveyed in a way that nice people are too polite to admit they understand. I'm grateful it's back in print."

—Ottessa Moshfegh, from the Foreword

"Startling . . . [A] classic that has lain dormant for fifty years. Ahead of its time, and now looking timeless, it has resurfaced with éclat. It is short and shocking . . . [An] alarming, accomplished tale . . . This tragic story may not arouse much pity, but it certainly knows how to arouse fear."

—Margaret Drabble, *Times Literary Supplement*

"This gripping tale of power, cruelty and all the consequences—the title's reference to Joseph Conrad's novel hints at the themes—was first published in 1973, and it seems extraordinary that it has been largely forgotten until now . . . This novel [is] full of horrors but energetic, funny and tense as a spring . . . *Lord Jim at Home*, inspired by a real story but full of the kind of truth only fiction can deliver, plants its devilish brilliance deep in the reader and won't let go."

—John Self, *The Guardian*

"Dinah Brooke's *Lord Jim at Home* . . . dwells unflinchingly, sometimes gleefully, on the way that scandal washes over a community, and the sorrow and schadenfreude that follow in its wake . . . We're in the vicinity of Philip Larkin and Pink Floyd—how can you have any pudding, etc.—and Brooke has as cool a hand as the former . . . Brooke has a limpid, assured style: cruel, yes, but not detached or apathetic . . . It's frigid fun."

—Dan Piepenbring, *Harper's Magazine*

"How bracing to read something as odd, nasty, unpredictable, funny and just downright different as *Lord Jim at Home* . . . The prose is cut glass, icily distancing us from Giles and everyone he meets until, gradually, it becomes clear that the novel is in fact a horror story of Patrick Melrose proportions . . . Finding out that the glittering sentences are all based on a true story makes it simultaneously better and worse. This book is a perfect martini with a razor blade at the bottom of the glass."

—Jayne Taylor, *The Times*

LOVE LIFE OF A CHELTENHAM LADY

LOVE LIFE OF A CHELTENHAM LADY

DINAH BROOKE

WITH A FOREWORD BY EMMA CLINE

McNally Editions
New York

McNally Editions
134 Prince St.
New York, NY 10012

Copyright © 1971 by Dinah Brooke
Foreword © 2025 by Emma Cline

All rights reserved
Printed in the United States of America

Originally published in 1971
by Barrie & Jenkins LTD, London
First McNally Editions paperback, 2025

ISBN: 978-1-961341-64-7
E-book: 978-1-961341-65-4

Design by Jonathan Lippincott

FOREWORD

Italy is not always the salvation of English-speaking people—but it does often seem that way. In film, in literature, in food, it's the place where you go to find yourself. The *real* you, the one whose blazing depths have been obscured by the cold crust of convention. In *The Enchanted April*—the 1922 bestseller that turned Positano into a tourist destination—Elizabeth von Arnim suggested that the Mediterranean climate could burn off the impurities of the English soul, as if by a kind of Italian alchemy. English travelers from Byron to E. M. Forster advanced a similar sort of travel magic as a means for getting in touch with one's soul. Keats, wracked with tuberculosis, went to Italy hoping to save his life.

While the sunny views may have limited curative powers, Italy, for the traveler not coughing blood onto their bedsheets, still seems to promise a kinder, more elemental world. Especially in contrast to the modern gray drizzle of England: in Rachel Cusk's memoir of her family's months in Italy, the decision to bolt from their Bristol suburb is prompted by an ad on the street with the tagline, "Is there more to life than this?"

Well, is there?

The life of Dinah Brooke suggests that she took seriously the idea that it is possible to change oneself by geographical means—she escaped to Paris when she was sixteen, moved to Greenwich Village in her twenties and, for six years, lived in Pune, India, where she was a follower of Osho, or Bhagwan Shree Rajneesh. For decades now, she has been Pankaja Brooke, her sannyas name. A resounding feat of self-transformation—or annihilation, or reconstitution.

Love Life of a Cheltenham Lady describes a more equivocal transformation. In one version of Italy, you find yourself. In another, to your horror, you find no self. Deprived of the context of home, thrust into the exaggerated pressures of vacation, you start to dissolve. In this novel of intense and often violent description, the more you pursue transformation, grasp at a different self, the more the possibility disappears from reach.

Miranda, the young English lady of the title, and her American actor husband, Louis, have brought their newborn to a house in the Tuscan countryside. The trip is an escape from dreary England, and a hoped-for salve for Miranda's existential disquiet. To the couple's great delight, they pull up to their rented villa and discover it's perched on a beautiful hillside with "heart-stopping" views. What luck—the trip is off to a wonderful start. Then they open the front door. The rooms inside are impossibly dark, the air is freezing, and there are no windows at all on the side of the house with the view: the villa's only windows look onto a field of "harsh, stubbly grass."

The house is the first disappointment. Things don't get much better from there. From the beginning, we are given signs that Miranda's psychic turmoil might be beyond the reach of a nice Tuscan vacation, or a room (or villa) with a view. And beyond the reach of a husband.

Louis recognizes the malleability of his wife, though he doesn't realize what it means for him: "Whenever she turned her face towards him Louis had the sensation of watching an actor manipulating a white mask on a long and slender stick." Who is this woman beside him? We quickly get the sense she wouldn't be able to answer this question either.

So what does Miranda make of Italy? Like the rest of us, she encounters the place and she sees herself encountering the place. There are the usual disappointments of vacation, when the imagined self and imagined place butt up against the actual. Like life, I guess, but in miniature. It's hot. The rented house with its non-view is also, it seems, actively rejecting their presence. When Miranda and Louis attempt to picturesquely dine outside, they get only a "mouthful of wasps." Miranda thinks, "I shall be able to read, and walk to the horizon across these ancient moon hills, and lose myself in the contemplation of Etruscan sarcophagi in the museum." But an instant later, she's in a butcher shop, where "suddenly the pale carcase of an animal loomed up intimately, hanging by the heels, flayed to the white fat, blood sticky on the sawdust floor—its identity as pig, sheep or calf almost lost, and organs exposed namelessly. Miranda took a breath, choked on the soapy fetid smell, and fled into the street again."

It's not rare, even in those soft-focus, Merchant Ivory memoirs—*Under the Tuscan Sun* or *Eat, Pray, Love*—to come across difficulties on the journey to a strange land, encounters that reveal the ignorance of the hero. But typically these turn out to be lessons, opportunities for wisdom to be won. Or opportunities for the distinction between self and other to be ratified: as in Cusk's memoir, in which she handily flays every bumbling tourist, boorish ex-pat, and ill-behaved child in her path.

Miranda has none of that cutting certainty about where she ends and others begin, and is unable to access any superiority or three-act wisdom offered by the genre of a foreigner abroad. Miranda is a foreigner everywhere. Days and nights, to Miranda, seem to last for years. All is incoherent, the self fractured. Very little is offered in the way of wisdom.

Except, perhaps, never to become romantically involved with actors. Timeless advice. Miranda not only marries an actor, but takes another as her lover: when Louis is unexpectedly called back to London for a part, he is replaced by the Italian Oreste, an aspiring extra in tight white jeans, a man who can "quote commentaries to his own moods from Shakespeare and Dante" but doesn't quite know how to drive a car.

Both her lover and her husband repulse and attract Miranda in rapid succession. Like the optical illusion of the crone and the young woman—gruesome, desirable—Miranda toggles between her perceptions with disorienting frequency. Even as Miranda experiences these men as false and lacking, she convinces herself to carry on: "She had always found it easy to live more vividly in fiction than in the confusions of reality, and allowed herself, in pure fantasy, to fall in love with him as he existed in pure fantasy, on the stage."

The performance, hers or others, allows a brief respite from those "confusions of reality." Vacation offers many opportunities to perform, and be performed for, Brooke describing the Italian waiters enacting their intricate "ballet" for the tourists, Louis comparing their villa to the set for a low-budget historical movie. Even Miranda's baby, who "allowed herself to be turned into an Italian baby," is roped into the production: in one of the novel's bizarre, surreal interludes, the infant is passed off as Miranda's lover's child for the benefit of his estranged parents, while Miranda pretends to be his wife. The ruse is ridiculous, even nightmarish. But for a moment, these fictions provide real comfort. To perform is a relief, a stretch of solid ground in the psychic morass.

When the self is ruptured, isn't it preferable to step into the comforting confines of a role? Put on the costume, stand up straight, hit your mark. "Being a hostess allowed her to be complete again," Brooke writes of her heroine, "and she totally forgot her hours of agony. In retrospect the day seemed short and pleasant." As soon as the curtain falls, reality rushes back in.

Only her infant seems to connect Miranda, intermittently, to the urgent needs of the animal self. The baby is sick, the baby is hungry, the baby is (in one extraordinary scene) in physical danger—these primal demands provide rare flickers of clarity for Miranda, experienced without artifice or projection. It holds out the promise of consequence, or meaning, concepts that she has so much trouble locating in herself. When she first discovers that she is pregnant, Miranda imagines the unborn child as possessing "a life that could never be replaced, never repeated."

But can Miranda's life be replaced or repeated? This is another of the book's sorrowful threads—the narrowing of Miranda's self by motherhood and partnership, the fact of her gender. Motherhood is another performance with its limited rewards, as is the role of lover, as is the role of woman and wife. So much of this novel sees Miranda trying and failing to find some footing in the world via these external, gendered roles, but only fracturing herself further, ceasing to function coherently. Brooke narrates from a mind that, even in total anguish, helplessly invokes the fashion wisdom for the savvy Englishwoman on vacation, like a glitchy *Woman's Weekly* copywriter in the midst of a breakdown:

"For holiday evenings sitting in cafés a light woollen shawl is a pretty alternative to the Englishwoman's ubiquitous cardigan. The young woman sat silent with tears running down her cheeks. In a mauve dress trimmed with white braid, with a headscarf to match, the young woman sat silent, tears running down her cheeks and splashing onto her hands. Have fun on holiday. Perfect for sightseeing. For sitting in cafés in the evenings a light shawl is a pretty alternative to the Englishwoman's ubiquitous cardigan."

Miranda's psychic turmoil is jarring, contagious. And, according to Brooke, is semi-autobiographical. She wanted to title another book *The Woman Who Almost Succeeded in Killing Herself*. The distress is so alive. It's no surprise that Dinah Brooke turned to a guru for some peace. She found it, and stopped writing entirely. In an interview, Brooke says of the Sannyasins:

"My life there replaced in me the need to write." She once told Osho that he had stolen her creativity. "His response was to hit me, really hard. The effect was to release my attachment to writing. This is what an enlightened master is for." I tell her that, to me, the story sounds tragic. "Not to me. To me it felt wonderful."

It sounded tragic to me, too, when I read this interview.

And yet. That despair she describes so well in this novel that my stomach tightens. The discomfort, the unease, life broken into unfulfilled wantings and failures, the deep confusion of a human being trying to survive the pain of consciousness. Sure, this misery becomes raw material you can shape into a narrative, into Brooke's lucid images—we tell ourselves that transformation has some value. But wouldn't you rather be happy? Free at last of ambition and costuming and artifice?

"If only (and for the first time the possibility did not seem to be entirely out of reach) I could lose myself, bury my self-conscious self in a life like that, where everything is what it appears to be, and I too am what I appear to be. A life was something seen from the outside, solid and complete in itself."

Dinah Brooke's Miranda is a foreigner everywhere, even to herself. If enlightenment is to be at home in the world, in a place where "everything is what it appears to be," Pankaja Brooke, on the other side of a writing life, seems to have achieved it.

Sounds pretty good.

Well. A writer is maybe always a foreigner. (Or that's what I tell myself.) From here in Babylon, deep in my projections and attachments, still groping in the foreign fog, I'm happy she wrote this book. The moments of startling observation, her granular descriptions of a blitzed internal world. Even just the many greens: *Eau de Nil*, which is less green, I learn, than celadon. The translucent green of a bunch of grapes. A dark green cake of spinach, the gray-green blanket of the English countryside.

If we can't have enlightenment just yet, I'll take the bracing experience of this novel and the singular visions of its author, a harrowing, howling report from the disintegrated self.

Emma Cline
New York, 2025

LOVE LIFE OF A CHELTENHAM LADY

I

Gently, gently, the afternoon shadows of the cypress trees flipped across the baby's face. Her eyelids opened and shut with a languorous movement, the unfurling of small waves which spread themselves at your feet like a fan opening. It gives me the sensation, thought Miranda, of running my hand along the railings of the park, on my way home from the afternoon walk, in my neat grey coat and round hat, beside the silent and anonymous nanny, to the empty house. The movement of the baby's eyelids gradually became slower and slower. Her lashes at one moment golden and full of light, dark and secretive the next, barely parted, and then with a final tremor, a rolling of hidden eyeballs, gave up their resistance to sleep.

Her parent's feet kicked aside white stones which gave off puffs of fine dust. The local industry was carving alabaster into sacred statues or profane souvenirs, and many of the country roads were gravelled with bastard, rejected alabaster. The dust (deadly to the lungs of those who had to work in it all their lives) and the fragrant, medicinal smell of the cypresses seemed richer and more dense than the air in which they existed.

The alternating heat and coolness made it difficult to breathe. Miranda felt herself gasp for breath as if she had plunged into cold water, but the next instant the balmy heat relaxed every muscle, and she leaned her head back and exhaled with the voluptuous abandon of death. Images of herself, Louis and the child in its pram strolling down the long alley of cypress trees, herself and Louis eating in restaurants, looking at pictures—the child changes nothing, nothing at all—riffled through her mind like a pack of cards. She put her hand over Louis's on the ridged rubber handle of the pram to make him walk more slowly. Low down, through the trunks of the cypress trees on the right the valley plunged away in a haze of blue and purple. They were silent.

They had rented the house because of the alley of cypress trees. Driving down from Volterra it had been the first thing they saw as they came round the edge of the mountain: long, dark, and not quite straight, it seemed almost possible that the trees had grown there naturally; they had been planted along the lines of a well worn path, following the arbitrary movements of the ground like a line in an oil painting drawn by an elderly Sunday painter, his hand shaky with rheumatism, extending on and on past the moment when it seemed impossible that the brush did not slip, or the stubbornly continued line shift the whole picture out of gear, to justify itself abruptly when the square, plain house pushed to the very edge of the cliff, detached itself from the landscape. In order to drive into the alley itself they had to make an awkward, three-hundred-degree turn on a blind corner, and bump up a steep incline between two small houses where several black-eyed children in maroon velvet dresses gazed at them sombrely, crouched by the roadside, caressing a cat. The road itself, which was the main road from Volterra to Pisa, was wide and well cambered, but there was no stretch in this hilly area where it ran straight for more than fifty yards, and Italians in small white Fiats swooped round every curve in the centre of the road with no warning of their coming except the squeal of tyres. For the first few days Louis waited for five or ten minutes to make the turn, expostulating in astonishment:

—These guys must be out of their minds. No wonder they believe in God.

However, by the end of the week he was swinging into the alley with just a quick glance to left and right.

The house, perched as it was on the edge of a cliff, should have had a heart-stopping view of the hills heaped on top of each other for twenty miles towards Florence, but since it had been built as a working farmhouse and not a pleasure villa there were no windows on that side except for those of one room, now boarded up, which had served as a chapel. The front of the house, square and uncompromising, with no steps or portico leading up to the entrance, faced a sloping orchard, fields of harsh stubbly grass, and the gentle rise of a hill on which the ancient Etruscan city of Volterra, itself invisible from here, was built. An effort had been made, when the owners first decided to rent the house to foreigners, to temper its sternness, which was so at odds with the grand, luxuriant, tawny landscape, and together with the bathroom and refrigerator a terrace had been added, on the far side of the drive, next to the orchard. Two cypress trees which used to shelter the pig pen and hen house had been cut down, so that now across the farmyard litter it was possible to see the view that had previously been reserved for Christ on his altar. A stunted oak tree in the middle of the paving stones gave some shade, and urns planted with flowers were placed at intervals on the low stone wall that had been built to correct the slope of the ground.

Louis, on their first arrival, peered round, anxiously, because he had been the one who chose this particular villa and made the arrangements—on Miranda's insistence—but half against his own better judgement, because the child was so young, and who knew what post-natal depression might descend on his wife in a strange villa in the Italian countryside? Her profile was totally inexpressive; not exactly inexpressive, but still to him, after more than a year of marriage, impenetrable. Outlined against the pitted, greyish, golden stone of the house it appeared luminously pale, the forehead so high that it reminded him of those Renaissance ladies who painfully plucked the first inch of their hair until they were married. Louis had bought several postcards of Pollaiuolo's portrait of a lady because they reminded him of his wife. The expressiveness of the lady in the picture was in the pattern of her profile and her puffed and jewel-entwined hair, rather than in her pale eyes and the full and tremulous modelling of her nose and mouth. It was the same with Miranda. However much her features might change, the impact of her face was the smooth, pale oval shape like the alabaster eggs that were heaped up in bowls in the shops in Volterra for sale to tourists. Whenever she turned her face towards him Louis had the sensation of watching an actor manipulating a white mask on a long and slender stick.

At the sound of the car on that day of their first arrival, a woman with a fine, square, classic face, brown and slightly wrinkled, came towards them from the farmyard, carrying eggs in her apron. Her neck was sunk into her shoulders and her steps dragged slightly with the weariness. Her husband came at the same time from a small whitewashed house tucked away behind the larger one. He was wearing a blue shirt and wide straw hat and his face had the gentle sweetness and strength that painters try to express in portraits of Saint Joseph. They learned later that he ate no meat and drank no wine; to him work was life, and life was hard and good and holy. A gift from him became something more perfect than itself—an egg was all the goodness of Heaven, and a bunch of herbs the abundance of Nature. These were Gina and Corrado, the peasants whom the bourgeois expatriate doctor (Milan is not Tuscany) who owned the house, referred to as the *brava gente*, of whom any service could be demanded.

They were led into the house, Corrado opening the door with an immense old-fashioned key. The heavy oak door, studded with nails the size of small potatoes, creaked painfully. As they entered the hallway, dark and cold as an empty church, Louis almost raised his hand to brush imaginary cobwebs away from his face. His eyes still dazzled by the sunlight outside he could just make out heavy, carved oak Victorian gothic furniture, and dim antlered heads waiting cocooned in silence on the walls. My God, he thought, it looks like the set for a low budget historical movie. He glanced at Miranda who was staring up at the wrought iron chandeliers and the nineteenth-century frescoes fading round the cornices. He sat down in a semicircular wooden chair, suitable for a Tudor monarch. Vassal, bring me wine! Gina held out her arms for the baby, who allowed herself to be transferred without screams or struggles. Miranda smiled with delight, Louis, with relief; it was going to be all right.

Upstairs there were three bedrooms, two with double beds, and one with two single beds, all four-posters with mattresses like solid rock, and a gigantic iron cot, recently scrubbed free of rust by Corrado, which squeaked and groaned as it was rocked, for the baby. Flowers and fleurs-de-lys were painted on every exposed surface, and the walls were covered, one above the other, with sentimental pictures of dogs and children, saints and watercolour landscapes, brown at the edges. The floors were made of polished red tiles, the lights were so tiny and weak that it was almost impossible to read by them, and every room, including the bathroom, had a high vaulted ceiling that sent back echoes, and echoes of echoes, of every word and footstep.

Inside the house it was always cold and dark; if they ate in the dining room it was difficult to distinguish between the sugar and the grated parmesan, and if they ate outside wasps homed in on every mouthful; outside, during the day the heat was unbearable, and there was nowhere comfortable to sit—but it was all right. For a week it was all right. Miranda breathed in deeply the pleasure of being abroad, and the baby was amenable to anything; she slept while they drove to Florence or Siena, absorbed without complaint jars of baby food in restaurants, and in museums stared silently with round eyes. The holiday was being a success.

But after a week a telegram arrived from Louis's agent, summoning him back immediately for a small but desirable part in a film being made in London. The postman, a boy of seventeen, had bumped his way past them with great speed and noise as they pushed the pram back to the house, made a wide turn at an acute angle to the ground, scattering gravel with his balancing foot, and posed to wait for them like a trapeze artist waiting for the applause. Louis tore open the telegram, horrors running through his mind. The postman sat on his dusty blue-grey scooter in his faded blue-grey shirt with his feet splayed out to support him, and the engine chugged and spluttered, sending out plumes of fumes or fumes in plumes to decorate the air. Louis handed the telegram to Miranda.

—Er . . . *bisogno di rispondere*, he gesticulated with his hands to amplify his meaning and improve his Italian.

—*Si, si*. The boy revved up his engine and gestured with his head to the pillion. I'm making it, I'm really making it, thought Louis.

—I've got to go.

Miranda looked up, her eyes shining with excitement. How marvellous, you've got to go.

—*No, grazie*, Louis shook his head and pointed to the car, and the scooter zoomed off. He looked at Miranda standing palely against the dark cypresses, and put a hand over his eyes in a spasm of guilt. Why the hell did it have to happen now? Should I turn it down? Miranda saw Louis looking at her and wondering if she was crazy. Well, I've never been in a bin yet, but I bloody well ought to have bin, ha ha. She said,

—You'll have to leave first thing tomorrow morning. We'd better find out if there's an early morning plane from Pisa. Louis put his hands on her shoulders.

—Do you want to come with me? She looked round at the hot stone, golden in the morning, white at midday, now beginning to take on a patina of mauve and orange at the approach of sunset, at the shimmering grey green of the olive trees in the middle distance, and the richer, heavier green of the occasional fig tree; everything, the deep, brilliant azure sky, the pecking chickens, Corrado sorting tomatoes into boxes, had a clarity which seemed to define her as she looked at it. Every image was complete and satisfying; it required no effort of the imagination to bring it into relationship with human life. She thought of the emptiness of their London flat. Louis, if he was working on a film, would leave at seven in the morning, and not be back till late at night. The last time he had worked on a film he had been away a month, in Rome, just after the baby was born, and Miranda had lain in bed, the nurse bringing the baby to her to be fed every four hours, in a stupor of rumpled sheets and torn newspapers, fingers sticky with breast milk and grimy with printing ink, drinking Guinness, ostensibly for the nourishment, and whisky from a flask under her pillow when the nurse wasn't looking. London, with no nurse and hardly any Louis. Impossible.

—I'll stay here. I've got the baby and the *brava gente*. I'll be all right. It's only for ten days.

—Maybe we could get your mother to come out?

—No. I'd rather be alone.

He put his hand under her chin and shook it gently from side to side. —You won't be depressed?

She pulled her head away. He understood nothing about her depression; he had assumed it was something to do with the birth of the child. He learned, but from experience and not through instinct. He saw and added up the exterior signs of her feelings and asked her to explain them; but she could explain nothing.

—I honestly don't think I will, not in Italy. She felt that if he loved her, as he said he did, his duty was to understand her better than she understood herself.

As they drove into Volterra Miranda began to feel very gay. It'll be better without him. I won't have to bother to cook. I'll become aware of the character and spirit of the place in a way that's impossible if there's anyone else around. Old hopes and fantasies from the fruitful time of her adolescence sprang up like the cut-out figures in children's books when the pages are opened. I shall be able to read, and walk to the horizon across these ancient moon hills, and lose myself in the contemplation of Etruscan sarcophagi in the museum without having to explain why I love them so much. Momentarily she forgot the child.

In the town they plunged from the dark narrow streets into tiny dark shops. Looking straight up it was possible to see the pure azure sky; further down a shaft of hot sunlight struck a patch of wall, then head down through the bead curtain at the entrance to a butcher's shop and suddenly the pale carcase of an animal loomed up intimately, hanging by the heels, flayed to the white fat, blood sticky on the sawdust floor—its identity as pig, sheep or calf almost lost, and organs exposed namelessly. Miranda took a breath, choked on the soapy fetid smell, and fled into the street again. Leaning against a wall she clamped down on her revulsion and called out to Louis.

—Get something nice, we'll have a feast.

Foreigners were always served first. Women dressed in black, after half an hour's gossip came out with impossibly small parcels wrapped in brownish tissue paper. An entire carcase was seen only once a week.

Louis bought huge quantities of groceries. He said to the woman who owned the supermarket,

—My wife will be alone for a few days, you'll look after her, won't you?

—*Sola, sola.* The woman and her daughter, black eyed and smooth skinned, nodded and smiled, and gave the baby a bag of sugar biscuits. Miranda smiled and nodded back. Louis left her choosing books, and went to the post office to send a cable to his agent. The ceiling was high and the counter topped with marble; it was cool and light in there. He stood with his elbows on the marble counter, chin in hand, while the assistant counted the number of words in his telegram, and rearranged the punctuation with slow, elegant flourishes more suited to a quill pen than a ball point. Mancini remembered me from Rome. I'll write every day.

The girl in the office where he bought his airline ticket was pretty and spoke good English. After half an hour on the telephone she said:

—You are lucky. There is only one seat in the flight tomorrow morning, and that is a cancellation.

He grinned,

—That's great. I'm starting work on a film on Friday. With Mancini.

She put her head on one side and smiled, raising her eyebrows,

—An Italian.

—When I was living in London I had to come out to Rome to work on a film with him, and now I'm on holiday in Italy I have to go back to London. They both laughed. The girl handed him his ticket. Her nails were carefully manicured, and red to match her lipstick. Poor girl, I guess she needs to cheer herself up in this dark little office. How do they manage it? They work such long hours, and yet look as if they spend the whole day in a beauty parlour. Miranda's beauty was more casual, which pleased him better. He heard the sound of a baby crying in the square. Oh my God, she's been alone for nearly an hour.

—That sounds like my kid. *Arrivederci*, and thanks.

—Goodbye. The girl smiled.

He hurried out into the square, but the crying was that of another child, his own was sitting on her mother's knee, at a café table, sucking, absorbed and ineffective, at a biscuit. Miranda sorted through a pile of books and magazines, with a glass of wine in front of her. She seemed animated, whole, content. He bent down to kiss her,

—Darling, you're going to be all right, aren't you? I'll write every day.

She looked up, pushing a piece of hair behind her ear.

—Honestly, what a selection of books, nothing but Agatha Christie and Harold Robbins. Will you send me some from London?

—Of course I will. Louis sat down and ordered a glass of Italian brandy. It was getting cold. Gusts of wind blew in from the side streets, chilling the sweat between their shoulders, and swirling dust around their feet. The sunshine had almost vanished from the square. Only the façade of the post office was still warm and golden. The square was so small and the surrounding buildings so high that it felt as if they were sitting at the bottom of a well.

The baby started to whimper, and her parents packed her and their purchases into the car and drove down the hill to the house. Dusk was falling rapidly. The baby was now crying in good earnest. Gina materialised out of the shadows; air, sky, stone were the same bluish grey, coarse grained, like the enlargement of a photograph taken on fast film; the texture of solid objects seemed no different from that of the air. Gina was carrying armfuls of soft, feathery grass and leaves to feed to the rabbits. The vitality of these uprooted grasses was far greater than that of the animal life surrounding them, of which they were soon to become a part, chewed, pulped, digested. They alone retained their colour, deeper and richer. Miranda could feel their juicy coolness as she stood next to Gina, her own arms burdened with the struggling child, feverish with hunger and exhaustion. She had an impulse to lay her head and her daughter's down on that soft, refreshing pillow. The cries of the baby, and Gina's voice came plaintively out of the dusk.

—*Piange, piange, a fame.*

—*Si, si, a fame.* The cries gained in volume and echoed back on themselves in disharmonic accompaniment as Miranda carried her into the hall, preceded them up the stairs, stretching out thin and forlorn to the bathroom, where the steam and the shining modern tiles, vaulted ceiling and refractive water made an orchestra, an organ, a scene of rape and carnage out of the purple thrashing infant in the blue plastic basin.

—Be quiet can't you, muttered her mother under her breath, Gina will think I don't know how to look after you. Down the staircase again, as high and wide as a passage in the London Underground, arms stretched out, body rigid in her yellow terrycloth suit, cries bubbling and disappearing behind her, like the sound trail of an aeroplane, till strapped into her folding chair on the kitchen table, ready for her supper, she fell silent. Louis who had finished putting away the groceries, gave his daughter a kiss on the top of her bald head, and placed himself in front of her, ready to amuse or be amused.

—At your service, Madame.

Her round, shining face, with a wisp of hair in front of each ear, stared back at him with an affronted expression. The flesh on her face looked as if it was still wrapped in tight little parcels, uncertain as yet of how they were going to distribute themselves over her skull. Louis snapped his fingers slowly, slowly, and then faster, going into an imitation of a Fred Astaire dance routine as he sang 'Singing in the Rain'. The baby stared in silent astonishment, but Miranda laughed as she warmed milk and mixed cereal. Louis was very conscious of their existence as a family in this small, light-enclosed world. The kitchen, like all the other rooms was large and high, shadowy in the corners, with a vaulted ceiling and floor covered with red tiles. A wooden table filled the centre of the room, and into a low archway, cut six feet deep along the whole length of one wall, an iron range had been built. The fridge, sink and three-ring gas stove perched on top of the range had no place in the life this room had been intended for, and he sometimes romantically imagined his wife scrubbing the wooden table in rhythmic spirals, and cooking slow earthy meals in the range heated by burning gnarled olive trees he had chopped down himself, and utilising all the doughnut shaped and conical cooking pots that were heaped untouched in the cupboards. But alongside this gentle fantasy lay the image of Gina's dragging steps, and even brighter, diamond hard, her description, imperfectly as he had understood it, of the cold bright days of January, snow sometimes lying on the ground, when she and Corrado, alone in the winter crispness of this landscape, worked round the roots of the black trees, breaking the hard earth, fingers bleeding and numb, she with a shawl wrapped round her head and shoulders which did nothing to protect her from the cold, doing he never discovered what, since Gina was interested only in communicating the pain and weariness of year-long labour. Miranda's small movements as she spooned Farex into a bowl, poured on the warm milk, and stirred gently, a miniature reproduction of the scrubbing movements he had been imagining for her, in the conical pool of light that dangled so precariously, a tiny, dim bulb at the end of a fragile and twisted flex from the high ceiling, were soothing and gentle. He and the baby, in their own wavering cone of light that touched Miranda's at the edge of the table, performer and audience bound together as they stared into one another's eyes (all his repertoire of charm and humour was unable to crease her face into a smile until at last their levels of apprehension met as he made balloons out of his cheeks and popped them loudly) were still apart enough, until she began to smile, for him to be very conscious of and very grateful for this moment of perception, all the clearer because it came as it were sideways into his mind, slipping in while his attention was engaged elsewhere, of the symbolic trinity, mother, child and father, of which he was now a part, and which was superceded by the ordinary and lovely reality of family life as Miranda turned round with the bowl and spoon in her hand, and the baby began to laugh, either at her father or the prospect of food.

It always gave Miranda a sense of comfort and relief, like finding her place in a book that she had put down several days ago, or realising that she had after all paid a bill, or sent a lost cheque to the bank, when Louis started behaving like an actor. It enabled her to establish some link in her own mind between herself as she had been before they met, and the still undigested image of herself as a mother spooning Farex between the gums of this self-absorbed and irritable creature sitting Buddha-like on its throne.

When she had first seen him she had been sitting alone at the back of the stalls of the Playhouse Theatre, in Oxford. It was the end of her last term; schools were over, the farewell parties were over, Oxford was almost empty of undergraduates, but Miranda lingered on, unable to tear herself away from this matrix in which she had been so comfortably embedded for three years. She had been living out of college, and kept her room in North Oxford on from week to week, waiting, perhaps, for all the promises of friendship and knowledge miraculously to fulfil themselves. In these last weeks she got to know several people more intimately while saying goodbye to them than she had in the previous three years of possibilities of daily contact. She bitterly regretted that she had acted in no plays, made no films, written no poetry, read too little and argued too little. Her life had been reasonably gay, she had gone to parties, punted down the river, climbed in late, but an infinity of possibilities presented themselves to her now, as they had done when she first arrived, except that now they existed only in the past.

All her friends seemed to have plans not only for the summer, but for jobs—for their lives. Miranda passively waited to be included in somebody else's plan, but rejected any suggestions that were tentatively made of sharing houses in London, going on trips to India by Landrover, or walking tours of Greece, because all she really wanted to do was to start all over again. This was the only period in her life when a personality, a place, an identity had been freely given to her, and now it was going to be taken away. She wandered round the beautiful, leafy town in the endless hot days of the end of June and the beginning of July, as one after another, groups of her friends left, full of vigour and strength, their future firmly clutched in their hands, with mounting emptiness and anxiety progressively paralysing her will. She often went to the theatre or the cinema, but particularly the theatre (college productions full of mishaps and marvels, operas in the Town Hall, touring companies or the resident rep in one of the two theatres) alone, making the most of a freedom which she knew she would not have the courage to enjoy in a larger community. But by the middle of July the college productions were over, her friends had really all gone, and would never be coming back, and she was beginning to admit panic, and to regret and reconsider the trips to Greece or India which would at least put off a little longer the need for more serious decisions. It was then that she had first seen Louis, on the stage, as she sat alone at the back of the stalls, in the Playhouse Theatre.

He was playing Segismund in Calderón's *Life is a Dream*; the more than romantic hero, the tamed Oedipus, who is sent by his father the King of Poland to be brought up in an isolated and rocky dungeon because of a prophecy that he would bring disaster to his own people. Being of noble birth, and therefore able to act nobly without benefit of education, at the moment when he should have slain his father he becomes the virtuous Prince, and all ends happily ever after. Triumph of civilisation. Miranda's heart bled for Segismund, the rational man, forced by the accident of his birth to deny all natural human needs. She had always found it easy to live more vividly in fiction than in the confusions of reality, and allowed herself, in pure fantasy, to fall in love with him as he existed in pure fantasy, on the stage.

But the following afternoon fact and fantasy met. She had been to the cinema, again alone, to see *Le Jour se Lève*, and had wept so continuously that she couldn't even read the subtitles. The foyer of the cinema was rectangular, and flanked on either side by the toilets. After the film was over Miranda went into the Ladies to bathe her face and splash her eyes with cold water; coming out again she put on a pair of dark glasses. The foyer was painted white, and was full of diffused, reflected sunlight from the street, people moved past her eyes like shadows, but at the moment when she saw Segismund, straight in front of her, coming out of the Gents, the moving figures stopped, and were retained in her mind for ever scattered in a pattern of arbitrary perfection. She paused, and tried to recollect what she was wearing: a deep blue dress with a sailor collar, and white high-heeled shoes—she looked good, she could take her place in this ordered creation. She smiled at Segismund. He smiled back, and walked towards her, pausing, and making Miranda's heart pause, to allow a couple to walk in front of him.

—Hullo, are you incognito?

She touched her glasses and laughed. —It's the film. I always cry in the cinema. They stared at each other for a moment, then started to walk out of the cinema and down the street together. Miranda felt the skin on the small of her back prickle with excitement. She felt an astonished pride. How many of her girl friends would have dared to pick up an actor? She said,

—I saw you in the theatre last night. I thought you were very good.

Segismund was walking in the street, because there was barely room for two people to walk abreast.

—Did you? That's nice. The house has been half empty every night. We've been very disappointed, it's such a great play. The students seem to have gone already. Miranda was grateful for the dark glasses as he looked at her.

—All except me.

He took her arm.

—Come and have tea with me?

Having successfully picked up her actor, Miranda was now at a loss as to how to behave. Life in Oxford was made very much easier by the fact that it was immediately possible to place anyone you came into contact with, and you yourself were immediately placeable too, in this small and rather static society. You had the option of either fulfilling or contradicting the expectations raised by a first year student of Eng Lit at St Hughes; but that, after the immense range of possibilities in the world at large, was a satisfyingly limited choice.

But so far as Segismund was concerned she was thrown back onto unfamiliar territory. What did he know about St Hughes, and what did she know about his expectation of female Oxford undergraduates? Seeing no way out of this situation she was struck dumb, and only just managed to reply with muttered monosyllables to his invitation,

—All right.

Louis was delighted with her. He had been afraid the whole week would go by without his meeting a single student, and this one was pretty, and the right sex. They stopped at a small antique shop, and Miranda stood in awkward and embarrassed silence while he examined and exclaimed over a pile of Victorian paintings. He bought two of them. The sun shone down warmly, and Oxford looked at its most perfect.

They wandered arm in arm round Worcester Gardens, paused to watch the ducks on the lake, walked down the High Street. Miranda was in the awkward position of someone who finds that having a fantasy fulfilled brings them more uneasiness than pleasure. What's the matter with me? she muttered fiercely to herself. She had captured a prize; not even a student, but a handsome, talented young man who had already achieved status in that outside world into which her contemporaries were sailing off so bravely, but her stomach cringed with fear at the possibility that some leftover friend or acquaintance might see and recognise her.

—What's your name? she asked rudely and abruptly. Louis smiled and pressed her arm comfortingly. He was flattered and touched by her embarrassment, which he took to be a tribute to the glamour of the stage.

—Louis Hahn.

Miranda blushed violently. How stupid. Of course she knew what his name was, she had read it in the programme. When he asked hers in return she mumbled inaudibly, and had to repeat it, feeling like a child at school being told off in front of the rest of the class. She looked at the slightly puzzled Louis with a suddenly critical eye. He was wearing beige jeans, and a linen shirt with wide orange and yellow stripes. He did not look like the majority of her student friends, whose jeans, when they wore them, were blue and dirty, and who otherwise were usually seen in baggy grey flannels and old tweed jackets. His hair was too curly, his neck too short, and his nose too long. When she looked away again she found that her retina carried a clear image of his cheek, the upper part fine and soft, the lower part aggressively bristly. The image dissolved slowly into a montage of shop windows, flashing glass and middle-aged merchandise, which dissolved in turn to a shot of his feet in tennis shoes and thick white socks. He was telling her that his mother had been born in England. His father was Jewish, a doctor, and they lived on Riverside Drive in New York. Louis always mentioned that he was Jewish early on in any conversation to avoid possible embarrassments, not that he expected the world to be rabidly anti-Semitic, but if the necessity for mentioning it came up later on it might seem that he had been keeping back this essential piece of information about himself for the sake of possibly scoring a moral victory. He thought a lot about his Jewishness (his mother was also Jewish), and felt that he was probably unduly sensitive about it.

They walked down the High, arm in arm, Miranda stiff as a board, staring at the ground, her English reticence outraged (and fascinated) by the ease of his self-revelation. His family, Louis continued, had been horrified by his decision to become an actor. He had given up Medicine just before he took his finals. To be a doctor was respectable, but an actor . . .

—You know what Jewish families are like.

I certainly do not, thought Miranda. They had struggled to dissuade him, which was partly why he had come to London, selling his car to finance a year at LAMDA. He led her through a doorway and up some stairs into a café.

—That's why I've got to make it, and quickly too, he said. He grinned with pleasure as he looked round the café. Two large rooms painted green, windows draped with *eau de Nil* curtains, tables laid with white cloths and heavy English tea-shop cutlery. In each corner there was a potted palm, and all the waitresses were elderly and bad tempered.

—Isn't this great? said Louis, I come here every day.

Miranda looked around. The place was neither familiar nor unfamiliar. To Louis a tea shop like this was an astonishing revelation, like men walking the streets of London quite naturally, wearing bowler hats and carrying rolled umbrellas, both of which were of course familiar to him from English movies, but he and his New York friends had always assumed these movies to be satires. They sat down at a table near one of the windows. A sour-faced elderly waitress, wearing a starched white cap and frilly apron, came up to them, notebook in hand and said,

—We don't serve after half past five.

—Ah, said Louis, but it's not yet twenty past.

She sniffed, scribbled something in her notebook, said, defeated,

—Two teas? and stumped off. Under her dress her ankles were lumpy in dark grey lisle stockings, and her feet, misshapen by bunions, burst out of cracked leather sandals. Louis said,

—I always sit at this same table, and leave her a huge tip, but I haven't got a smile out of her yet!

Miranda smiled faintly, without looking directly at him. So far as she knew this place had not been the haunt of anyone she considered desirable among her fellow undergraduates, so she found it totally devoid of interest.

Louis, after a short silence, started to talk about how he had first become interested in the theatre. While he was at Medical School, a friend had offered him a part in a student production, and to his immense astonishment he had come to realise during the three weeks of rehearsals and week of performances, that he could never be happy doing anything else.

—There's a special sort of intoxication about being up on stage there in front of an audience.

Miranda played intently with her knife, which though it looked heavy was in reality extremely light, or rather top heavy, because the handle was hollow. The metal had a strange, non-metallic texture, that appeared to be rough, but was smooth and greasy to the touch. The waitress came back with the tea. Louis smiled at her and said,

—Beautiful day, isn't it? but she only gave him a look of the deepest hatred, and managed to slop some tea onto his jeans. He winked at Miranda, who laughed, and offered him her napkin, but she really identified with the waitress, and found herself thinking, you can smile all you like, but that doesn't change the fact that you're foreign. She poured the tea. Louis tried asking her about her family, but she answered so briefly that he didn't press it. She realised with slight surprise that no one at Oxford had ever asked her about her family, and she had felt no need to volunteer more than the barest essentials. Father in the Foreign Office. Divorce. She thought about her family as little as possible. She suddenly achieved a new vein of fluency, and started to attack Louis for his clothes, and for being American.

—In this country people stop wearing white socks when they're five years old, she said, biting into a soggy tomato sandwich. Was it with other students or her mother that she had laughed at the ridiculousness of Americans who ate peanut butter and jelly sandwiches, and wore loud shirts?

—Oh yeah? said Louis.

She went on. —And generally it's only queers who wear shirts like that over here.

Louis was half annoyed and half amused. Her nostrils quivered, she was intoxicated with her own daring.

—Do you really like being an actor? You have to be a fantastic exhibitionist, don't you?

He decided it was funny, and laughed.

—As a matter of fact I'm not sure how much longer I'll be able to go on being an actor, at least in this country, it's very tough for an American citizen to get a work permit. This is a LAMDA production, not a professional one at all.

Miranda took a piece of fruit cake.

—Well why don't you go back to America?

—Yankee go home! I might have to, but I like it better over here. I guess the only way I can stay is to marry an English wife!

He grinned, and Miranda's heart sank into her stomach, she thought, how ghastly, he thinks I want to marry him. Her face became stony and she retreated into monosyllables again, pushing her plate aside.

—Have you finished?

—Mm. Louis couldn't decide whether he was interested in this girl or not. He picked up the bill which the waitress had deposited by his elbow on the stroke of half past five. Miranda was seized with panic. She had had the courage to pick up this obviously desirable young man (now he seemed desirable again), he had found her attractive enough to take her out to tea, and she was throwing it all away by being so rude and unpleasant that he was not going to ask to see her again. Did she want to see him again? Yes—no doubt about it, the thought of Louis saying goodbye, leaving her on the pavement with a wave of his hand, and disappearing into his unimaginably strange and exotic life made her feel like a small child left behind while everyone else goes on a picnic. She searched desperately for something to say that would persuade him that she really did like him, she meant well, her rudeness was merely sophisticated playfulness. The waitress came with the change on a heavy silver tray and slapped it down on Louis's thumb.

—Do you like Oxford? asked Miranda. Have you been punting on the river? She gazed at him so anxiously, so pitifully, that Louis heard himself asking,

—Will you have dinner with me tonight? What am I doing? he thought. Do I really want to play around with this kooky kid just because she's a student at Oxford? He counted out a large tip.

—Oh I'd love to, said Miranda with exaggerated cheerfulness, but I'm meant to be having dinner with my tutor and his wife. They both stood up.

—I don't get out of the theatre till late anyway, so why don't you come round for a drink afterwards. About eleven thirty?

—O.K.

He scribbled his address on a piece of paper and gave it to her. I know, I know, he thought, but she is pretty. They walked down the stairs together. On the pavement Louis waved goodbye.

—See you tonight then, and walked off towards the theatre.

II

Miranda went home to change for dinner. Her room, in a house off the Banbury Road, was small and untidy. It contained a bed, a table and chair, a cupboard, a chest of drawers, and a dusty, manure green Victorian chaise longue she had bought for four pounds at a junk shop. Every surface was piled high with clothes, empty Guinness bottles, and saucers full of cigarette stubs. She pushed some clothes off the chaise longue and sat down to have a cigarette. The trees in the street grew so close to the house and were so heavy with foliage that her room was always in greenish, underwater shadow during the summer. She leaned back, gazing at the gently moving shadows on the ceiling, and muttered to herself—it's bloody stupid to be a virgin at twenty-one. Just plain bloody stupid. Her watch said six thirty, too early to start changing. She picked up an old newspaper and read part of an impassioned correspondence about the proposed new design of fish knives in the proposed new dining hall of St Catherine's college. My life is a permanent adolescence, she thought. She sat looking at her newspaper until the cigarette burned her fingers, then put it out and lit another. The conscious surface of her mind was blank, but underneath it thoughts and images scurried about like ants at the debris of a picnic. She remained in this trance-like state for nearly an hour. In fact she spent most of her time and a considerable amount of energy in refusing to become aware of the mice in the night, the scurryings behind the wall.

At seven thirty (she was meant to go to dinner at eight), she suddenly thought, perhaps I should take a nightdress, and leaped to her feet. Searching through piles of half-worn clothes she realised that she only possessed two night garments, one flowered flannel with a high neck and long sleeves, and a pair of nylon pyjamas, faded and torn, the elastic sagging at the waist. She tried to stuff the flannel nightgown into her handbag, but it was too bulky. Cursing—you bloody fool— she threw it on the floor and changed into a pretty red and white silk dress that her mother once brought back from Paris, and made her face up heavily with rouge, lipstick, and black lines round the eyes. She smeared vaseline on top of her lipstick to make her lips glisten, and combed her hair forward. But it would not stay there naturally, and the white, domed expanse of her forehead above the highly coloured features made her look like a doll. She slapped on cream and hurriedly wiped it all off, dabbed powder on her nose, and pulled her hair back, fastening it with a rubber band—the first one snapped and she searched for another, holding a fistful of hair at the nape of her neck with one hand, could not find one, and eventually tied her hair with a piece of crumpled ribbon.

Geoffrey Gale was a large, ponderous man in his late twenties, with smooth dark hair and square jowls. He had been a Rugger Blue, and got a First in English, but looking at his heavy-lidded, sleepy eyes, and his usual posture, slouched so deep in his chair that his head and his knees were on the same level, it was difficult to imagine that either his mind or his body had ever been agile. His tutorial method was to listen to his pupils' essays with eyes entirely closed, open them a fraction to satisfy the demands of the particular situation by saying: If you work a bit harder you might just get a good degree—and then go on to talk about his wife, who had been his best pupil and also got a First, his other students, and which of the male ones would be suitable as boy friends for her and Annabel, the friend with whom she shared her tutorials, and his collection of Sèvres china. He and his wife lived in a small, cramped, attic flat at the top of a Victorian house further down the Banbury Road, with two small children. Geoffrey usually ate in college three nights a week, and brought colleagues home for dinner on the other four. His wife also had smooth dark hair and a large jaw, and her brilliance was dimmed by the exhaustion of her present way of life. To this end of term dinner party had been invited one of the much touted students, whom she had not previously met, and who seemed to Miranda, without any question of doubt, to be queer, and a bachelor don who had sunk into the role reserved for bachelor dons, in which nothing is interesting or even noticeable about him except for his hobbies and his eccentric habits. In this case his hobbies were walking tours and collecting china, and his habits mainly that of always wearing knee breeches instead of trousers.

The dinner of goulash and rice was punctuated by cries from a sleepless, snuffling child. Its mother left the table with guilty relief at each whine of—Mummy—her departures and returns ignored by her husband, taking no part in the conversation. Miranda looked at her with pity, but no sense of identification. It seemed impossible that such a destiny could lie in wait for her. She realised that she was meant to be the star turn of this party, and endeavoured to give satisfaction by retailing anecdotes about acquaintances of hers at other, better colleges. For the first hour or so she talked continuously, feeling extremely gay and witty—febrile? suggested another mental voice—possibly—she conceded. She was tempted to tell them that she had a date with an actor after dinner. A date with an actor, almost at midnight! How far from their lives, how infinitely strange such an event must be. She felt the cold dark breath of the unknown before her, and drank another glass of wine. After dinner Geoffrey and his colleague discussed china with the slow thoroughness of the trained academic mind. Miranda, still feeling herself the centre of the party, listened without hearing to her fellow student analyse his chances of future advancement. After some time it occurred to her that he too was talking about china, and hoped for a job in the Victoria and Albert Museum. By half past ten Jennifer Gale, having cleared the table and done the washing up, was asleep in her chair. The undergraduate turned to Miranda and said,

—Well I've got to be going now; can I give you a lift? I've got my car outside.

Miranda looked at her watch. It was only half past ten. There was an hour to go before she met Louis. What should she do?

—No, no, thanks very much. I live very close, I'd rather walk, she said, getting up and looking round in despair at the white painted, beamed ceiling, the Mexican blanket on the floor, and the anglepoise lamps.

—It's such a lovely night. The don of the walking tours struggled to his feet, and Miranda realised that she had made another tactical error.

—If you would allow me, I'd be happy to accompany you. I always walk myself on these balmy summer evenings. This man, too, was not much over thirty, though he must have given up in despair, some time during the course of a prolonged and stifled puberty, any attempts to live the life of a young man. Having sedulously perfected his cover of elderly eccentricity he could go through the motions of flirtation with old world gentility, with no danger of his being taken seriously. Miranda looked helplessly from one man to the other, and then at the pale, angular, collapsed figure of her sleeping hostess. She turned to the don,

—All right, we'll walk together. Geoffrey shook hands with them all from his chair, and then struggled ponderously to his feet. He placed a meaty hand upon the shoulder of each of his two undergraduates, and said:

—I'll be interested to see what sort of degrees you two get.

The three guests descended several flights of stairs, still in a warm cocoon of noisy footsteps and sociable exchanges. Out in the street the younger man got into his red Triumph, and said to Miranda, puzzled,

—Are you sure you wouldn't rather come in the car? She wasn't playing her appointed part.

—No, thanks very much.

It was true that it was a beautiful night. The sensation of the warm air against her skin was so gentle that it was barely possible to separate the two elements, the air, filled with the scent of leaves and gardens, and herself, breathing it in. They walked slowly back to Parktown. Miranda's companion entertained her with an account of his latest walking tour, in Austria. She thought, if he really belonged to the generation he is pretending to, he would be talking of the poetry he read and the friends he made rather than his boots and his feet and his food. They walked down the street in which Louis was staying. Miranda took care to avert her eyes from the house—she even allowed herself to remain uncertain which house it was—and made no effort to work out the position of his room from his description. Physical processes which were certainly involuntary and should have remained decently below the level of consciousness made her walk more quickly and wriggle like a child wanting to go to the lavatory. The hairs round her nipples rose on end, the nipples themselves were constricted into hard balls, the processes of digestion made her intestines flap against her bladder like fish in a bucket, and residual turds jumped around like pieces of mercury in her rectum, causing it to itch intolerably. She longed desperately for the release of physical sensation. Her mind dwelt on soothing images of running, leaping, climbing, bathing, excreting, avoiding with care the one physical sensation that had provoked her present state.

Suddenly she thought—perhaps he got home early and saw me walking past with another man, in which case he'll just think I'm a bitch, and certainly won't want to see me again, how can I explain it? She noticed that they had already walked past her own gate, and stopped. The don walked on a few paces with his heavy boots and reliable tread before he noticed that he was unaccompanied. He turned round, peering uncertainly from a pool of lamplight. Miranda laughed.

—I'm here, this is where I live. Thanks for your company.

He walked back towards her,

—Oh, er, the pleasure was mine. But she was already halfway up the garden path. He leaned over the gate,

—Perhaps we'll met again at Geoffrey's new house?

—Perhaps. Goodnight. She went in, closing the door with a firm click. North Oxford remained unchanged; balmy, scented, secretive. Inside, the house smelled of old linoleum. Miranda felt as if she had shut herself for ever out of the Garden of Eden. I daren't go out again. Maybe that damn boy scout'll still be there, pacing round the crescent in his hobnailed boots. She ran upstairs to her own room, but it seemed intolerably small, musky, stifling; it smelled like a public lavatory, of old ashtrays. There was still forty minutes to wait. She daren't go outside or even open the window for fear of passers-by who might guess her guilty secret.

She decided to have a bath, went down half a flight of stairs to the bathroom and turned on the antique geyser. Even on this warm night the bathroom was draughty. The window would not shut properly, and the door did not fit. In winter it was purgatory. The unshaded electric light bulb poured a yellow glaze over the white bathtub, brown linoleum floor, broken cork bathmat. Miranda lay like a statue in the bath, covered with gooseflesh, staring at the uncovered window, changing the focal length of her gaze from the reflection of the wall, door and towel rail, to the rising moon and silvery re-creation of roofs and trees beyond, occasionally punctuated by an agonisingly tight, pulling of focus onto a speck of dirt or an insect on the surface of the window itself. She indulged in this exercise until the water was cold and she had a splitting headache, then leaped out of the bath, half rubbed herself dry, pulled her dressing gown round her and ran upstairs. What am I, Delilah or something, powdering and scenting myself for the kill? She pulled on a petticoat, and the dress she had been wearing that afternoon, and looked at her watch. It was eleven thirty. An awful stillness descended upon the town, the house, the movement of her blood. She slowly picked up an old cardigan, her handbag, a packet of cigarettes. Each gesture looked to her like the gigantically magnified, slow motion leap of a ballet dancer. The hands of her watch did not move. She started slowly, movements laden with dignity, to descend the stairs again. O tempora, O mores, why the hell didn't I get this over when I was twelve years old? She had the firm intention of walking round the crescent for a breath of air, and then coming home to bed.

A sense of duty led her to the street where Louis's house was, but she kept in the shadow and looked firmly towards the houses on the other side. It was now eleven forty-five. It wasn't my fault; I couldn't find the wretched house. As she neared the far end of the road she began to feel a sensation of vast triumph and relief. She had screwed herself up (Freudian pun) to the point of making a reasonable effort to fulfil her social obligation, and it was not her fault if she was able to return, virgo intacta, innocent, unsunk, to her home port.

A man's voice echoed down the street:

—Hey Miranda, is that you? She stopped dead as if he had hit her with a bullet in the back. She took another tentative step, but the voice called again,

—Miranda? This time it was a harpoon. She turned round slowly, and felt herself being reeled in. She crossed the road and walked back along the other side. Louis was standing on a small iron balcony outside his room, with a glass of wine in his hand. He waved the glass at her.

—Did you get lost?

—Ssh! hissed Miranda loudly, her eyes on the ground. Louis looked around, could see no one, shrugged his shoulders and said in a half whisper,

—I'll come down and let you in.

She stood outside the garden gate, waiting, wondering if she dare seize these precious seconds to run away, escape, but crucified to the spot by fear of that penetrating, alien, voice. Louis opened the door.

—Come on in and have a glass of wine.

She moved up the garden path like a zombie, cardigan clutched round her, face white and set, pushed past without looking at him, and waited like a prisoner ready for the final interrogation, a martyr whose faith is not quite equal to the lions, at the foot of the stairs.

—Go on up, it's the door on the right.

She obeyed mechanically. The door on the right was open. On a table by the bed, which was covered, oddly enough, by a Mexican blanket, was a light with an orange shade, which gave a soft glow to the whole room. The smoke from a cigarette in an ashtray curled peacefully upwards, a small portable gramophone was playing some jazz which sounded warm and welcoming. A half-finished bottle of wine stood next to an empty glass on a round table in the middle of the room, beside the remains of a sandwich and a book lying open, face down. The thought flashed in and out of Miranda's mind, how lucky he is, he can read while he is waiting. Louis followed her in and closed the door behind him.

—Sit down. He indicated the one armchair. —Have some wine. He handed her a glass, and sat down on a stool opposite her. —I began to think you weren't going to come.

In the dim orange light he looked more like Segismund again, and she made a conscious effort to switch into the mood of emotional indulgence she had achieved so effortlessly while watching him on the stage. She took a sip of wine and began to feel a very slight relaxing of tension.

—You've still got make-up all round your eyebrows.

Louis laughed. —I hurried home. He reached out and took her hand. —Are you afraid of me?

Miranda gave a false little laugh, after the manner of Millamant in a recent college production of *The Way of the World*,

—Of course I am, I had an English education.

Louis squeezed her hand and thought, poor kid, she's probably still a virgin.

—Why did you tell me to be quiet just now? Surely it's not so terrible to come visiting after dinner, it's not even term time. Don't people ever give parties in this place?

—Well, said Miranda, taken aback, this isn't a party. She started to describe her dinner party to him, being as witty as she could, but extremely conscious of his hand holding hers. After a few sentences she realised that her brand of wit was carefully aimed at Oxford ears, and almost became aware of how provincial and snobbish it sounded. Louis kissed the back of her hand, turned it over and kissed the palm, then stood up and pulled her up from her chair. She smiled nervously, unnaturally conscious of her teeth. I'm all bone. I have no flesh.

He gently caressed her forehead and her cheek, and then kissed her, feeling like a most true and chivalrous knight rescuing a beautiful maiden from the horrid toils of sexual ignorance. He kissed her for several minutes, at the same time exploring her back and buttocks with his hands, and she responded eagerly if somewhat spastically, with convulsive movement of the lips and tongue. Nudging with his knees he moved her over towards the bed, and removed his mouth from hers to say,

—It's not so bad, is it?

Miranda frowned in irritation; she had at least been kissed before. He started to kiss her again, before she could articulate her annoyance, and laying her down on the bed thrust his hands inside her dress and started to explore her breasts and groin. Miranda's little sighs and gasps enabled her to express, at least to her sastisfaction, thoughts such as, come on, get on with it, enough of the foreplay, stick it in. Louis undid his flies, and searching for her hand, wrapped it round his penis with a groan of pleasure and the whispered injunction,

—Stroke it. It felt like the long upper lip of a horse, as Miranda stroked it with a stiff and nerveless hand; infinitely soft, wrinkled flesh over solid, self-sufficient muscle. Louis stood up suddenly. Have I done something wrong? wondered Miranda. He stripped off his shirt, trousers and underpants. He was very hairy and his penis pointed diagonally upwards, like a piece of sculpture, with no visible means of support,

—Take off your dress, darling.

Miranda, frowning stubbornly, teeth tightly clenched, forcing herself to stare at Louis's naked body, took off her dress and bra and pants, but kept on her petticoat, which she had had since she was at school. She turned out the light and crawled under the blanket. Louis felt his way towards her, outlined in the cold light from the window. Nothing was any longer bathed in a romantic orange glow.

—I want to see you.

—I like the dark. He slid under the blanket, but crouching over her belly lifted it off her with his body so that she was no longer protected even by those brown and yellow stripes. He pushed her petticoat up to her shoulders, pulled it over her head and started to pasture on her breasts, licking and sucking each nipple with exquisite sensual enjoyment, descending slowly, his long tongue leaving a chilly trail behind it, to her groin—she immediately covered her cunt with her hands; he spread her legs apart, and slowly worked his way, with his lips and tongue, up and down the inside of each thigh. Humph, he's settling in for a long run, thought Miranda, and rolled her eyes unseen to the ceiling. Her violent sighs of boredom, resentment, humiliation, and astonishment approximated closely enough to sound of pleasure to encourage Louis to continue towards his own apotheosis. He prized open her hands and thrust a finger up her vagina.

—My God you're hot if this is your first time. Miranda bared her teeth in hatred. —This may hurt a little. He thrust two fingers in together and started to work them from side to side to break her hymen.

—Ouch! She sat bolt upright with a screech of pain, banging her chin on his forehead.

—It's all right, baby, lie back, this is where the fun starts. She turned her head desperately from side to side. He pushed her down again, and started to lick and kiss the lips of her cunt and her clitoris, worrying them with little grunts like a dog with a bone, while she flailed limply at his head with her hands, her face in a rictus of misery, sobbing silently to herself. Louis seized her hands and imprisoned them behind her back, and thrust his tongue up into her vagina as far as it would go; please, she whispered soundlessly, please. Suddenly he leaped forward with the whole weight of his body, gave a quick suck at each of her breasts (that'll keep them quiet), nuzzling, nibbling, almost swallowing, gagging, then panting heavily he raised his buttocks to get a good aim—his cock had grown to a foot long—he plunged into her body. Miranda had a mental image of herself as a fishwife, standing arms akimbo, sleeves rolled up, white apron, looking at the goings on down below. Well I must say. Her body suddenly took the initiative and rose up to swallow Louis entire. Her movement was so sudden and violent that it jerked him from his moorings with the sperm still pouring out of him—Oh God—he struggled to get back in, but she was still heaving from side to side, her knees twisted round him so tightly that he had no room to manoeuvre.

—Oh, oh, oh, he groaned and buried his head in her stomach. Miranda lay back quiet and still, her hands clutching the sheet, legs pressed together, cunt throbbing, teeth and eyes tight shut. Louis raised his head for a moment,

—It wasn't your fault.

Miranda became slowly aware of the wetness of their limbs, and a pool of liquid under her bottom. She withdrew herself from the sensation of Louis's body touching hers. I suppose I ought to stroke his hair. She touched it; it was as wet as if he'd been swimming. His scalp felt hot and fragile, as if there was no flesh between it and the bone.

A sensation of extreme restlessness took possession of her, as if there were insects crawling over her body under the surface of her skin. She jumped up from the bed, letting Louis's head fall back into the exudations of his own body. Air and cool light from the window flowed over her damp skin causing it to shrivel slightly, faint contractions of the tiny network of surface muscles and capillaries, but the blood in its deeper tunnels pounded through with a dark roar. She went over to the window and pulled the curtains right back in an orgy of exhibitionism, exposing herself entire to the gentle stirring of plants in the garden, the pulsing life of the trees—contained, restrained, hidden behind the crusted bark until it burst out in a soft delirium of leaves; to the blue grey of the asphalt, coarse textured, smelling of tar, buckled and wrinkled from the warmth of many days and the cool of many nights, retaining the night's chill for the feet that trod upon it in the freshness of the morning, and still at night giving off, even up here to her pale body so far above it, the warmth and odours of the day.

Louis raised his head to say,

—There's a bathroom down the hall, and my robe's on the back of the door.

Miranda thought, if I wash myself much more today my skin will come off, but she obediently went over to the door, and picking up the dressing gown slipped out onto the landing with it thrown round her shoulders. The landing hummed with darkness and silence. Blueish moonlight from one high window outlined four closed doors, the banisters, several pictures of framed shadows, and a piece of worn carpet. The dark triangle of her nipples and pubic hair led her past the closed doors, and the open stairwell, from which at any moment young men, landladies, dons, schoolmistresses might surge, to the bathroom. She splashed water from the basin ineffectually over her thighs and bottom, unwilling even to get her feet, let alone the rest of her body wet. My poor old body's had enough for one day. On the way back she paused for a minute, digging her toes into the carpet, listening to the floorboards creak; she felt like a fly at the heart of a piece of clear amber, preserved in the perfect stillness. She could step through any one of those four closed doors, forward or back in time—she was no prisoner of the moment. Each door appeared to be created equally of enticement and rejection, shuddering in its frame from the pressure, within and without. Then an outline of yellow light was drawn round the one she had come from, dulling, by contrast the mystery of the moonlight. She felt like the rich man being pulled through the eye of the needle, and the process was painful and ridiculous. She opened the door, sidling in through the narrowest possible space, and pulled it shut behind her.

—I almost forgot which was your room.

Louis had been sitting on the edge of the bed examining the soles of his feet. He stood up when she came in, his penis dangling soft and weak, and walked over to her. They stood by the door looking at one another. To Miranda their looks seemed to be blank. He took the dressing gown from her shoulders and wrapped it round his own body like a towel. She stared at the wall behind him. He said,

—You're beautiful, and kissed her left breast gently. I'm going to have a quick shower, well, bath. Pour yourself some more wine. He patted her on the buttocks and went out.

Miranda felt cold, empty, let down, foolish. She pulled on her pants. Her feet were yellowish and the toenails needed cutting, and her shaved legs were bristly against her palms. She searched the rumpled bed for her petticoat, and finally found it pushed down between the mattress and the wall. She pulled the bedspread up to cover the sheets, got into her dress, cardigan and shoes, and flopped down in a chair beside the fireplace. I shall never move again. The wine tasted acid and dry. Louis came back from the bathroom glowing with a different dampness. He started to get dressed. Miranda picked up the book he had been reading, and looked at it. It was a book of poems by W. H. Auden.

—You made the bed, how sweet, said Louis, refilling both their glasses, putting another record on the gramophone, and sitting down opposite her. But I didn't she thought, I just pulled the cover up over the rumpled sheets; he'll discover later on that I'm not sweet at all. He leaned towards her.

—Don't look so forlorn, Miranda, you had to lose it some time. You're not a kid any longer.

She didn't look at him, and shrank, mummified, into the stuff of her chair: faded chintz and old, sagging upholstery. Louis, accustomed to female kookiness being expressed in terms of excess, was touched by this silence and withdrawal. He picked up Miranda's limp left hand and gently stroked the inside of each finger.

—I'll tell you a funny story; I want to see you smile.

Miranda frowned anxiously. Oh God, what if I don't see the joke?

—This chorus girl was introduced to Tallulah Bankhead at a party as the only showgirl in New York who still had her cherry. Louis lowered his eyelids sexily and put on a Tallulah growl—and she said, 'Oh that's marvellous, darling, but doesn't it get in the way awfully when you fuck?'

Miranda's anxious expression didn't change, she shrank even further into her chair and turned her head away; then realising that something more was required of her, she gave an unhappy little smile.

Louis thought, I think she's blushing. He squeezed her hand and shook it gently.

—Don't you know what a cherry is? It's what you've just lost, your virginity. Now come on, cheer up! It happens to everyone—if they're in luck.

Miranda pulled her hand away and reached for a cigarette. Her mind was a total blank—or rather it was full of such confusion that she was unable to pull out a single coherent thought, for fear of committing herself in a way she did not fully understand. Even such neutral statements as—it takes a bit of getting used to—appeared so dangerous that she remained stubbornly silent. Louis's presence began to exhaust her so that she longed to burst into tears. He said,

—Would you like to spend the night here, or would you rather go home?

—I'd better go home. She stood up thankfully, stubbed out her cigarette and finished her wine.

—Miranda—Louis stood up too and put his arms round her—I'm not going to let you go until I see you smile. She smiled pathetically, huddled in his arms, but did not respond to his kiss. He waited for a moment while she absorbed the warmth of his body, the soft glow of light, the music, then said, gently,

—Come on, I'll take you back.

She allowed herself to be led through the door, mute and passive, like Eve out of Paradise, an orphan child thrown out into the snow from the only home she had ever known.

Louis walked with his arm round her shoulders through streets that were now blank, echoing, empty of life. She was as cut off from the lives around her—the fragrance from a garden full of night-scented stocks on the corner—as if she was in prison. It must have been half past two, nearly three in the morning. There was a faint sensation of lightness, of dawn in the sky. I must be in, I must be hidden before the light comes. She was aware of the image and the truth that they represented, two lovers walking back, their arms round one another, from a night of love; but it had nothing to do with her. She was only truly herself when she was alone, body numb, mind a blank, inert in her lair, protected from the possibilities of love and rejection.

At the gate of her house they stopped and Louis kissed her again.

—Do you want me to come up?

If he had really wanted to he would have come without asking. She shook her head.

—When am I going to see you again? She didn't answer.

—The whole company is going up to London at the end of the week. We've got the Arts Theatre for a six-week run. If you want to see me you can always find me there.

She smiled and said, —O.K., suddenly like the girl he had met coming out of the cinema again. This is obviously a girl you've got to go gently with, he thought, you can't push her. She skipped and ran up the garden path as if she'd been released from captivity, fumbled in her bag for the door key, turned to wave, and was swallowed up inside. She ran up the stairs two at a time, laughing under her breath, and kicking off her shoes took a running jump onto her bed without bothering to undress and hugged the sheets and blankets round her body, rubbing her face in the pillow, smiling idiotically, continuing to wriggle and wrap the covers more tightly round her until within five minutes she was asleep.

The next morning, by the time she woke up, Miranda had decided to go to Greece. She finished throwing the accumulated junk of three years into a motley collection of suitcases and took an afternoon train to London.

Her mother was away and she had lost her keys, so the porter let her into the small flat in Marylebone. The flat appeared, as it always did when she returned to it after an absence, cold, empty and featureless. They had lived there for ten years, ever since Miranda's mother had left her husband in Moscow and come back to start a new life alone with her daughter. All the pieces of furniture, pictures, books, objects which were connected with her past seemed pathetic, sordid and unfriendly. They remained hunched in their ugliness as if to say—your love should have enriched us in the past so that we could enrich you now. Ignoring them, she helped the porter dump her suitcases in her bedroom, and then went straight to the telephone and rang Annabel. Yes, Annabel would love her to come to Greece; the party at the moment consisted of Annabel, her boyfriend Julian, and two other young men, Robert and Anthony, and her parents were being difficult. Another girl would make them feel much happier. Miranda went to dinner at their flat in Eaton Square. The parents, whom she had met several times without being able to establish any sort of relationship with them, were delighted and grateful that she was going to accompany their daughter and her gaggle of young men, and were kind to her.

Three days later they were in the train, and three days later still, in Greece. Miranda's impression of their stay was patchy and confused. She was aware of the harsh modern buildings, the dusty streets of Athens, of walks, exhausted from the heat, along paths of blinding white stone, the sad, narrow streets of provincial towns, isolated bare mounds of ancient tombs, the valley of Delphi like a dark and devouring bowl. Robert and Anthony vanished in the direction of Mount Athos; there were plans to meet on an island for the last few days.

Annabel and Julian held hands, virginal and absorbed, with total lack of sensuality. I could never love an Englishman, thought Miranda. She kept the idea of Louis at the back of her mind, with triumph and satisfaction. She had escaped by coming here, but she could go back and pick him up again, imprisoned in the role of Segismund like a butterfly under glass, any time she wanted.

They went to Hydra sooner than they had intended, to wait for the others. There they spent most of the day sitting in a café by the harbour playing gin rummy. Friends of Julian's parents had a villa on the island, and they went to several parties there, and one day joined a trip by mule to the monastery on the hill in the centre of the island. As they swayed up the stony hill, buttocks aching, knees rubbed raw, the scent of pines in the air, Annabel confided to Miranda her worries about whether to sleep with Julian or not. Miranda's role, she had realised from the beginning, was for Annabel not only that of a chaperone to soothe her parents' fears, but also a sexual pundit who could be turned to for guidance and practical advice; a role she had achieved because unlike most of her contemporaries she had been ignorant even of what she was ignorant of, and having no way to define her ignorance, had never admitted it.

—How, asked Annabel, turning round on her mule and leaning backwards, her forehead wrinkling with anxiety under her floppy red sunhat, does one keep from getting pregnant? Miranda had no reaction for a moment. Her mule stumbled over a stone.

—Well, she said, her mind racing back over images of Louis stripping off his trousers, poised above her, you've got to have a contraceptive. What was a contraceptive? Was it a sort of balloon a man stuck on his penis? Had he done anything, or couldn't it happen the first time? Did he expect her to have taken precautions, and if so how? What? Her mind shied away, in imitation of her mule. Turning a stony face to the stony mountainside, Miranda said,

—Well obviously you've got to take precautions. I mean it isn't worth the risk, is it? Did you bring anything with you?

Annabel stared back over her shoulder, admiring, embarrassed and relieved, and shook her head.

Robert and Anthony telegraphed to say that they would be on the train at Salonika, and after a month they all found themselves back in London. The two young men vanished, bursting with news and excitement, to a friend's house in Chelsea, Julian and Annabel went to her parents' flat in Eaton

Square, and Miranda returned to Marylebone. Nothing had changed. She sat down in the silent, empty, green and white flat. There were several postcards from her mother, and a note: Terribly sorry darling, to miss your hols like this, but you would *not* tell me what your plans were. Had to go to New York for three weeks, for work. *Do* be here when I get back.

Her mother was buyer for the dress department of an Oxford Street store. She was also beginning to look for a second husband, having recovered, or so she felt, from the wounds of her first marital experience.

Miranda couldn't be bothered to unpack. The rest of her life stretched emptily ahead of her. It had been divided up into terms and holidays, terms and vacations for so long that the disappearance of this whaleboning of time left her sagging loose and blowsy, her life devoid of shape. She sat slumped on the sofa, staring at her bare sandalled feet, covered with the grime of a long journey. She needed a bath. The thought of a bath reminded her of Louis, and she allowed thoughts which had been somewhere below the level of her consciousness for several days to float up and reform themselves complete on the surface. She had not had a period since she had slept with Louis nearly five weeks ago, and her breasts during the last few days had become heavy and painful. Was it possible that she could be pregnant?

What do people do when they're pregnant? They go to doctors; they have abortions; they get married. Her mind wheezed to a halt like an old clock. I don't want to think about it. I won't think about it. She hadn't slept much for the last three nights in the train, and the shape of her skull and the sockets of her eyes were defined by a slight ache on the inside. But the idea of lying down on her bed and going to sleep seemed terrifying, to be avoided at all costs. If she let go now she might never find herself again. Anyhow the bed was covered with suitcases. If you don't sleep you should eat. She looked in the fridge, but it was empty and turned off. She heard her mother's voice—it's no use leaving food to go bad, darling, if I've no idea when you're coming back. You can always pop out to Leon's.

Just as well it's not the middle of the night, and I'm not starving to death. Miranda sniffed; she was abandoned by her mother, her lover and her friends. She washed her feet, face and hands, and went out. Marylebone High Street was bright and full of bustle in the afternoon sun. Women pushing prams piled high with infants and shopping negotiated pavements and doorways with expressions of glazed concentration. Miranda picked up a wire basket in Leon's grocery and delicatessen, and greeted Mr Leon.

—What a lovely tan, where have you been?

—Just came back from Greece this morning. Miranda's spirits lifted a little. She bought milk, butter, yoghourt, bread, paté, bananas and a tin of lychees, and put them on her mother's account. Out on the street again in a mood of defiance she decided to buy a new dress, and walked over to a boutique in Baker Street. While I've got a tan, and I've still got my waistline I might as well.

There were two cheques left in her cheque book, and she had a few pounds left in cash. Every month her mother paid an allowance into her account at the bank, and every month she had an overdraft. How much her overdraft was after the trip to Greece she dared not think. I don't care if the cheque does bounce, I need a new dress.

She shuffled through rows of garments, and took several into the tiny fitting room to try on. The first one was white, with a low-cut back, and looked good with her enlarged bosom and her tan. The second had puffed sleeves, and was dark red. The colour of blood. They stick a knitting needle up you and scrape it around inside; they can easily push it too far and puncture the womb, and then you start bleeding. She put one hand over her stomach and one over her mouth and sank down onto the floor. There was a sharp pain in her bottom as she sat on a pin, which prevented her from losing consciousness completely. A salesgirl peered round the curtain.

—Are you all right?

After a minute Miranda moved her hand from her mouth far enough to say, bit faint, then replaced it. The two salesgirls half lifted, half dragged her onto a chair, and draped her own dress over her shoulders as another customer came through the door.

—I think she fainted. They pushed a cold glass against her lips and she took a sip of water. The edge of the glass felt too thick for her lips and teeth to negotiate, and the water tasted tepid and flat and bitter, as if tin cans had been soaking in it. She sat with her head between her knees for several minutes and then got up, shaking her head and rubbing her eyes.

—I'll have the white one. She took out her cheque book.

—Are you sure you feel all right? Can you get home by yourself? Shall we call you a taxi?

Sometimes you died; sometimes you could never have babies again. This poor sickness in her belly might be a life that could never be replaced, never repeated. Another customer came in, silhouetted darkly against the bright street outside.

—I'll be all right thank you. It's not very far. She picked up her parcels and walked home with exaggerated care. Of course I'm not pregnant, she said to herself. I'll probably get the curse tomorrow.

That evening, sitting at the back of the stalls in her white dress, with the whole weight of the circle pressing down like anxiety from above, she watched Louis on the stage for the second time. During the afternoon she had stoked up her resentment against the invulnerability and callousness of men, but as she watched the play, she began to weep, and continued weeping until she was completely drained of all emotion. She sat wiping tears from her cheeks while the rest of the audience filed out and the life of the play which had filled the auditorium shrank and sagged like the air dying out of a balloon. Ordinary life made itself felt again. Footsteps and shouting could be heard backstage, and people turned lights on and off. Miranda got up and walked out of the theatre; she stared for a long time at the photograph of Louis outside, and then went back and asked if she could see him. The lady at the Club Members' desk was packing up to go home.

—It's the door up the stairs on the right, ask the porter. She climbed the stairs and saw a middle-aged man in uniform.

—I want to see Louis Hahn.

—'e's probably gone 'ome by now, but we'll 'ave a look and see. He knocked on the door, and when there was no answer pushed it open and motioned to Miranda to follow.

—If 'e's not in 'ere 'e might be in the bar. He knocked on a door on the left of a long corridor. You're in luck Miss. He opened the door.

—Visitor for you.

Louis was putting on his jacket. He paused with one arm awkwardly behind his back, half into a sleeve. The porter's steps echoed back down the corridor. As he stared at Miranda, Louis felt what had been partly a fantasy and partly a game becoming reality. He shrugged his jacket on and put his hands on her shoulders, pushing the door shut behind her and staring into her face.

—Do you know I've been looking for you? Every weekend I went back to Oxford, looking for that damned house? I couldn't remember which one it was, and I never knew your last name, and everyone was away.

The mother.

—I've never been more astonished in my life. I come back from New York, and there she is, engaged. I'd never even heard of this young man, let alone met him. She'd only met him herself two months ago.

—Oh Lord, thank goodness I haven't got any daughters! I suppose it's a shotgun wedding.

—Nobody was forcing her to get married. I'd have given her the money for an abortion, or she could have had the child if she wanted. It seems to be all the rage to have an illegitimate baby these days. But the young man seemed very keen, and he really is rather nice.

—Did she meet him at Oxford?

—Well yes, she did. But he wasn't an undergraduate, he's an American, and an actor. I must say I was a bit dubious at first, but he does seem to be doing quite well. And he's Jewish, of course. Not that I mind that in the least, but I had rather hoped she'd marry one of those nice undergraduates she used to go around with. Oh well, he's awfully sweet to me, and I shall love having a grandchild.

III

In the morning Louis, with Miranda beside him, and the baby, asleep after her early breakfast, in her carrycot in the back seat, drove into Pisa airport. After the first few miles of descent from the series of hills upon which Volterra was the crown, the rest of the journey was a dull, flat plain; tantalising small hills with towns or villages poised on top of them visible in the far distance on either side of the road. At half past eight everything close at hand was very bright and clear; the asphalt road glittered like silver; men in blue shirts worked in green fields turning rich brown earth; the occasional farm buildings were brilliantly whitewashed, and old women dressed in black fed cocks with scarlet combs under small, circular, golden haystacks. Directly above their heads the sky was bright blue, but it became milky towards the horizon, and the distant hills and towers were faintly outlined against it in pearly, opalescent green.

Louis drove quite fast, although his plane was not until ten, and they had plenty of time. Frowning slightly, and not taking his eyes off the road, he went through the things that Miranda must try to do, or remember, while he was away.

—Get Corrado to tighten up the brakes on the pram, I meant to do it before I left . . . Don't just hang around the house all day; it should be all right for you to drive with the baby in the back like this. Go out to lunch sometimes. You could go back to that restaurant in Florence where they were so nice to us . . . I've left the doctor's name and phone number pinned to the kitchen wall. You can telephone from the church, apparently. Corrado could drive you up in his truck if there's any emergency.

Miranda felt absolutely unconcerned about her approaching solitude. She looked out of the window, listened to her husband with half an ear, slightly irritated by his thoughtfulness. This mood continued as they arrived at the airport. She watched, without interest, while Louis weighed in his suitcase and checked his passport and ticket. She held the baby, balanced on one hip, and bought some more books.

They sipped black coffee from tiny cups of thick white china with a gold rim. Louis gave her the car keys and made her promise to drive carefully.

—The petrol coupons are in the glove compartment. He ordered another coffee, and pulled at his fingers anxiously, wondering if he had forgotten anything. The baby, having taken in the cool, low, grey green space of the new airport building and the muted sounds of travel, transferred her attention to her bottle filled with fruit juice. As the time for the plane to leave came closer, however, the atmosphere changed again, and the teat bumped against her parted lips as she watched people hurry in with sharp movements and strident voices. Louis jumped down from his stool, and hugged his two women in one embrace. He kissed the baby's nose, and his wife on the mouth, gently describing the line of her closed lips with his tongue.

—I love you darling, he said. —Miss me, but not too much.

Miranda followed him to the barrier; a kindly official let her through, and she straggled with the passengers out onto the tarmac, but the roar of the engines frightened the baby, who began to cry, so she retired inside the building again, and waved through the window.

The group of passengers swelled out raggedly, then came together again and were funnelled into the body of the plane, and the plane in its turn widened, and its roar increased as it turned towards the runway, gathered power, then speed, and then with a marvellous smoothness of motion rose from the ground and became a silver decoration on the calm blue sky.

Miranda sat rocking the baby in the sudden silence and emptiness for a few minutes. Then she felt in her pocket for the car keys, made a gesture of farewell to the kindly official who failed to look up from his work, and went out into the carpark. The car seemed to have a suitable compactness and neatness for her and the child. She felt a pride of ownership which she had never had while sitting in it beside Louis. She drove into the centre of town, and thought of visiting the leaning tower, but didn't because there were too many tourists. She changed some travellers' cheques, had lunch in a nearby restaurant, drove home.

What on earth do I need a husband for? she thought, turning into the cypress alley without hitting anything or stalling the engine. I can do everything perfectly well by myself. She gave the baby some mashed banana for tea, took her for a long walk in the pram, across the busy main road, past a farm, through a small, unexpected pocket of beechwood which smelt damp, leafy and English, further than she and Louis had ever walked together. Like Mother Courage, a dark, slowly moving figure against the reddish dust and large undulations of the countryside, she jauntily pushed her wheeled burden along the empty, rutted road. She achieved her purpose of arriving back late, tired, in the dark, with a sense of triumph and adventure, changed and fed the child, put her straight to bed, and made a salad of tuna fish, tomato and black olives for her own supper. As she sat in the cone of light, eating, drinking wine and reading one of the novels she had bought in Pisa (with the dark spaces of the kitchen around her) she felt perfectly casual, contented. The pattern and colours of the salad pleased her; every action she had undertaken since Louis left had been efficient and satisfactory. She felt alert and in control. Things are really very easy, she thought. Life, pleasure, they're very easy.

In the morning she woke up with a sense of doom, and couldn't for a moment locate it. Then she remembered—I'm alone.

The previous night's optimism seemed absurd, crazy. She was divided, like Gaul, into three parts. One writhed in anguish screaming, why did I let him go? Why didn't I remember what it was like to be alone? Another lay motionless in bed, leaden and inert, arms flat to the body, eyes staring straight ahead at the corner of the ceiling and the wall and part of a window where sunlight was streaming in through slits in the shutters. The third was aware of the baby in her iron cot by the bed (Louis had brought it into their room before he went) who was at that moment gurgling contentedly, amused by the bars of light and shade and the motes of dust that magically appeared then disappeared, but who would soon require changing (*again*), and feeding (*again*). The weariness of these demands united Miranda, and she turned over on her stomach and cried the dry, helpless sobs of a child who knows that it won't get her anywhere but is trying it on all the same.

After a few minutes she levered herself off the bed, put on her white nylon and lace dressing gown (which suddenly appeared so ugly and vulgar that even its texture changed and the smoothness caught on the skin of her fingers like burrs) and went to open the shutters. The brilliant landscape was like an insult to her eyes, and Corrado, sorting tomatoes down below as he did every morning, throwing the bad ones to the chickens and washing the others and packing them into boxes, was inexpressibly alien. She stared at him with hatred. He looked up, smiled and waved.

—*Buon giorno.*

Miranda went to fetch the child and held her up for Corrado to see. This had become a morning ritual. He pointed the dog and chickens out to her. *Cane, pollo,* and held up a tomato, *pomodoro.* He relished each word with love.

Miranda twisted her face into the grimace of a smile and thought, shall I throw her out? She waved to Corrado again, took in the laughing child, changed and washed her, responding with no smile or kiss to the blandishments of this daughter, and took her downstairs for breakfast. Each movement, though it took minimally longer in the physical world than the same movements last night, felt heavy, weighted, slow as a wasp drowning in honey. The heating and pouring of milk, the stirring of cereal was as bitter and endless a task as that of explorers who drive themselves on to the limits of human endurance without ever discovering America or the source of the Nile. She turned away from spilled milk and spat out food with disgust, unable to muster the energy to wipe it up, or to make a cup of tea for herself. Food seemed deeply repulsive. She ate two or three spoonfuls of congealed cereal.

The dark, cold kitchen with spiders' webs, she only now noticed, in the high corners of the ceiling, and unwashed dishes in the sink was more in tune with her mood than the bright day outside, but she forced herself to put the baby out on the terrace in its pram, wearing just a nappy and a light cotton top, with a rattle and the pattern of the oakleaves against the sky for entertainment, while she went upstairs to change into a bikini (pulling in her slackened stomach) and came down again, armed as if for a delicious lazy day in the sun with Ambre Solaire, mattress, towel, sunhat, dark glasses and novel.

Lying on her stomach, oiled and bronzing, she was very conscious of the image of luxury she presented, exposed to the envy of Gina, Corrado and the postman; but as if to prove her human solidarity with them, inside her mind was black and her bones hollow and cold. Rather than raise her head, open her eyes and read a novel, she concentrated her awareness on those parts of her body which were hidden from the world, pressed against the ground. Her toenails scratched the paving stones, and she wriggled further up on the mattress, searching for a position in which they could be allowed to vanish from consciousness. Kneecaps flipped awkwardly from one side to another, in their loose bag of skin. Thighs and stomach were prickled gently by the roughness of the towel, and her left cheek and the undersides of her arms against the yellow and white plastic mattress which formed part of the child's playpen, collected heat and formed liquid sweat quite independently.

She remembered lying in the sun (not in a bikini, she would have been too embarrassed at fourteen) in the garden of a hotel outside Cheltenham the summer after her mother had come back from Moscow. She had had the same sensation then of everything being perfect on the outside—charming old Cotswold mansion, ponies grazing in the paddock, mother and daughter in pretty cotton dresses on the lawn—but black, evil and corrupt underneath. She had, in fact, written a poem about it, using as a symbol the smooth green turf with worms writhing and turning in the dark earth (a simile that couldn't be carried too far, as she thought about it later, but it seemed at the time that only her mother's lack of literary sensibility made her say—what a horrid poem! Why don't you go riding this afternoon with that nice boy at the next table?). Every holiday, from the time she was three until they got the flat in Marylebone, had been spent in hotels or with relatives, or with nannies in rented houses.

Memories of childhood were snapshots of herself in school uniform, trudging alone through the grey green blanket of the English countryside or across stony winter beaches, pale, uncomprehending, weighted with misery. She could form no coherent chronological picture of her own life, and when her mother reminisced about pleasant times they had had together Miranda rarely remembered any of the incidents or the people, and was insulted and astonished at the notion that she could have been enjoying herself, or even appearing to enjoy herself. Her hopes of happiness had always been in the future; vague, undefined, and far in the future.

There were times before that, of course, times she couldn't remember but had been told about, when she and her mother and father had lived a normal family life together. And there were photographs to prove it. As a one-year old her smiling Daddy held her proudly on his knee, beside a lake. At two her parents swung her between them, one chubby hand clutched in each of theirs, wearing an embroidered pinafore dress and shiny patent leather strap shoes. At three she pedalled proudly round the lawn in a scarlet racing car her fond Daddy had given. This idyll took place in Sweden. She was born in Oslo while Daddy worked at the Embassy there. She had been a privileged and triumphant child.

Then things changed. Everywhere things had changed. Daddy was sent back to London and Mummy followed him, but Miranda was not allowed to go. She remained in the laps of nannies, coming and going, and the houses of friends, with no place of her own, her triumph and uniqueness slipping through her fingers. After a couple of years Mum fetched her back to gloomy post-war England, and they lived in a dank little cottage in the country. Daddy was in Lisbon. Sometimes he reappeared for a few weeks and they would have parties and picnics (margarine and carrot jam sandwiches, their egg ration used to make a cake), but nothing was the same. She herself could no longer charm her father, and he and her mother drank gin and shouted at each other after she had gone to bed.

Things will get better when we all live together again, her mother promised. But things didn't get better, they got worse. Daddy was sent to Moscow, and they trailed after him, full of hope. Daddy was colder and more distant than ever; he must have been protecting himself, she worked out painfully many years later, from the loathing and terror he felt at these female extensions of his own body, because Father, her own darling Daddy, was queer.

After an eighteen-month siege of his masculinity in Moscow the army retreated in disorder, first Miranda, sent away as if in disgrace to boarding school, then a defeated mother who didn't give up for several years, making courageous sorties to try and retrieve her former position.

A jumble of schools, nannies, furnished houses, hotels, friends, relatives; years of alien floorboards, and possessions dismally overflowing suitcases. Just before she went up to Oxford Miranda's mother had told her, in a stilted jolly voice, as if it was a slightly too adult joke, her version of the story. Apparently poor Daddy had been dismissed from the Foreign Office because of a spy scandal. Well, of course he wasn't actually a spy, but photos had been taken of him in compromising situations. They're always doing that sort of thing, the Russians, and of course the poor dears are usually quite innocent. But the

F.O. has to let them go because of the possibilities of blackmail. Can't take the risk.

Miranda had taken this story at its face value. She had asked no questions, and worked nothing out for herself. It wasn't until the end of her first term that she unwillingly learned the truth. Her mother's sister had come up from Suffolk; Miranda had spent several school holidays there, unable to join with much enthusiasm in the chilly and energetic pastimes of her two older cousins, Nicholas and Andrew, who were now in the army. Mrs McCullough had just been to the hairdresser and had her hair cut short.

—Honestly Jean, anyone would think you were still after poor Maurice. I wish to goodness you'd let it grow again—you want to find a normal man next time, don't you?

—Shh—Mrs McCullough made fierce grimaces towards Miranda who was sprawled on the sofa, sipping adult gin and tonic before dinner. Aunt Liz stared at her sister in astonishment.

—Do you mean to say you still haven't told her?

—Oh yes, of course I've told her. After all she's grown up now, she's nearly twenty-one. Aunt Liz turned towards Miranda.

—You knew that your father was a bit unusual in his . . . er sexual preferences, didn't you darling? He, well, liked boys better than girls?

Miranda said with cool sophistication, —Of course I did.

She turned towards her mother, who was sitting with her head turned away, her face buried in one hand. The newly cut hairs on the nape of her neck looked harsh against her reddened skin.

—You're very bad at hiding things, darling. I've known for ages.

This scene was encapsulated and hidden deep in Miranda's mind, like an indestructible plastic object swallowed and lodged in a child's intestine. Occasionally, no, quite often, it was played through on about the third or fourth screen of her consciousness. She did at one point ask where her father was now, and was told that he had last been heard of in the sexual outer darkness of the Middle East. Mrs McCullough was so relieved that her daughter had known the truth all the time and had experienced no horrible psychological shock, that she became quite flirtatious. Aunt Liz said,

—It's much better to have things out in the open, isn't it?

But oddly enough, after that evening Mr McCullough was never referred to again between mother and daughter. Miranda redoubled her efforts to persuade her still attractive Mama to marry again, and Daddy retired to the world of fantasy where he had become so much at home.

The demands of the baby did at least provide some framework for the day. Miranda was dragged out of the state of semi-consciousness by her cries. It was very hot. She turned over and sat up. The backs of her calves were red and burned, but the rest of her body had been protected by the moving shadow of the oak tree. Her cheek and arm were raw from contact with the mattress. The baby was wet, dirty, smelly, hot, thirsty and uncomfortable. Miranda lugged her upstairs to the bathroom and stripped, wiped, washed, powdered and changed her; then threw away the dirty nappy, washed out the plastic pants, put the sheet, pants and top which were also wet and stinking with the dirty washing to add to Gina's burden and prepared a bottle of juice. It was only eleven o'clock.

Inside the house it was too cold to sit comfortably unless one opened the shutters, and then the flies came in. Outside it was too hot, even in the shade. Miranda opened the front door and pulled one of the heavy wooden chairs and a table towards it so that she could sit with her head and body in the shade and her legs in the sun. It was uncomfortable in her bikini, so she went upstairs again and left the baby in its cot while she changed into a cotton dress.

Settled in the Tudor Monarch chair she gave the baby her bottle while trying to read a novel lying open on the table beside her. The trouble was if she held baby and bottle with one hand and used the other to manipulate her book she got an ache in the bottle-supporting wrist, and if she used one hand for infant and one for bottle the pages of the book turned slowly according to their own whim or the faint breeze that drifted in through the open door. She stared out at the oak tree and the terrace and the olive trees beyond. Occasionally Gina or Corrado would pass slowly by on their way to the orchard or the farmyard, turning to smile, but not changing their pace. The idea of going out to lunch as Louis had urged her to do passed with a slow, stately movement across her mind. She mentally went through the process of getting ready, without moving a muscle. By far the easiest and best course seemed to be to let her whole life take place in the mind without ever moving again. Her natural reactions seemed to bypass her body. The path of response between instinct, feeling and action had been severed. She thought that this was a fairly general characteristic among the English. It seemed to be the most arbitrary chance that the cries of her baby produced in her the response of getting up and attending to its needs. She imagined a disaster happening; the house catching fire, the infant swallowing a pebble, or being stung on the mouth by a wasp, her tongue swelling so that she choked. What would she do? As in a nightmare Miranda saw herself, the flames licking round the iron cot, or the child coughing, spluttering and turning blue while she watched in a frenzy of mental activity, but physically paralysed.

Soon after twelve the postman came, and the baby, who had fallen asleep in her mother's lap, woke up. The postman brought a loaf of fresh bread and a telegram from Louis. It said: ARE YOU ALL RIGHT DARLING STOP HAD A GOOD JOURNEY STOP START FILMING 7 AM TOMORROW MORNING STOP KISSES TO MY DAUGHTER ALL LOVE LOUIS.

Miranda smiled and hugged the baby and wrote on the reply paid form that came with it: BOTH FINE. She paused, sitting on the stone bench by the front door, and using it as a support for the telegraph form so that her writing appeared wobbly and uneven, each stroke composed of tiny dots, like an amateur brass rubbing. She looked up at the sky for inspiration.

The sun blazed down, and she screwed up her eyes against it, and pulled the baby's sunhat further down over her nose. She continued: ENJOY THE FILM AND BE GOOD. She meant act well, rather than do not chase other girls, but could not think how to elucidate, so left it and added: WE MISS YOU A LOT BUT NOT TOO MUCH LOVE MIRANDA.

The postman zoomed off, dead centre through the wrought-iron gateway and down the avenue of cypresses. She stayed on the stone bench, flattened white by the sun against a white wall until the baby began to whimper, then decided to give her an early lunch.

In the cool, cavernous darkness of the kitchen she looked through the tins of baby food; *manzo* would be the one, with a few *piselli* on the side, and some *pesce*—what the hell was that? Oh yes, peaches if it wasn't fish, to follow. The *manzo* really tasted of beef . . . Mm . . . much better than Heinz, lucky little so-and-so. The baby stolidly opened and shut her mouth, and worked each mouthful over with her tongue, gums and two teeth.

Miranda stood poised with each spoonful, waiting for the judicious moment to pop it in—trying to achieve the right balance between approaching too soon, to be greeted with tightly closed lips and a glare of fury, and forgetting her loaded spoon, allowing her mind to wander, to be recalled by snuffles, grunts and occasionally piercing yells of frustrated hunger. The main trouble was that the baby took far longer to ingest each mouthful than Miranda did to load the spoon; and though they had on the whole achieved a fairly good rhythm, they still had their moments of tension. Together they got through the beef and half the peas, and finished off the peaches. Then the baby had a drink, and satisfied, started to doze. Her mother took her upstairs to the cot, changed her nappy again, came downstairs, finished off the tuna fish salad, now going hard and brown at the edges, and drank two glasses of wine. She stacked the washing-up with the breakfast things for Gina, who came in the afternoons, and wondered whether to sunbathe or go back to bed. It seemed altogether easier to go to bed.

She dozed for an hour among the rumpled sheets, opening the shutters halfway to let in a little air. When the baby woke up again it was still only half past two. The day seemed already to have lasted for several years. Miranda stared at herself in the mirror when she took the baby into the bathroom. Every hair and pore and wrinkle was unnaturally clear in the direct and reflected white light. She made a grimace of misery and despair, stretching her mouth wide, like a mask of tragedy. Help, help, she mouthed silently, I can't bear it, I shall die, and her thoughts boomed and reverberated round the room like a cannon shot.

What would they have done with the afternoon if Louis had been there? Driven up to Volterra, perhaps, to sit in the café in the square and eat ice cream, and wait for the shops to open; or explored another of the nearby hill towns or taken blankets and cushions out to the fig tree half-way down the hill in the orchard, defying the prickly stubble and the insects. As she tried to imagine him Louis seemed small and remote. She thought of him on the film set, busy, involved, absorbed. Her own life, in contrast, drained away. I no longer exist. I am empty. Uneasiness mounted during the afternoon from her legs to her stomach to her throat. She moved from the terrace to the kitchen to the hall carrying the baby, giving it bottle after bottle of juice to stop its crying, to stop Gina from approaching with sympathetic cluckings. She felt that if anyone came near her she would start to scream, and could easily scream for the rest of her life.

When, after two or three hours of this restless and wretched moving to and fro the heat started to fade, she took off the baby's clothes, and let her sunbathe naked, exposing her poor damp bottom to the air. The change from stifling heat to pleasant warmth was made a little sinister by the sudden lengthening of the shadows. The shadow of the first cypress tree already reached the middle of the terrace. Miranda looked up and saw a young man walking down the cypress alley. She knew from experience that an Italian, seeing an infant naked in the sunshine would immediately accuse her of exposing it to the dangers not only of sunburn, but also of pneumonia and typhus, so hurriedly dressed the child. The young man, who was wearing a blue denim shirt with the sleeves rolled up, tight-fitting white jeans, an ornate belt and white canvas shoes, came through the gate. He paused to look uncertainly about him before seeing Miranda on the terrace, then smoothed his hair with one hand, and walked over towards her. As he came closer she saw that he was very small, several inches shorter than herself, and that he had beautiful, perfectly classical features. He paused on the other side of the low stone wall that divided the gravel drive from the terrace and said, standing with his feet together, and bowing slightly,

—Good afternoon Madame. Is Mister Louis at home?

—No. Miranda shook her head. —He's in London.

The young man did not seem to understand her. He said,

—I come from Rome to see him. He invite me.

—I'm awfully sorry, said Miranda, but he's gone back to London for a week.

The young man didn't move. He had not even glanced at the baby. Miranda thought that she needn't have worried about his attitude to child care.

—You are Madame Hahn?

—Yes, I am actually.

He came down the steps and held out his hand, bowing again.

—I am Oreste Mira. Your husband I meet in Rome. I tell him how beautiful is the Toscana. He come, he bring his beautiful wife and child. He send me a message. I travel by train and bus to visit.

—Oh dear, I am sorry, repeated Miranda shaking his hand which was small, fine-boned, soft-skinned and damp with sweat. He had after all noticed the child.

—Were you working on the same film in Rome?

Oreste made a grimace of world weariness and cynicism.

—I was . . . assisting.

What could she offer this young man in place of Louis, or a part in a film?

—Let me get you some . . . wine, at least. You must be awfully tired after your journey. She went into the house. Oreste, on the terrace, sat down, took out a cigarette and lit it, his hands shaking. He was extremely tired, and also hadn't eaten for two days. Louis's message had been a general invitation on a postcard to a mutual acquaintance, but Oreste had just been thrown out by the girl he had been living with. She was a starlet, and had managed to catch the eye of a producer. Every sign of Oreste had been banished from her flat within an hour, although they had been living together for eighteen months. Oreste had assumed when he met Louis that he was an established actor, possibly on his way to becoming a star. After all here he was, this good-looking young American (tall, certainly with a lot of connections, and a rich English wife) flying over to Rome for a month to work on a film with one of the most prestigious Italian directors. Oreste himself had been studying, living, occasionally working in Rome for over ten years on the fringes of the cinema world without ever getting so big a job. And already now his marvellous Italian features were beginning to look a little ragged. His hair was thinning; there were dark shadows under his eyes and bitter lines at the corners of his mouth. His pride was more involved with his talent than with his looks, so this would not have disturbed him much if he had not realised that beauty was an asset he could ill afford to lose. To him, Miranda, sitting on the terrace in front of her large house casually rented for the summer, foreign, pale and cold, seemed the epitome, the very symbol of the haute bourgeoisie, that world where all the connections were made, and which he had never been able to enter, light years away from his upside down world of sex and intrigue in Rome, where the famous might sleep with you but would never employ you.

Miranda came out carrying a tray on which she had put a bottle of white wine, some ice, two glasses and a packet of biscuits. Oreste was sitting with his elbows on his knees smoking in nervous, rapid puffs. On one wrist he wore a gold chain and identity tag, and on the other a watch with a white leather strap. As soon as he noticed his hostess walking carefully across the gravel he leaped to his feet and took the tray from her. His hands were trembling so much that the glasses chinked together, and she was afraid he was going to drop it. He reminded Miranda of a whippet he was so slender, tense and nervous, and his eyes had something of the same dark luminosity. He put the tray down on the round table (marble and wrought iron, too pretty for the garden, but chipped and old now) and they sat down. The chairs were made of plastic, brilliant red and blue, and were comfortable and ugly and could be bought in the local market. He offered Miranda a cigarette.

—No thanks, I hardly ever smoke.

—Please.

—No, really. She couldn't fail to notice it was the last in the packet. She poured out two glasses of wine, added ice, and pushed one over towards Oreste. As he picked it up he smiled a surprisingly cheerful grin, and bowed again, half getting up from his chair,

—You are very kind.

Miranda smiled back.

—It must have been awfully hot in the bus.

He drank his wine in a series of long, sensuous gulps, leaning his head back and shutting his eyes. His Adam's apple moved rhythmically up and down the line of his throat. Miranda poured him another glass and they exchanged another smile. She sipped her own wine. Her loneliness and uneasiness had disappeared the moment Oreste spoke to her. She was concerned that he had travelled so far (by car it would have taken three hours, but looking more closely at Oreste she noticed the sweat stains on his shirt, the dust on his shoes and jeans, and the fact that he had not shaved for at least a day; he looked as if he had been travelling all night) to see Louis, and missed him. Being a hostess allowed her to be complete again, and she totally forgot her hours of agony. In retrospect the day seemed short and pleasant. She had done exactly what she had intended to do; read a little, sunbathed, looked after her child. She looked back on herself with derision.

They sipped their wine in silence for a few minutes. Oreste seemed to be more relaxed. He shut his eyes again, and leaned back in his chair,

—Is good.

Miranda said to make conversation, —Is Oreste a very common name in Italy?

—Oreste sat up and leaned towards her, frowning, his face seeming suddenly heavier and more masculine.

—My name is the name of a Greek hero. He paused, staring at her, and shook his head slowly, adding with great weight and bitterness—a very unhappy man. I too am a very unhappy man.

Miranda was touched and embarrassed. She turned away and saw that the child had rolled off her mattress and was trying to eat one of the tufts of grass that had pushed its way between the paving stones.

—Stop it, naughty girl! She swooped down and picked her up.

—I ought to be giving the baby her bath now, and putting her to bed.

Oreste nodded, but made no other response. Miranda wondered how he would get back to Rome. She thought that he didn't look prepared for a very long stay anywhere because he had no luggage, not even, so far as she could see, a toothbrush in his shirt pocket.

While she was bathing the baby she looked out of the window and saw him eating the biscuits one after the other. My goodness, he's probably starving. I ought to ask him to stay for dinner. After all, Louis did invite him. In fact I suppose he could stay the night, there's plenty of room. She felt her vagina and nipples contract, first sign of any sexual intention that she was aware of, and said to herself with round-eyed innocence, shut up.

When she brought the baby down again, wrapped in a shawl against the evening freshness, Oreste had finished the biscuits and was smoking his last cigarette. The sky was still a clear blue, and the western sides of the hills golden, but the shadows of the double rows of cypress trees had covered the whole of the terrace. Miranda said,

—Why don't you stay for dinner? I'm sure Louis would want you to.

—You are very kind, said Oreste, turning his head aside and screwing up his features almost as if he wanted to cry.

—Come and sit with me in the kitchen while I feed the baby.

He followed her back into the house, carrying the tray. His apprenticeship in being of service to women had been long and harsh.

As Miranda fed the baby Oreste prowled round the kitchen. He stopped in front of the range, touching the top of it gently with his fingers, and said with his back to her,

—All her life my mother she cook on a stove like this. Now she is old.

A Dickensian image came into Miranda's mind of a strong, smiling woman, smooth black hair pulled back in a bun, sleeves rolled up, white apron, plump muscular arms slapping and pulling dough on a scrubbed wooden table, while behind her numerous savoury smelling saucepans steamed and bubbled on the range and at her feet small children with faces like Oreste's stared and played.

—Do you have many brothers and sisters?

Oreste answered without moving,

—My sister she is married and my brother dies when he was a child.

—Oh, I'm sorry.

His voice took on a fatalistic and bitter tone.

—They are old now, and they are alone. There was a silence, broken only by the baby's rhythmic sucking at her bottle. To cheer him up, Miranda said,

—What shall we have for supper? There's some spaghetti, but I haven't got anything to make sauce with. And there are some escalopes of veal in the fridge. Oreste's lopsided smile as he turned round at last, said quite clearly, this is how you eat, you, the rich and innocent, who know nothing of life. But hunger? youth? friendliness? triumphed and he said out loud,

—I will make you a real Italian spaghetti. Not like you have in London. I have been in London. But simple. He made a gesture of perfection, index finger and thumb describing a circle and the other fingers fanning away to give it weight and balance.

He washed his hands carefully, taking off his watch and identity bracelet, and put a huge pan of water on the stove to boil. He tied a cloth round his waist as an apron, and when Miranda went upstairs to put the baby into her cot she heard him go out into the deepening orange sunset, and talk to Corrado. She heard the words—*amico, Signor Hahn*, and then a burr of conversation in which the only familiar word was *giardino*. She stood on the balcony outside the window of the large drawing room upstairs for a few minutes watching the orange light die out of the sky. There was a patch of kitchen garden over by the orchard where Corrado grew potatoes and onions. She watched Oreste and Corrado walking back from there together, talking familiarly, more easily distinguished by their voices than by their visual presence from the surrounding vegetation. When she came downstairs to the kitchen Oreste had thrown a bunch of leaves onto the scrubbed table, leaves as long as fingers, but wider, fleshy, a dark greyish green, a little like the leaves of primulas. He chopped them intently and skilfully, using a curved, two-handled knife and pushing the chopped leaves into mounds with the hollowed palm of his hand.

—What's that? asked Miranda.

As he glanced up reflected light flashed and winked in his dark eyes as it did off the knife.

—Salvia.

—What a beautiful name. She picked up a leaf and smelled it. Oh I know what it is; it's sage. Memories of sad, stuffed birds. In England we make it into a stuffing that smells of dust.

He formed the herbs into one rough pyramid, turned to the pot of water which was now boiling furiously, and carefully, delicately, bending it with the will of the water, lowered in a fistful of spaghetti. On one of the other gas rings a quarter of a pound of butter slowly melted in a small pan and on the third the veal escalopes, well floured, sizzled slowly.

—I think it will be good that we eat outside, under the moon, said Oreste.

Miranda felt absurdly, childishly grateful. The turning of a meal into a celebration is one of the great gifts, she thought, hurrying between the dining room and terrace with handfuls of cutlery and glass. She and Louis had never thought of eating outside in the evening. This is what living in an Italian villa should be like. She still felt a perfection of innocence within herself, and hoped for many more Roman guests. In a cupboard in the dining room she discovered two old iron candlesticks and some candles, and placed them on the table. The small flames wavered and danced when they were first lit, but the air was still enough for them to burn straight up towards the stars, making the night darker, occasionally bending in a slow and excessively graceful angular movement. Miranda went back into the warm heart of the kitchen. The sage and butter steamed together, melting into one another, and Oreste was draining the spaghetti into a huge earthenware bowl.

IV

Herself at seventeen, staring into the eyes of a boy at a Bible Reading. In her fantasy they meet, exchange a long look, he says: Will you marry me? she says: Yes, and they drift slowly, like clouds, into one mingled body. Dark sloe eyes float in her dreams, black and shining, among the orange wooden benches with initials surreptitiously tattooed into them with ink and pen point.

The clasp of a hand, warm, dry and firm, and the candid gaze. Those were the secret signals, she had read; the signals whereby one human being conveys the offer of love to another. She gave herself to many hands, her own warm, dry and firm, the hands she clasped as often as not limp and soon withdrawn; to many eyes, shifty and uneasy, making excuses to leave the room, or indulging in conversations of polite idiocy, unable to see that there were more important things to be said, or that nothing need be said at all. Bible Readings and Church were the only chances she had to stare into the eyes of young men. If they weren't concerned with love they should at least be concerned with God. There must be some level of sympathy on which they could meet, in human understanding at least, if not in sexual passion. What sort of creatures were these who could switch their thoughts so easily from the great mysteries of life to inane chat about cricket or tennis or the vocal peculiarities of the vicar? I do not want to see your thin neck and chin thrust forward in an effort at self confidence, the pimple at the left corner of your lower lip that will soon be ripe for squeezing. I will stare into your eyes and clasp your hand. Do you not understand? I am offering love. I am offering a soul. I have put on my best dress with the gold buttons, and my amber brooch, given to me by my father. I want to play according to the rules. I know the body is the garment of the soul, you don't have to take one without the other, I am offering both.

Oreste was so used to having women fall into his bed like ripe figs, that it was second nature, part of his social behaviour, to shake the tree. But with Miranda it never occurred to him to regard her as a sexual object. She was the wife of a friend; a mother; she was not in Rome, and he had met her not at a café or restaurant, but in her own house. She fitted one of the few stereotypes he still respected. Part of his mind could not fail to register her hot and melting gaze, her movements that became as supple and voluptuous as spaghetti against his tongue, the fact that though she watched him devour enormous quantities of food she ate nothing herself. He took all this in with his usual mixture of cynicism at the exceedingly simple and venal nature of women, practicality (her husband was not in the house) and pride, and at the same time he discounted it utterly.

After dinner they cleared away the dishes with the minimum of efficiency, leaving a bottle of wine half empty, a corkscrew, ashtray, candlesticks on the table as mute witnesses to their feast, and dishes, plates, forks, piled haphazard in the sink. Desire raged in Miranda's body. Oreste was nothing to her but eyes, lips, tongue, hands, penis. The muscles of his back and the softness of his stomach (under the tight blue denim shirt) made the root of her tongue ache with desire. She imagined the soft and hairy indentation of his navel. She longed to feel, to crush, to swallow, to absorb him. She continued to play the role of thoughtful hostess.

—Do stay the night, Oreste. It's getting late; the last bus will have gone. We have plenty of room. Her conscious will expected her to show Oreste the spare bed, and then retire to her own. He followed her upstairs.

Miranda put out her hand at the top of the stairs to turn on the light but Oreste said,
 —No, wait. He ran back down the wide, vaulted tunnel of stone across the hall, and unbolted with hollow clanging the heavy oak door. Miranda stood poised in the darkness, her heart beating strongly, breathing in oxygen through her mouth, like a runner at the start of a race, with every faculty at its height. Oreste banged the door shut again, and began to climb the stairs, preceded by a faint glow. Like an acolyte he rose, carrying a candlestick with three guttering candles on it, only his face lighted against the blackness of the night. Staring at the curve of his nostrils, the wise and melancholy droop of his eyelid, the free and beautiful line of his jaw and brow a voice in Miranda's layer of consciousness number two said, My God, I could even fall in love. As he approached she turned and led the way across the upper hall which was also the drawing room, feeling her way by the brownish, coarse grained light and moving shadows of the candles, and the conflicting still, pale light of the moon through the open window. Lifting the lid of a heavy wooden chest she took out an armful of sheets, and went into the room next to her own, where the baby usually slept. There were two narrow four-poster beds in this room, placed side by side, but the ornately carved legs made a six-inch gap between the two mattresses. Miranda motioned to Oreste to help her pull them apart, and he put the candlestick down on the dressing table. The legs of the bed screeched as they moved across the tiled floor, and Miranda paused,
 —Hush! Her hand on her mouth. Silence, secrecy, formed an element that must not be destroyed. She took off the old, torn lace cover, unfolded a sheet, and threw it, crisp and clean, across the bed. She squeezed in between the two curved pillars at the bottom of the beds, pulled it taut, and leaned over to

tuck it in. Oreste, unable to resist so clear an invitation, but at the same time more than half expecting Miranda, in her role of hostess and mother, to turn him down, perhaps flirtatiously, but still to turn him down, put his hand on her waist as she stood up. They remained looking at each other for a moment, their faces dramatically lit by the candles, and reflected, small and impersonal, in the mirror. The top of Oreste's head came just above the level of Miranda's chin. His hand on her waist made Miranda feel as if her clothes had melted and run off her skin like water. Her own breath smelled of flowers. As she leaned down towards him Oreste fastened onto her lips with a hungry and contemptuous stab of the head. But as they kissed the warm flood of her desire rolled over and into him so that hardly knowing what he was doing he fumbled at his belt and jeans to release his cock. It was longer than Louis's, and uncircumcised. My tower, my tree, my forest, thought Miranda, thrusting down her pants and catching the life-giving organ between her thighs; she rolled it like a child's piece of plasticine, and sucked his tongue into her mouth in great gulps. They wriggled round the corner of the bed and fell back on it. She kicked one foot free of her pants, and her knees bumped her shoulders as he dived into her, wave after wave of sperm and orgasm hitting, meeting, bursting in a cloud of spray. She rubbed her head from side to side, and laughed silently, imagining Gina and Corrado, the baby, Louis, the priest, the doctor, the whole town of Volterra outside the half-open door; she wished they were there. Her freedom was so great, that pleasure would have been given an extra edge by the presence of other people—not watching, but just about to discover them. To discover her lying back on the bed, her mouth open, her cunt gaping as Oreste withdrew himself and stood up.

He had not even touched her breasts. He slowly tucked his shirt and penis back into his pants, frowning. If she had been coy, if she had been ashamed of her passion, if she had hurriedly covered herself and said: oh, what do you think of me? he would have responded with self-righteous disgust. But he had not been long enough in England. His expectations were Latin and Catholic. Miranda's appetite had barely been whetted. The long years of innocence had finally come up for their reckoning. She stood and started to kiss him again, licking his brows, his eyelids, his lashes, rubbing her breasts and thighs against him as if they had not yet made love at all. Oreste's masculinity could not resist this new challenge. This time they stripped off their clothes, and in the liveliness of their movements found the bed too small.

—Where is your bed? whispered Oreste.

Miranda leapt to her feet and led him into the next room, her fingers on her lips as the door creaked and groaned on its hinges. She tiptoed over to the cot with movements of exaggerated caution, and gestured to Oreste to pick up one end. Naked and hot with anticipation they carried it, heavy and awkward, the iron legs hitting their shins, barely scraping through the narrow doorway. Oreste's erect penis rose diagonally over the edge of the cot, from time to time shedding drops of liquid onto the coverlet of the sleeping infant. Thank God, thought Miranda, I'm no longer breast feeding. She had done so for three months until the birth pill dried up her flow of milk. Her breasts had been as large and round as footballs, and as feeding time approached they squirted milk of their own volition, with every movement she made. Louis had never shown any desire to drink this richest of all gifts, and she fleetingly regretted that she could not offer to Oreste those huge, voluptuous and overflowing tits. She could have competed with any Italian then; but now her breasts seemed shrunken, flat and empty, and erotic sensation had not fully returned to them. Oreste picked up the candlestick, and Miranda pulled the counterpane over the damp and wrinkled sheet on the abandoned bed, and, giggling like schoolchildren, they crept back into her room, carefully shut the door behind them, and threw themselves onto the double bed (*letto matrimoniale*), Miranda on top this time, bumping and grinding with the best. An orgasm or two like that, and then she started to browse down his body, burying her face in his chest, and then his stomach, pursuing with her tongue the long soft hairs that grew anti-clockwise round his navel, nuzzling into the very core, the centre, down to the rumbling intestines; she took his penis, momentarily soft, into her mouth, tasting the mixed flavours of their two bodies; playfully she tried to swallow his testicles, moved on and circled his anus, protected by two goosefleshed cheeks, and soft hairs like the navel.

—No. He pushed her away, and sitting on the edge of the bed impaled her on his body like a bun on a toasting fork, then rolled her over and fucked her good and proper for several minutes. After that they lay side by side, breathing heavily.

Miranda suddenly started to shiver, and pulled the sheets up over them. Oreste playfully kissed her nipple and her cheek, and said,

—You have make love in the bath?

Miranda sat up, arranging the pillows behind her back, and pulling the sheet so that it covered her from the neck down, and shook her head. The first tide of her lust was beginning to recede. She felt as if all sensation had been rubbed and battered from her. Oreste swung his feet over into the pool of shadow that was the red tiled floor. He was relaxed and at home, expecting no surprises. He slipped his shirt over his head, struggling his arms into the sleeves, and tiptoed over to the door. The shirt just covered his bottom, making him look like a caricature of an American cover girl. From the back his head looked oddly flattened above the ears. He opened the door and peered out, as if he too expected crowds of people to be gathered, waiting, then he turned, with an elaborate gesture.

—Wait, and tiptoed out.

Miranda remained on the bed, hunched under her sheet. Drained of his existence as a sexual object, Oreste had become a small, thin man with a few spots on his shoulders, hairy legs beneath his rumpled blue shirt, and clownlike feet that splayed outwards. There was something oriental about the height and flatness of his cheekbones which gave his face a wolfish, stupid look from certain angles. And yet with this man she had been leaping and bouncing on her husband's bed, and would likely continue to do so for the rest of the night. She heard, muted through space and closed doors, water gushing and rattling into the bath.

Oreste crept back into the room, smiling eagerly, his hands full of new candles. She imagined another woman, warm and glowing with sex, pulling her hair forward round her cheeks to make herself look prettier, saying: You look so cute in your little shirt. The soft light hid the skin drawn tight over his cheekbones and the thinning hair, and made his ears look pointed and his eyes rounder. They should curl up together, bathe, eat, drink, talk, sleep in their own warm world, excluding everything outside. She said nothing. Her face was pale and bony. She looked lost, cold, and distant.

He padded over to the bed on his bare feet and put his hand round the nape of her neck, shaking her gently from side to side, as one would do to a puppy or a kitten, looking down at her with quite a different expression. Now he was a man. His jaw and chin, thrust down into his neck, were heavier; the line of his mouth (emphasis on the lower lip, slightly thrust forward, whereas before his eager smile had raised the upper lip high and vulnerable over his teeth) weary, tender and responsible, his eyes full of an understanding beyond cynicism. This was no promiscuous and sophisticated woman, searching for pleasure alone, her sexuality was something simpler and purer. He understood that her relationship with Louis was nothing; a shadow. The child was the product of an immaculate conception. The burden of her ardent sexuality, of her love, was his alone. Miranda still said nothing, but hatred welled up in her. Like an unrepentant heretic with her head on the executioner's block she meekly allowed his hand to rest on her neck. But in her heart she exulted in the fact that he was nothing to her. He was her lover for a night. In the morning she could throw him aside like a used Kleenex. She had a husband, and a life, self-contained and self-sufficient, apart from him.

One of the candles flickered out, and a pungent, pleasant smell of burned cotton drowned in wax drifted across the room.

The other two had only a moment of existence left. Oreste, his expression still heavy and serious, dipped and turned the rounded ends of the smooth, white candles in the flame; wax shone and liquefied, and spluttered into life. He screwed them down into the sockets of the candlestick, and old wax spurted out in slow motion and added to the dripping stalactites. Carrying a candle in one hand to light their way, and grasping Miranda's arm with the other, Oreste led her to the bathroom. The blinds were already drawn, another candle was balanced on top of the lavatory cistern, and water continued to gush into the tub with a noise like a pile of tin trays falling down stairs. Steam billowed out and condensed on the shiny walls, Oreste stretched in luxurious sensual anticipation, spreading his arms as far as they would go, and rolling his head in deep semi-circles from side to side to ease the muscles in his neck. He slipped off his shirt, and perching on the edge of the bath offered Miranda his back.

—Massage me. He pointed to the pads of muscle on either side of the base of his neck—there.

Is this one of the things you have to do? thought Miranda, looking with distaste at his flesh. She touched him with nerveless fingers, still clutching her bedspread round her with one hand.

—Harder, harder. She dug in sharply, viciously, hoping to give pain and not relief. He groaned with pleasure.

—Yes, yes, that is good.

She stopped abruptly. He rolled his head round in a full circle several times and then picked up one of her hands and kissed it. Noticing that she was still wrapped in the bedspread he said,

—You are cold? I will fetch some fire.

The only form of heating in the house was a paraffin stove which Louis had filled one afternoon when there was a thunderstorm. During the winter, they presumed, the inhabitants either moved, or froze. Miranda turned off the bath, feeling raw and exposed in the sudden silence. The idea of making love in the water excited her not at all. For some reason she had regressed emotionally to her schooldays, and she longed for a reassuring phalanx of ignorant girls with whom she could giggle at Oreste's funny foreign ways. He came back carefully carrying the lighted stove, and put it down by the bath. On the side, stuck down with elastoplast, was a note in Louis's handwriting, in capital letters and underlined: *Never carry while lit.* Miranda's army of supporters turned on Louis now and giggled at him, also foreign, fussy, peculiar.

Oreste tested the water with his foot, added some more cold, and then stepped in, gallantly holding his hand out to Miranda, like a courtier leading her onto the ballroom floor for the first stately movements of the minuet. Her adolescent self climbed into the bath with a splash and lay down, awkward, sexless and uninviting. Oreste settled himself on top of her, smiling his boyish smile. He kissed her cheeks and nose and lips, but when she failed to respond, settled down to more serious business. Miranda, her bottom, back and skull, not to mention one sharp protruding vertebra at the top of her spine pressed uncomfortably against the hard enamel, was filled with a mixture of rage and schoolgirl hysteria. Oreste, hitching his thighs and knees carefully into position, reminded her of a batsman at Lord's, adjusting his bat with little swings and taps, and shuffling his feet in front of the wicket. She imagined suddenly wriggling out from underneath, and leaving him floundering in the water.

All the bodily juices which make the entry of one human being into another smooth and easy had dried up, or been washed away by the hard water; her vagina was tightly closed, as if her hymen had suddenly reformed itself intact. Oreste couldn't understand it. He looked at her closed, masklike face for a clue, and struggled to enter her, finger by finger. Suddenly it seemed to him that he did understand. She was becoming a virgin again. She was showing him that all her previous sexual experience had been nothing, and she had only been born as a woman under his hands. Deeply moved, he gave a little sob, burying his face for a moment in the hollow at the base of her throat, which was covered by a film of water, and redoubling his efforts, at last succeeded in thrusting himself into her body.

His bumping and pushing shifted Miranda slightly against the bottom of the bath, like a large rock rolled this way and that on the seabed by the movements of the waves; her pubic hair floated in the current like seaweed. It was cold, in spite of the oil stove. Miranda's breasts, rising above the level of the water, but washed over by the occasional wave, were covered with gooseflesh. Oreste's buttocks rose and fell, and his knees bumped against the side of the bath. His face was set in a grimace of concentration. Miranda ignored any sensations inside her body and looked round the room as well as she could within her limited field of vision. Was it her imagination or was the brownish flickering light of the candles becoming darker and grainier than before? Oreste's shoulder, just in front of her chin, was almost black. She wrinkled up her nose in disgust, then looked down at the water. It too was black. Interrupting Oreste just as he reached the point of orgasm she sat up with a shriek,

—Oh! My God!

Clouds of thick, oily smoke were pouring out of the stove. Oreste too sat up, turning his head from side to side with a pathetic expression of loss and bewilderment. Particles of soot like ashes or black snowflakes wavered through the air to descend gently on their heads and shoulders and the surface of the water. As they watched it was possible to see the pale areas of their flesh slowly darken, spot by spot. The far side of the room was almost invisible. Every flat surface was black, and the smoke continued to billow out. Miranda rubbed at her forearm with one finger, leaving a greasy smear.

—Oh my God, she said again.

Oreste clambered out of the bath, leaving a hollow in the water, and black wave crests momentarily slapping against the sides of the tub. He knelt down in front of the stove, shaking his head. The flame was burning yellow. He twiddled at the knob, but the flame continued to burn yellow until it went out. He said,

—The wick she is old, no good.

Miranda climbed out of the bath too, warily approaching the stove.

—It's not going to explode, is it?

—No, no, she is safe now. They looked at one another, sheepishly, guiltily, confronted with this scene of desolation. The air cleared slowly, leaving its pall of filth and shame over the room and its two shivering inhabitants.

—Jesus H. Christ, said Miranda suddenly, pulling herself together, let's get clean at least.

Her audience had changed. She was no longer acting out her exotic erotic experiences for the benefit of a group of breathless sixteen-year-old girls, but trying to explain and justify herself to spinster schoolmistresses, middle aged and grim. She shook Omo into the bath (from a black packet), scrubbed it round, and ran in clean water.

—Here, she handed Oreste a flannel and a piece of soap, and started to scrub her own skin furiously. Oreste watched this transformation of virgin into Girl Guide in silence. He slowly soaped himself, his expression once more heavy, masculine, thoughtful. He allowed himself to remember nostalgically the games he had played with his starlet. She would have laughed herself into hysterics at this scene, and then they would have made love again, all black and greasy, on the floor. Miranda gave herself a second scrub and a second rinse and washed her hair, and then, groping for a towel, remembered that they too were covered with soot, and ran dripping into the dark and draughty hall to grab a handful from the linen chest. The towels were mostly two foot by four. She wrapped a couple round her body, and one round her head like a turban, and threw the rest to her lover. She did not look at him directly. From time to time exhausted sperm trickled down the inside of her thighs. When she was ready she picked up one of the candles, first wiping it clean with lavatory paper, and walked out of the room, stepping delicately on the cleaner patches of floor, and leaving Oreste to follow as best he could. She went into the room where the baby was sleeping. Oreste followed close behind, a towel wrapped round his waist like a sarong. Miranda turned towards him and whispered coldly,

—Will you help me move the cot back into my room, then you can sleep here? Oreste seized her by the arm and led her into her room. He took the candle from her, set it down on the table, and slapped her hard across the left cheek. He stared at her, his face dark and furious, his hand still raised.

—You are a stupid, ignorant little girl. We are lovers, we will sleep together.

Miranda stared back, anaesthetised by pain and shock, and started to cry silently. The night had lasted too long. It had already lasted for an unnatural length of time; far longer than could be borne.

—Change the sheets.

Oreste sat down on a chair by the dressing table, leaning his elbows on his knees and tapping his fingers together. After a moment he rummaged in Miranda's handbag, took out a packet of cigarettes, and started to smoke. Miranda, no longer an adolescent, but a six-year-old on her first day at boarding school, abandoned by everything familiar, completely at a loss, ignorant of all the rules and patterns of behaviour, with tears running down her face, pulled off the dirty sheet and threw it in a corner, and painfully, slowly, fetched a clean one, put it on, tucked it in and when the bed was all fresh and clean, prepared for a new life, an honest, marital love, said in a choked, resentful voice, not looking at Oreste.

—There.

He came over to the bed, sat down, and pulled her down beside him. Holding her chin he turned her face towards him; he put the cigarette into his mouth, and eyes half closed against the smoke, leaning his head back, he pulled off the turban and smoothed her wet hair back from the white dome of her forehead. He said,

—You are a woman, you must behave like a woman. He gave her the cigarette and she took a drag, wiping the tears from her cheeks and sniffing. It tasted very good. Oreste unwrapped the towels from her body and passed a hand over her breasts and stomach, not caressing, but judging, like a trainer looking at a horse. Then he pushed her down on the bed, adjusted a pillow under the small of her back, laid the cigarette carefully in an ashtray, and fucked her again, thrusting hard and viciously. Miranda lay still, and raised her knees when told, passive, childlike, slavish, sobbing internally with pain and weariness. The rest of her body was incapable of reaction, but her vagina still shuddered and squeezed. When he had finished Oreste pulled himself out of her, wiped them both with a towel, snuffed the candle with his fingers, took a last drag at the cigarette and then stubbed it out, and settled himself down for sleep, with one arm heavily over Miranda's breasts. Miranda lay rigidly awake, her eyes open in the darkness, until Oreste was unconscious, then she slipped out from under his arm, curled up in the foetal position with her back towards him and went to sleep.

In the morning the cries of the child wakened her. She leaped out of bed, pulled up the sheet again, almost covering the other head on the pillow, and put on her white nylon nightdress and dressing gown. With these added layers of protection she began to feel autonomous. The bright morning sunlight, in horizontal stripes decorated at the edges with polka-dot motes of dust was streaming in through the half-closed shutters as it had done on the previous day. She struggled to remember the anguish and despair of solitude, but the gaps in her perception had closed up, and the previous day existed smooth and round, without a flaw or crack between herself the young mother and Corrado looking up from his tomatoes to wave at the child, the slow rhythm of spoon feeding, tuna fish salad, the waving patterns of the oak leaves against the sky, and the smell of sun and dust. Today she picked up the damp and hiccoughing infant and hugged her close, but did not open the shutters. Creeping downstairs barefoot she felt the same exultation in silence and secrecy as the night before, but this time it enclosed mother and child, and her lover was left out. She could not have slept more than four or five hours, but had never felt so intensely awake. Every muscle throbbed gently, and her head was hollow and clear. She washed in the downstairs cloakroom, changed and fed the baby, then carried her through the echoing, churchlike hall, unbarred her castle gates, and peered out into the morning. Corrado and Gina were nowhere to be seen. Miranda took deep breaths of the intoxicating air, and stretched up her face to the sunshine. The sky was a fresh clear blue. Every leaf and stone was doubly outlined, first by the darkness of its contrast to the light, and then by a halo of sunshine; backlit like the heroine of a silent movie. The wrought-iron table with its burden of ashtray, wine bottle and lumps of candlewax shimmered in the perfection of its being. A clanking of pails round the corner suggested that Gina was on her way to feed the hens, and Miranda ran round the corner of the house, her bare feet shrinking from the gravel. She ran past the well, past the car parked on the shady side of the house, and hid in a small, scrubby patch of pinewood. Underfoot layer upon layer of faded brown pine needles felt damp and rough, like sodden rush matting, hiding an occasional rusty and collapsing length of barbed wire fence, or forgotten pile of rubbish. The trees were dusty and brown for half their height, and then a dusty, greyish green.

Miranda squatted on her haunches, staring at the strips of countryside—small, wrinkled hills miles away and below her—through their trunks. Gently patting the baby's back as it lay with its chin hooked over her left shoulder in the after feed position, she imagined jumping into the car, bare feet, transparent nightgown and all, driving off to another town, far away, and staying in a hotel there until Louis came back, leaving Oreste to explain himself and disappear any way he could. Would he go? Or would he lie there, not moving, like a spider in his web, until she returned? Gina's voice could be heard calling the chickens in the farmyard. Guiltily, like a guerrilla darting from tree to tree, Miranda slipped back into the house.

Here she was, back in the kitchen, the child on her hip fed and contented. She made a pot of coffee and buttered some slices of bread, then precariously balancing the tray on one hand, the child tucked under the other arm, she mounted the stairs, her bid for freedom over. She settled the baby with rattle and dummy in her cot, and carried the tray into the bedroom. It was cold after the morning sunshine, and the air smelt sickly and stifling. For a moment the darkness and thin strips of sunlight dazzled her, and she could see nothing. She inched her way over to the bed. Oreste was not there. Miranda's feelings underwent a violent reversal. She was no longer, and of her own free will bringing some breakfast in to her lover and preparing to go on to the next stage of life. She was abject, abandoned, whimpering. She shrank into a heap on the bed. Oh God, oh God, I'm not good enough, he hates me. She lay there for several long minutes and then heard the lavatory flush. The door opened and closed. Oreste padded back into the room. He paused, put his hand on her shoulder and turned her over. He said,

—I thought you were gone.

Her eyes had become accustomed to the twilight now. He was wearing his blue shirt, and looked like a man ready for the morning, tired but friendly, anxious to please. She buried her face against his thigh in exquisite relief. He sat down beside her on the bed and tenderly stroked her face. She felt for his hand and pressed it between her thighs. When he bent to kiss her, his mouth tasting freshly of toothpaste, their tongues lay against one another quivering gently, and their blood pounded powerfully, slowly, like signal drums deep in the forest. She felt her eyes roll with infinite languor up into the darkness of her skull, and her body became so liquid that she could not even tell when Oreste entered her, time neither stopped nor changed but remained forever, motionless in their bed. Decades later she took a breath and let it out so slowly, so slowly, that the air did not even move.

—I love you, I love you, muttered Oreste, and she muttered in return, crossing her fingers, with many mental reservations,

—I love you, I love you.

They went to sleep, and when they woke up the coffee was cold, but Oreste said, you are sweet, and they drank it, and made love again, and went to sleep again. Every time one of them awoke they would turn to the other and the slightest movement would set them diving into each other's flesh as if they had not yet touched. As the squalor of the sheets and the weariness of her muscles increased Miranda felt more and more deeply, with a mixture of relish and disgust, that she had found at last the element which was most truly hers, swamped with the smell and darkness and secret intimacy of sex. Momentarily she was astonished and proud, I'm a very sexy lady, and imagined showing off this accomplishment to, for instance, her mother and Louis: look what I can do. At last she had discovered the secret. All the empty, cold beds of the past thronged into her mind; chilly school dormitories, grey light making an oily gleam on the linoleum floor, allowing no grace to the chipped paint on the iron bedsteads. Hunched figures of other girls, infinitely solitary and distant under their blankets. Every texture rejecting sensation. The floor and the iron bedsteads so cold, so cold to the touch they even smell cold. Every object too old, too much used, too little loved. Unclean. The small rectangle of carpet rejects her feet and the blankets and sheets reject her body; chair, cupboard, chest of drawers, today hers, yesterday and tomorrow someone else's, reject her eyes, and she in turn rejects her slippers, dressing gown, pyjamas. There is no comfort to be found. Life and warmth shrink into the inmost confines of her body where nothing can steal them away. Her own body is the only thing she can be sure of, it at least has never yet deserted her. Sometimes pants, pyjamas, sheets, pillowcases, deeply impregnated with her own smell after a week or so become comforting objects and give back a little of the warmth bestowed on them, but then they are seized by the steely-eyed wardress and new ones, stiff with cleanliness and hatred are forced against her poor numb shivering flesh. Look, come, poor grey bodies, flickering souls, dying in the cold, this is the way to be warm, to be no longer alone. Oh you mean just like that? It's quite easy really, isn't it? Thanks awfully, Miranda. I wish I'd known before. Army upon army of starved nerves to be nourished, bodies to be assuaged, old weary fantasies, lank and unkempt, to be laid. They cling to this other warm, responsive body; texture of flesh, muscle, hair. Liquid solid. Cold warm. Sheets woven, a little rough, wrinkled, crumbs from the bread, impressing their pattern onto flesh again. Darkness itself solid, tangible, breathed in. Speech an unnecessary abrasion.

Like a fish pulled violently out of his pond by a hook in the friendly worm, Gina's voice and a knocking at the door land her floundering and gasping on the hard ground. She stumbles round the room, every passage in her body constricted with terror, looking for her dressing gown. Clutching a garment in front of her, she feels her way over towards the banging, the crying, the apocalypse and opens the door an inch.

The room next door is pale burnt siena and cream in the afternoon light. Gina holds the child, wrapped in a white shawl, in her arms, rocking it and soothing it, her brown cheek pressed against its head. Her expression anxious and kind. She does not fling open the door and scream accusations, there is no malevolence in her eyes. Gentleness, calm and order are in the colours of the room, the pattern of tiles on the floor, worn and smooth, the figure of a woman with a child. They are no longer in Italy, but in Holland, the peace of eternal afternoon lunch cleared away, odours of food slumbering and dissolving in the air, the light milky and diffuse. The child has stopped crying now, and hiccoughs gently to itself, rubbing its face against Gina's arm. The two four-poster beds, dark carved wood, heavy and solid, speak also of bourgeois interiors, of life dreamed away in the fumes of food and wine, the sensuality of the slow, unchanging pattern of days. One is still pulled out from the wall, its cover rumpled from some heated dream.

Gina's lips move. She is saying something that Miranda cannot understand. She repeats one word several times.
—*Medico . . . un medico.*
Violently Miranda shakes her head.

—No, no. My skin must be grey, my hair wild, my eyes absent; I'm a scarecrow, a madwoman. Hamlet with his stockings round his ankles. On the far side of the disarranged bed, beyond the door, is the bathroom. Pompeii petrified under a rain of filth and ashes. Downstairs are the dishes, mute testimony of dinner for two. Oreste has been seen to arrive, and has then disappeared, swallowed up by this pale Englishwoman, who is now sick with digesting him.

—*. . . Oggi non posso . . . bambina . . .*

She puts her hand to her throat and closes her eyes. Yes, I am sick. My life has made me sick. Gina nodded, and holds the baby closer.

—*Io . . . Io.* She strokes the soft, furry scalp with her lips. Miranda says,

—*Domani va bene.*

—*Si.*

Miranda shut the door. Darkness enclosed her. Her eyes were bright. She felt the pupils widen like an animal's. Her world was enlarged, she could move with confidence in her own demesne. Oreste pushed on the dim yellow bedside light, a tiny button on a lamp like a small inverted mushroom, bulb an inch high, parchment shade. The flesh was still on their bones; their faces still recognisably human. He held out his arms and welcomed her back to bed like a schoolboy at a midnight feast when the footsteps have paused outside the door stopping all breath—hands held hearts thumping—and then continued on their way. They clung to each other and rocked to and fro, stifling giggles. They wondered, under their breath, how Gina would account for the sickness of Miranda and the disappearance of Oreste. Miranda lay stretched out, naked, relaxed, sensation reaching to the end of her fingers and toes. She had come into possession of her body at last. The English numbness had left her. Blood flowed through her cheeks. The two bedside tables, narrow wooden cupboards (each containing a commode) topped by small squares of pinkish marble, the bed, dressing table, chest of drawers, the ceiling, the walls covered with their

Madonnas, kneeling Saints, children and dogs were friendly, and agreeable to forming a part of her visual universe. There was nothing that could destroy her in this familiar space.

Her lover, however, was becoming restless. They had eaten nothing all day except for a few pieces of stale bread and cold coffee, and they had run out of cigarettes.

—If you want I go fetch some food, wine.

—No, wait. Please. She felt as if they were the defenders of a besieged city, safe within the confines of their walls, but unable to move freely until night fell.

Love. Sleep. Love.

Towards evening, lying on his back with his hands clasped behind his head, in this old house, beside this woman who was not his wife, Oreste was overcome by deep, sentimental, Mediterranean anguish. The corners of his mouth turned down in a wry grimace. He stared at the ceiling. Miranda slept. He thought of his parents in their crumbling farmhouse by the sea. Half of the land was sand, and the other half marsh, soured, and made stagnant and infertile by the effluent from factories in the neighbouring town. The dunes and lagoons had been the playground of his childhood, stretching away grey and dull, or pale gold and blue, sea and sky reflecting each other infinitely. The farm was the place for long summers. It had been in his father's family for three generations, but no longer a farm after the death of his grandfather, and the building of the factories. A few chickens. Dogs and cats. Year by year it became more derelict. The peasants had all left the land to work in the factories. His father too. Educated, secure, he spent his life in the offices of the Provincial Administration up in the hills. Schools, offices, shops, streets. And in summer the freedom of water, sand and sky.

Oreste had this freedom to himself. His brother had died as an infant, and his sister was five years older, and wanted none of it. His father's life, the life of the family had been secure. His mother had clutched this security round them like a blanket, and could only watch her son's carelessness of it with the same wistful incomprehension as she watched the slow pollution and death of the lagoons, the creeping wilderness which lapped around her home. There was a flaw in the nature of this last, this only son; a fissure, a deep crack, which had seemed in his youth to be the source and well spring of his strength. He aimed too high. He despised the mould that would have supported and strengthened him. He scorned the possibilities open to him, refused the strings that were his to pull, rejected the position, salary, wife, children that could have been his. He was not content with the slow continuation of a family, the patching up of a home. Ten years ago the future had seemed to him as simple and self-evident as truth itself; he would go to Rome and become an actor, and when he was rich he would come home, rebuild the farm and drain the land.

He smiled wryly as he thought of his own innocence. He had seen enough of life now to understand, as Dante, Shakespeare and the Greeks—after one of whose heroes he was named—had understood, that the world was corrupt, and that merit and talent were rarely rewarded. In the bitter realism of his philosophy he felt himself closer to these great men of the past than to the naked, ignorant, struggling, pleading crowd, reaching and yearning hopelessly to be lifted out of the pit and into the light. The pride which had been his impetus and undoing was his salvation as well. He had despised and hated the bourgeoisie in his youth and he still despised and hated them as time narrowed down in front of him. He was still complete. He had gambled and—here he could almost admit that he had lost; in Rome he lived on hope, but here at this moment he could wallow in the unctuous dissolution of regret. A father, immobile in a chair; able to move slightly his head, one side of his face, one arm; paralysed by three strokes. A mother, nearly blind, peering to guide her large and wandering letters onto the page as she writes to her son: *Quattro anni, mio figlio, quattro anni.* Four years since he had been home.

Miranda half woke to see tears running down his cheeks and into his ears, and his face trembling.

—What is it, Oreste? She lifted herself up, leaning on one elbow. He put his hand over his eyes and wept, mouth open, tears staining the pillow. He clutched Miranda like a child, took comfort from her, buried his face in her bosom. But she was a woman and a foreigner, and could not understand what it was for a son to see his father die, and have no son.

V

Mid morning. Ten o'clock. The morning shadows of the cypresses long and crisp. The air already hot. Oreste Mira and Miranda McCullough (nonsense, Miranda Hahn), are sitting in the small green Fiat. Oreste, eyes closed, face and knuckles white, turns on the ignition and stamps on the nearest pedal. The car does not move. Miranda:

—I think that's the brake. The accelerator's the next one along. She eases off the handbrake as Oreste opens his eyes for a moment and shifts his foot. The car jumps like a gored horse, and zeros in on one of the gateposts (iron). Miranda grabs the wheel just in time to aim them through the gate,

—Lift your foot!

He lifts his foot, and the car, bouncing and zigzagging in the rutted driveway shudders to a walking pace. The road is blinding black and white, zebra stripes. Heat drums on the roof of the car. The cypresses enclose them on either side with a straight black wall. On the back seat the baby sleeps. They are on their way to visit Oreste's parents.

They negotiate the rest of the drive at five miles an hour. Oreste sits low down on the small of his back like a racing driver in the cramped bucket seat, which means that in order to see the road at all he has to lean forward so that his nose is almost touching the steering wheel. The car bears down like a juggernaut upon pecking chickens and sunbathing dogs, who lazily cluck or roll out of the way at the last moment. The intensity of Oreste's posture does not change. As they approach the steep incline to the main road, the turn, the two white houses, the little girls and their cats (one has recently given birth to seven kittens) Miranda starts to shift in her seat and glance from side to side. Oreste looks neither to right nor left. The Fiat, still rolling forward with portentous slowness, approaches dangerously close to the group of wide-eyed children; as they come into his field of vision he jerks the wheel to the right and the car slews away and abruptly changes angle as they start down the slope. They gather speed. Miranda, looking wildly round, realises that Oreste is not going to pause or brake—she seizes the handbrake; but the road remains empty. As he feels the car run away with him Oreste instinctively puts his foot down on the accelerator and they shoot across the road towards the ditch on the other side. Miranda can see the facts of speed, ditch, and the mechanical possibilities of the car slowly coalescing in his brain. At the last moment he pulls the wheel down to the left and they swerve half-way across the width of the road, back the way they had come, right themselves, and bucket to a stop on the inside of the blind corner. Oreste goes limp. Miranda pulls on the handbrake and turns off the engine.

—This car is no good.

Miranda lights him a cigarette.

—Why don't you let me drive while the baby is asleep? Oreste shrugs his shoulders, and swallows deep lungfuls of smoke, sucking it in with hollowed cheeks.

—I know only the big cars. He was still trembling. Miranda paused to let a lorry roar by, jumped out, and ran round the other side. Oreste slid over to her vacated seat and she got in behind the wheel. As she turned the ignition, checked the road before and behind, snapped on her directional signal, tested the comfortably familiar pedals with her foot, engaged first gear, and slowly releasing the handbrake, moved off, she felt marvellously calm, benevolent, full of forbearance. Not for an instant had she experienced panic, or acted in a way that might further upset Oreste's precarious control, or undermine his pride.

—Did you ever learn to drive? she asked, as they took their appointed place in the widely strung necklace of moving vehicles.

—I was poor. Oreste rolled his window right down and leaned his elbow out, like the bronzed young drivers of sports cars in movies, so that the wind whipped smoke from his cigarette into Miranda's eyes.

—My family have no money for a thing like that. His jaw and the droop of his lips became heavy as he felt the weight of his family's poverty again.

—You are rich, you cannot understand.

Miranda, revelling (but humbly) in her skill, admitted that she could not.

—I know to drive the car of my cousin Cola. His father is rich. Bourgeois. But he is a good boy. His car is very good. Better than this. Alfa Romeo.

Later he described how he had driven his cousin Cola's Alfa. He often used to stay, in the summer, to escape from Rome, in his uncle's villa near Brindisi. Groups of his cousin's friends, pretty, laughing rich girls with the characters and appetites of bitches (dirty little girls), who spent long afternoons in their bedrooms trying to make themselves look like Kim Novak, and bronzed, simple young men, formed and reformed themselves round him. Even among these materialistic youngsters he had glamour from his association with movie stars, and his ability to quote commentaries to his own moods from Shakespeare and Dante. That he did not know how to drive was never mentioned between the cousins. These rich children had grown up knowing cars as intimately as they knew their own bodies, and they found it as impossible to conceive of a male who did not know how to perform this simple mechanical operation, as of a man who did not know what to do with a girl. Oreste felt the same himself. He saw and imitated the gestures of these boys, younger and less intelligent than himself, rolling down the window of the car when he got in, settling himself low in his seat, leaning his left elbow casually out of the window and steering with his left hand while holding a cigarette in his right. Cola, his cousin, tactful and perceptive in his way, had pointed out, as if he was mentioning the features of one particular car as opposed to another, where the clutch, the gear shift, accelerator and brake were to be found, and sitting beside him Cola changed gear for his cousin, sometimes, without the benefit of Oreste's foot on the clutch. Oreste, however, barely listened to the explanations, feeling in his bones that understanding had nothing to do with the facts.

He managed several times, in his highly sensitive interpretation of the role of driver, to get the beautiful red sports car in motion and direct it along the straight and empty roads, pretty girls at his side relaxed and laughing, chiffon headscarves blowing in the wind, until one day, driving alone, he found himself suddenly hurtling down the long main street of a small town, low white houses shuttered and blank in the midday heat giving him a horribly increased sense of his own speed. The street was narrow, white and still. For an eternity he hurtled down it, his foot paralysed on the accelerator. For an eternity he watched the wide, tan and chrome American car approach like a monstrously distorted mirror image of himself. Several instants before the crash he was able to watch the mouths and gesticulations of the elderly couple in the other car as it screamed to a stop. After the crash was silence. He could make no explanation (though he ranted and raved as he knew one should in such circumstances at the monstrous size of this American invader). The two cars, clasped in an unseemly kiss, took up the whole width of the street. There was barely room for a pedestrian to squeeze through on either side. From the beige and black crowd which had instantly materialised, someone telephoned for the police, and Cola's father. The American couple were unharmed, and Oreste himself was miraculously unharmed; but Cola's father, though he managed to save his nephew from prosecution, and bought his son a new car, forbade Oreste to drive it, and Oreste, feeling his welcome cool, left his uncle's house.

Early morning. The light still pale, misty, flat. Olive trees, terrace, dark bulk of cypresses, distant hills all had the same density, and had been rearranged on a flat surface, like a Japanese painting. The young man crept out into the cool, dewy air, across crunching gravel, the smooth stones of the terrace, down through the orchard ducking his head under black knobbed branches, small fruit and leaves slowly recreating their daytime forms, to the fields. Green shoots of autumn wheat pushed their way up between calf-high stubble; canvas shoes slipped and twisted on the uneven ground. Fifty yards above the café (which was only open on Sunday evenings; it materialised out of a small concrete shed by the bus stop, and transformed the dull weekday corner with coloured lights, a table, a few chairs, men shaved and relaxed, and women in their Sunday dresses, talking and laughing) the young man scrambled up onto the main road, panting with exertion. He paused for a moment, looked up towards Volterra, then down to the bus stop, where two old women, black scarves round their heads, baskets on their arms, were waiting quietly. He brushed some pieces of straw off his jeans, tucked in his shirt, and sat down on a small white rounded fence post.

—One of the foreigners from the *fattoria*.
 —*Si*.
 —Funny.
 —What?
 —That he should walk through the fields, to wait for a bus. The young man tried to clean some of the earth out of his nails, scraping with the nails of the other hand. He folded his arms and rubbed them to keep warm, wishing he had cigarettes, watching the pale greens and greys turn to high definition blue and gold.
 —His shoes are wet.

—His shirt is too big.
—The trousers too.
—They don't know how to cut good shirts.

The tempo of the day increased, and the first morning bus came rocketing down the hill from Volterra. He waited while it disgorged a few black-clad ladies, and picked up the two who had been waiting, then, clanking, hissing, smelling pleasantly pungent like an old railway engine it rattled on its way. Now, decently, respectably, openly for all who cared to watch, Oreste could walk back to the house.

Miranda Hahn washed out her lover's blue denim shirt in the kitchen sink, and scrubbed at his jeans with a nailbrush and detergent. In the dim light she was unable to see if she was doing as well as Gina with her bar of soap, scrubbing brush and washboard, on the stones by the well. As she scrubbed and rinsed satisfying fantasies burgeoned of a life marvellously circumscribed by its physical content. A house small enough to fit its occupants, creating no unnecessary problems of categorisation. Shall we use this room for dining, or watching television, or reading? If there's only one room, no problem. Simple tasks. She imagined inhaling the savoury odour of steam rising from drying cotton; the slap of the iron, smoothness left behind, cause and effect. If only (and for the first time the possibility did not seem to be entirely out of reach) I could lose myself, bury my self-conscious self in a life like that, where everything is what it appears to be, and I too am what I appear to be. A life was something seen from the outside, solid and complete in itself.

When the clothes were washed she hung them by the range to dry, and started to cook dinner. Oreste sat at the table in Louis's shirt, and watched while she fried some eggs. His mood had mellowed into sentimental nostalgia. His voice shook as he said,
—I love that you cook for me.

Sodden but clean, his clothes hung over the back of a chair. His patient mother, and Immacolata, the simple-minded maid-servant, staying up late and rising early would always have his clothes washed and pressed for him when he awoke at noon, as is the privilege of the prodigal son; folded on the bedside chair, with a few notes slipped into the pocket of his shirt, carefully, lovingly hoarded from his father's meagre pension.

Miranda served the eggs and bread, and longed for more trials of her female strength. They held hands across the table as they ate. Pressing Miranda's hand Oreste said,

—Why we not go and see my mother, and my father before he die? He stared at her anxiously across the pale colours of the table and the food. Creamy brown, the wooden table, white china, eggs yellow and white, butter yellow, wine greenish gold. Beneath the long, delicate curve of the lids, his eyes were round and black. Cheeks hollow, dark with a two-day stubble. Thin hair, standing on end. Louis's shirt, red and white check, was too big for him. So were the jeans. Why should she go to see his parents? He nervously squeezed and pulped her fingers. He was not her husband. And yet here they sat, bound to one another (surely) by ties of love.

—We go in your car.

After all why shouldn't she go to see his parents? What was so wrong about a trip by car to visit friends. She imagined describing the trip to Louis, leaving out, perhaps, the fact that she and Oreste were lovers.

—What about the baby?

—Gina will look after him.

—It's a girl. Miranda reached for an image of motherhood. The only one she could find had been formed from a ragbag of articles and advice columns in women's magazines, occasional remarks let fall by her mother, her sense of abandonment as a child. It is bad to leave your baby.

—No, we'd have to take her with us.

Oreste shrugged. If not Gina, Immacolata could care for the child. He saw already the triumphant arrival, the astonishment, the cries of greeting, the tears, the embraces. Miranda watched herself in astonishment. A Girl Guide voice, all common sense, said in her ear: My dear girl, you're out of your bloody mind. You can't go traipsing off with your baby and your lover. It's . . . You . . . You simply can't do it. The Girl Guide shook her head, speechless.

Miranda started to plan. She would have to take Milton for disinfecting the bottles, disposable nappies, a plastic bag for dirty clothes. Louis wouldn't be back for at least a week.

Oreste's eyes filled with tears again.
 —My father's life is over. He has nothing. All his life he work for the Government. He work, he struggle to get money for his family. There come the Fascistos, the war, the factories . . .

Miranda mentally checked through the clothes she would take for herself and the baby. The baby could travel in the back seat in its carrycot, the transporter wheels folded up and stored on the roof with the suitcase. Anything was possible with a child. You just had to be organised.

—The life of a man is hard. He struggled all his life for what? For fame? for money? Is nothing. Is shit. Oreste released Miranda's hand to take a draught of wine, and then reached for it again.
 —The only thing, it is love. That I have understood. Love. The word flew round the room like a soap bubble, or Tinkerbell imprisoned. LOVE? Love? love? Miranda turned her head, faintly interested, to follow its flight. Love? It burst in a delicate shining spray, and vanished.

The baby woke with a gulp and a yell. Miranda automatically slowed down.
 —She must be thirsty, I'll have to give her a bottle.
 Oreste grunted. —Mmm.

They had swooped down in large and luxuriant curves to the plain on the far side of Volterra. Miranda stopped the car and got out. As the noise of the engine ceased there was a faint buzzing in the middle ear as the air cleared, and the countryside noises moved gently in to fill the vacuum. The faint hum of animate and inanimate life stretching away into the distance. She sat on a pile of neatly broken stones by the roadside with the baby on her knees, and a red and yellow plastic bag containing bottles of juice, warm milk in special containers, spoon, bibs, jars of food, tissues, nappies, plastic pants by her side. The cries of the baby, the slam of the car door, Oreste's voice, fell plummily into the soft haze of indistinguishable sounds. The infant gulped hungrily at her bottle of orange juice; avid, determined, exact. This is what I want, and I've got it, and ain't nobody going to take it away. Miranda sat prim, straightbacked, knees together, a faint smile of satisfaction on her face. The bottle of juice had been ready when needed, as planned. She was coping. She was in control of the situation. She could do what she wanted.

When she tried to put the baby back into the carrycot there were yells and screams and struggles.

—Oh dear, I think I'll have to hold her on my lap. Do you think you could drive? How cool she was. Miranda congratulated herself. The only way to give people confidence was to trust them.

—I no like this car. But I will drive.

Miranda sat in the front seat beside Oreste, the baby safe in the curve of her arm, pointing out again, casually, the brake, the accelerator, the clutch. They drove very fast, in the middle of the road, just like all the other small Fiats. As soon as the baby was quiet, Miranda put her in the back seat and took the wheel again.

With a sudden shock they left the quiet empty roads of the countryside, and found themselves in civilisation. Their journey ceased to be particular; they were swept into a higher gear. Confronted by an endless row of cars overtaking one another, their motives began to disappear. Driving off on an impulse to see aged parents, in no desperate hurry, became frivolous. Sentiment, unless it was a sentimental attachment to a particular brand of spaghetti, had no meaning in this Italy. They stopped to buy cigarettes. Miranda watched Oreste exchange a few sentences with the boy at the kiosk. They seemed to enter with no difficulty into a masculine, fraternal relationship. Oreste's heavy expression lightened. The two men laughed. They were in a service area which sold petrol, and Miranda suddenly realised that the tank was almost empty. She looked in the glove compartment for petrol coupons. There they were, exactly as Louis had told her. It was too easy. She drove up to a pump and handed some coupons to the attendant.

—*Benzina, per favore.*

The attendant was dark, with thick black eyebrows, quick movements and blue overalls. Oreste turned from his purchase and looked around for the car. As he walked over to it he tapped out a cigarette with a gesture that said: it is enough in itself to be a man, to smoke a cigarette, to be among men. He stood watching the attendant fill the car with petrol. The litres and lire ticked up. Oreste held out the packet, and the man laughed, and jerked his head towards the 'No Smoking' sign. Oreste made a comment, and they both laughed again. Miranda noticed that her hands and lips were trembling, and yet she had thought that she was enjoying this masculine freemasonry. That she was included. When the attendant handed her some coupons back she tried a flirtatious smile, but it died, stiffly. The anonymous cafeteria suddenly seemed like a haven, but already Oreste was climbing into the car and signalling his readiness to move.

Before they left the house, cursing, sweating, banging their shins, they had struggled to move the two single beds into her room, and the double bed out into the hall, and then into the bedroom next door.

—I do not want that you sleep with that man. Now the thought of Louis slipped in and out of her mind like an unattainable image of home. Rescue me.

—I can't drive on this road. I must go into the country.

Oreste said, —This is the way. When they came to a turning Miranda swerved down it and stopped to look at the map.

—We can go this way, she said, pointing out a wiggly green road. Oreste shrugged his shoulders and turned his head away.

He became more sullen and abstracted as the day progressed. He made no move to proffer help when Miranda suggested lunch. Like a good tourist she preferred picnics to restaurants, and this was after all a pleasure trip through unknown country. She bought bread, cheese, wine and fruit, and chose a patch of shade under a bridge by a stream as the place to eat it. Oreste found this habit unnecessary and bizarre, but made no protest. He smoked and ate in silence, lying supported on one elbow, thighs, feet and torso in an attitude of extreme relaxation like the statue of an Etruscan enthroned on top of his own sarcophagus. Miranda served him and fed the baby, fetching and carrying from the car, her voice nervously tinkling on, like the noise of the brown and golden waters of the stream, falling endlessly over rocks and into pools beneath the small, sturdy single arch of the Roman bridge. After some time Oreste said,

—When you chatter like that you sound like a stupid woman.

Tears came into Miranda's eyes. How could she be a stupid woman? She had been talking of things which Oreste himself knew nothing about, or else he would surely have discussed them with her. Bending her head she wiped her nose and eyes on the baby's short-sleeved stretchy blue and white terrycloth rompers. She hadn't yet managed to eat anything herself. She took a mouthful of bread and cheese and a sip of wine, but could scarcely think what to do with it next. The idea of swallowing this dry lump made her eyes fill with tears again. She made another sandwich for Oreste, shook a few tears onto it, and wiped her eyes by lifting a curtain of hair up on one shoulder, and rubbing her face in it. She offered him the sandwich with an expression of extreme pathos and humility. Lying in the most comfortable patch of shade he had on his heaviest and most lowering expression of masculinity—a masculinity which implied higher, wider and more important concerns with the world than she as a woman could possibly understand. He shook his head without looking at her. Clearly at the moment she was not even much good as a woman. Sitting marooned on her island of stone, surrounded by water and disapproval (nothing so positive as contempt), she felt herself incredibly light and unconvincing. The stone bridge, against part of which she was leaning her back, and which had continued to exist and perform its useful function in the same solid and undemonstrative way for two thousand years; the water, minding its own business, incidentally cooling their wine, gay, busy, repetitive and quite certain of its own value; the round, smooth, old, white pebbles were what they were, no existential problems, no role confusion there. Miranda was less and less. She withdrew from herself to a point some twenty feet nearer the blazing white centre of the blue sky, and the few skimpy pine trees on the hill above the road. She looked down at this empty, shrill and hysterical figure, sitting awkwardly cross-legged (legs paler than the stones, sharp shins, bumpy knees, sagging thighs. In gym classes at school, ten years ago, she had sat on the wooden floor in her blue serge knickers condemned, she knew, to a life of solitary despair because of those same purple, bumpy knees, and those thighs, so surprisingly fleshy on her skinny legs, which spread out in a great cushion when she sat down) in her red linen dress with white stitching.

Elaborate fantasies of humiliation and contrition caused her to lower her head until she was folded over the child on her lap like a penitent over her rosary. She grovelled in the water, stripped off her clothes, naked, bleeding, half drowned, coughing, choking, retching, trying to dig herself into the fine, soft river sand as if she was a worm. Oh, to go down, down, to vanish, to disappear—but she could not. She wriggled over, blindly testing with her worm's head to the huge, heavy, immoveable feet of the masculine statue, butted and pushed blindly against them, rubbing her body against their yellow callouses, tearing her face on those nails as hard as stone, creeping up a trouser leg, burying herself in a hairy forest, sinking into a navel—but there, exposed, with a gasp and soundless shriek of horror was a bare white bum and cringing goosefleshed legs—oh knocking knees, tightening sphincter, flaccid flesh—exposed, exposed, the worm's head had vanished, headless and bodiless flailed and trembled this obscene white tail.

Oreste flicked his cigarette end away and stood up.

—We go now.

He waited while Miranda, creeping, she felt like an old bent woman, her head on a level with her knees (below, below) picked up the picnic things, and the baby's things, and stowed them away, and crept into the car. In silence, they started on their way again.

The last hill town before the Adriatic was compact and beautiful. After some searching Oreste Mira and Miranda Hahn found a hotel whose third floor and their room was on a level with the main road (through a Renaissance gateway) into the town. The tiny road which tunnelled downhill past the entrance to the hotel, and the façade of the building, were old; but inside, the hotel was modern, curiously light, curiously empty. When they arrived, there was no one at the reception desk. The open, rectangular box of faintly transparent yellow plastic which formed the reception desk, the key rack, telephone, switchboard, all plastic, formica or pale teak appeared so insubstantial that Miranda expected with every blink that when she opened her eyes again all would have melted and vanished away, and what would be in its place—Renaissance palace? rat-filled tenement?

A middle-aged man, smooth skinned and heavy lidded with thick black eyebrows and a dark suit appeared, and after flicking expressionlessly through the pages of his register for several minutes said he had one room, number fifty-eight. He gave them their registration forms to fill in, and took the woman's passport. She filled in her form with a bright and casual expression. They sat on a spongeable plastic sofa, also pale yellow, and wrote on a black plastic table. The floor was made of thick, sound-proof white tiles. There was no natural sound. Voices and footsteps had the resonance taken out of them. The scratch of biro on paper was pleasantly loud and comforting. The young man paused, his pen making abortive sweeps and passes over the line where he was required to write his name, like a cat turning in circles to prepare the place where she is going to sleep, and finally wrote in a dash of illegible flourishes.

Several minutes after the manager had rung his bell a pretty maid appeared. She was wearing a black dress, and starched white cap and apron. Her hair was black, and there was one white lock in it, in the centre of her forehead which made her look like Circe. The manager handed her a key, and she smiled, picked up the suitcases of the young couple, led them to the lift (pale green plastic panels that gave slightly to the touch) and along an empty, pale, clean, shining, light, noiseless corridor to room No. 58.

Why was Oreste Mira, in the country of his birth, in the town where he had spent his childhood, less than fifty kilometres from the home of his parents, spending the night in an hotel? Why had he acquiesced when the English tourist, the pale anonymous despised tourist, ignorant of everything that makes a man and a place, and binds them together, why had he acquiesced with a silent shrug when she suggested staying in an hotel?

There were twin beds, and furniture carved out of some putty-like substance that might once have been wood. The maid went to fetch a cot. The English girl put her child down on a bed, opened the window and leaned right out onto the harsh stone ledge, breathing in the sulphurous stink and noise of the cars whose chassis were on a level with her nose ten yards away.

The young man sat on the edge of one bed with his elbows on his knees, nervously tapping a cigarette between his fingers, stained with nicotine like walnut juice. An inch of delicate, hairy wrist showed beneath the sleeves of his blue shirt. When Miranda had come down that morning, many hills and valleys ago, his clothes had gone from the chair by the range. They reappeared after breakfast, folded and ironed on the hall table—by Gina? in her own house (small, with a modern kitchen, a large fridge, an electric stove and its own quota of formica)?

Suddenly he got up. The woman, pale, anxious, uneasy, was unpacking clothes and infantile impedimenta. He said,
—I go now to see a friend.
The young woman spun round. —Don't leave me alone. She dropped a packet of nappies and ran towards him.
—Don't leave me alone here. He put his arms round her and patted her shoulder, gazing absently out of the window,
—When I am a boy this town is mine. It is war. I know everyone. I take messages, I ask questions. All the boys of my school, we are not pupils, we are spies. Fighters. *La Resistenza*. He looked round the room. Now the bad and the good are the same. Who can tell any more?

Up the Corso Garibaldi, towards the Piazza della Repubblica, in search of the heroic past. A cool summer evening possesses the town. Shops are still open, caverns of light carved out of great cliffs. The buildings are solid, monolithic; generations of people have tunnelled into them for living space. Only nature is capable of such warrens inside such solidity. Further up the hill in the Ducal Palace, space has been tailored to the proportion of man, and then contained with stone. There, in titanic and insupportable struggle men had lifted up their heads to see what they were, and had built what they needed. But ease and clarity are misleading. Who wants ease and clarity? Proportion to fit his size, light sufficient for his eyes? Back, back, back, into confusion, fantasy and darkness.

Down a narrow, steep, unlighted alley, soft slap of rubber shoes on uneven paving stones, a green neon cross: a *Farmacia*. The counter is carved dark wood; there are cupboards panelled in glass with gothic frames, huge curved glass jars containing substances necessary to the well-being of the citizenry.

—*Leone, come va?* White coated, plump, bespectacled, Leone who at twelve roamed the hills in the bitter winter of '43-'44 bringing food to Allied prisoners escaped and in hiding, guiding them to the local units of the *Resistenza*, warning of the movements of the Germans and the Fascists, given a superhuman, godlike quality, Mercury with wings on his heels, by youth, innocence, agility, opportunity. A chin and several fingers are raised in a Papal gesture of greeting. Leone Bevilacqua serves a middle-aged insurance assessor on his way home from the office with bismuth, and then embraces his old friend Oreste Mira, his old friend, closer than a brother, friend of the streets, the classroom, the mountains, of long races across the shifting sand dunes to the shallow and murky sea.

Enlaced like lovers, the old friends walked slowly up the Via Raffaello to the Piazzale di Roma, the highest point of the hill and the town, talking in desultory bursts, because it is after all several years since they have met, and they have little enough to say to one another. But of their affection and loyalty, each towards the other, they can always be certain. They leaned over the balustrade, arms crossed on the parapet, facing east towards the sea. The mountains and the distant blur of the coast change slowly in their relation to one another as the twilight deepens and darkness fills in the valleys and flattens the hills. Eyes straining to cling to the last familiar outline are surprised by one light, then another, forming a new pattern. Do they try to trace with their eyes through the dimness the valleys and flanks of hills where the partisans' exploits reverberated with heroism to their twelve-year-old ears? Do they try to make out the lights of the farmhouse where the Englishman had hidden for two months, who came back after the war to marry Leone's sister Graziella, and take her off with him to Canada? Leone Bevilacqua and Oreste Mira turn away from the indistinguishable sea and sky and land, and walk slowly down another angle of the hill, past the place where five partisans, one of them the uncle of their classmate Giambattista Bono, who had been treated with reverence and respect after this event, until it had become a habit, and who was now a lawyer, had been shot, until they come to the Piazza Duca Federico.

The café in the Piazza Duca Federico stretched across one entire side of the square, at least the chairs and tables belonging to and served by the café did. In fact there were not one but two cafés; one a dark and welcoming cave with upholstered benches covered with tartan cloth, and waiters making quick and purposeful movements like ballroom dancers as they dispensed steaks to tourists. The other was light and bright, with a long, covered counter for displaying pastries, and a few tables with pale green formica tops. At these tables, sipping grenadine or Coca-Cola, groups of plump or gangling girls were always sitting, friends of the black-eyed girls behind the counter. There were no trees in the Piazza Duca Federico, and no cars either, because the last few yards of the Via Vittorio Veneto were so steep that they had been carved into steps, and a car park built below the Ducal Palace, where during the day coaches slumbered like camels waiting for the evening caravan. So the Piazza Duca Federico had a pleasant atmosphere, with people strolling around it arm in arm, pretty girls in pairs, and parents relaxed after dinner, dressed in clean clothes, wheeling their infants, also washed, combed and prettily dressed, staring round them with wide eyes, their little boots unsullied by the ground. On the steps of the cathedral, opposite the palace, groups of young men gathered, their voices sounding intimate and close. The darkness was city darkness, that is—not darkness at all, but a circle of light in which people can see each other and be seen, clinging together, protecting one another from fear and solitude, and the huge dark emptiness of space.

VI

The two friends sat and talked for an hour. Then Leone went home to eat with his wife and three daughters. The hotel and the Englishwoman waited. Oreste sat on in the café, playing with an empty cigarette packet. Held gently between thumb and forefinger the packet was placed upright on the table. The fingers slid down, lifted it up by the bottom corner, it swung round so that the bottom corner was now the top, and the movement was repeated. Had he forgotten them? Was he wondering why, to this familiar town he had brought this strange woman? He sat for half an hour, and then walked back, down the Via Vittorio Veneto, across the Piazza della Repubblica. Slowly, very slowly. More slowly than necessary. The hotel was still empty, still silent. Far away at the end of a corridor two men in dark suits came out of a room. He opened the door of number 58. It was dark. There was no sound. He pressed the light switch. Miranda was sitting up on one bed, leaning against the pillow, her feet up and the child on her lap. She stared straight in front of her, and did not turn her head immediately towards the door. The child was asleep. Now, under the window, to the right of the washbasin, was a cot. On the washbasin were dirty spoons, bib, bottle, and half-eaten jars of food. Otherwise the room was unchanged. The wardrobe, straight ahead and sideways to Oreste as he opened the door, was still empty. The suitcase still full.

—You are not ready? he said. Now we go out.

Miranda turned round with a start and a bright smile. She got up carefully, balancing the sleeping child. I won't be a minute. I was just putting the baby to sleep. The baby was placed in her cot, and a pink woollen blanket tucked round. —The maid said she would listen for her; at least that's what I think she said.

—I go ask.

Miranda hummed under her breath as she pulled clothes out of her suitcase. Here was a lilac cotton dress, trimmed with white braid, with a matching headscarf. She tied the headscarf on, looked in the mirror, took it off and put it back in her bag.

Oreste came back. —She will watch.

The streets were dark now, empty and silent. This was no great metropolis, but a provincial town. Shops were closed. Restaurants empty, or hidden away in the labyrinthine bowels of the buildings. Miranda's high heels clacked awkwardly on the cobbles. She was lagging behind Oreste. He walked with his head slouched forward, shoulders hunched, and hands deep in his pockets. A small, fat, middle-aged couple stared at them as they passed. The woman was wearing a white suit with a black shawl over her shoulders, and her hand was laid neatly on her husband's arm. Miranda stopped abruptly by a lighted shop window. She put on her cardigan, doing up all the buttons, and a prim, cold expression. Out of the darkness and into the light. Up the steps and into the Piazza Duca Federico.

The piazza was more animated than it had been an hour ago. All the café tables were full. Oreste threaded his way to a table in the second row, outside the pasticceria. Miranda followed meekly. Three men were sitting there, Leone Bevilacqua, his brother Aldo, and Mario Piombelli. Mario was tall and gaunt, with greying hair cut short, and Aldo had smooth olive flesh like his brother, and dark hair. They all wore grey suits and were drinking cups of coffee. Many smiles, much shaking of hands and arms thrown around shoulders. Oreste's teeth were stained with nicotine. Leone turned to Miranda and introduced himself, and Aldo and Mario shook hands politely. Miranda smiled, but said nothing. Oreste threw himself down in a chair. Leone ordered two more cups of coffee and pulled up a chair for the young woman, the foreigner, the visitor whose status had not yet been defined.

Scraping of iron on stone. Hum of conversation, light and sharp in tone, with a bouncing rhythm swooping down and jumping up again with a healthy bang and overspill of white light like the soft pencil of light describing a cardiograph. One of the daughters of the owner, plump cheeks, black eyes, freshly washed hair, shy smile, brought the coffee. Oreste, no longer fastidious as he had been when he first arrived at the villa outside Volterra, lounged unshaven in his chair. The others in their dark suits, tieless, shirt collars open at the necks, looked relaxed but respectable. No one mentioned food. Those who had eaten were secure in the fullness of their bellies. Oreste showed no signs of feeling hunger. Miranda was not hungry herself, but longed for the ritual of a meal to create some order in the day, to justify her place at the table.

Outlines of sense detached themselves from the conversation. They were talking about the war. The foreign young woman took a deep breath and turned to Leone.

—Once I read a book about the war in Italy by an Englishman, an escaped prisoner.

Leone turned towards her, cradling his coffee cup in his hands, one elbow on the table and one on the back of his chair.

—There were many English hiding in the hills. We are good friends with many of them. You know Major MacKay? He has a red moustache, and red hair. You know him?

Miranda shook her head. —This other Englishman described how he was walking towards a river one day, to cross on the ferry, and he passed a peasant woman. They said *buon giorno*, and walked on, and then the woman turned round and called out to him, 'Oh young man, if you are one of those I would not cross. There's a German patrol waiting on the other side.' Miranda's hands were sweating and her heart drumming anxiously as he told this story.

—Yes, said Leone, who had been brought up on stories more dramatic than that, —the peasants they help a lot the Allies. The English they like especially.

—But just think, said Miranda, leaning closer, if that woman hadn't turned round and called out to him he would have been killed.

—Perhaps she thought at first he was a peasant.

—But supposing that when she had that second thought she had just shrugged her shoulders and said to herself, 'Oh well, it's nothing to do with me'? I'm afraid that's what I should have done.

—Of course not. Leone patted her hand with a slight frown. You would have been afraid, but you would have acted bravely.

—If she hadn't been there at all then it would have been the same as if she hadn't called out, then she couldn't have saved him. Miranda paused. Oreste was looking at her with a dark expression. Her voice had become shrill. Leone Bevilacqua said to the unknown woman who was playing a part, how large? and what? in the life of his friend,

—We have been good friends with Oreste since we were a child. The ones you have known since you were a child, those you always love.

—It is nice to have good friends, said Miranda.

The conversation rose and soared above her. She carefully placed two lumps of sugar in her coffee, stirred, then lifted her cup and drank in small sips, leaning her head back to swallow. The cup was so small that after three swallows it was empty. Composing her features to bright attention, she placed the cup carefully in the saucer without too noticeable a chink of china, and inclined herself again to listen if not participate. The figures on the far side of the square moved dimly among pools of soft light and shadow. Those sitting at the tables near her were bright and clearly outlined. For holiday evenings sitting in cafés a light woollen shawl is a pretty alternative to the Englishwoman's ubiquitous cardigan. The young woman sat silent with tears running down her cheeks. In a mauve dress trimmed with white braid, with a headscarf to match, the young woman sat silent, tears running down her cheeks and splashing onto her hands. Have fun on holiday. Perfect for sightseeing. For sitting in cafés in the evenings a light shawl is a pretty alternative to the Englishwoman's ubiquitous cardigan.

When, later on, Mario said *buona sera*, and went home, and the square began to empty, Oreste came to sit beside Miranda, and leaning close to her muttered,

—Give me your money. Miranda obediently opened her bag and handed him all she could find, not surreptitiously, under the table, but openly, so that everyone could see, hoping that his humiliation was greater than hers. Oreste bought cigarettes and insisted on paying for all the coffees. There was not very much money left. A few travellers cheques. Most of them were in Louis's name. What do you need money for when you go to stay with someone's parents, a family, in an old family house? (guest bedrooms with a water carafe and books on the table by the bed, and a bunch of flowers in a china mug).

Walking back through the dark, empty, echoing streets.

—What shall I do if you leave me alone, with no money?

Oreste, shoulders slouched, hands in pockets. —You are a bourgeois. You should not care about money. If you love me, everything we have is together.

—I suppose I should have to go to the Consul. There must be a Consul somewhere near. What should I say? I'd look such a fool. I can see myself sitting there silently, shaking my head, not answering his questions. Just silently sitting and shaking my head.

She glanced at Oreste who was walking slightly in front, and had not turned his head towards her. He would be sitting at his desk, urbane, and slightly impatient, thinking, 'Oh Lord, I'm so sick of these repressed Englishwomen who come to Italy looking for a lover and then get taken for all they've got. What in hell's name do they expect?'

Oreste seized her arm and swung her round to face him, his other hand raised in a threatening gesture. —Be quiet. I do not like you speak like that. You must have respect.

Miranda put on a naughty little girl face and said, —I'm only imagining the Consul. Inside her head she was jumping up and down and yelling, Yah! Yah! Who could respect you, you tiny little wog gigolo? Raising her face to the dark, starry sky she continued, in affected literary tones,

—Behind him there's a window, and outside a garden with a fig tree. His hair is dark and thick and neatly combed, and he's wearing a good suit. He is a man who likes facts, who understands the sensual pleasures of life, (what on earth is he doing in this town?). His fingers have full, pulpy tips, warm with blood, cushioning his neatly manicured nails, and they lie firmly, solidly, on the green speckled leather and polished wood of his desk. They descended the narrow, tunnel-like road that led to the hotel, and the sky was reduced to a narrow strip above their heads. —And I just sit there, hunched in a small chair, legs crossed, shaking my head endlessly in silence. As they entered the hollow sound vacuum of the hotel Oreste, too, shook his head.

—What are you talking about? You talk too much. Women should not talk so much.

In bedroom No. 58 a solitary infant slept, cot screened to protect her from the bright light. The beds were separated by a low teak cupboard and an orange and black nylon rug. The sheets were turned down, and Miranda's nightdress laid out. She undressed with her back to Oreste and slipped the nightdress over her head. He said,

—What you do that for? Take it off.

—Aha, thought Miranda, contact is going to be made again. Now I shall remember what I am doing in this strange room with this small man. She turned round. Oreste too was naked, cock at the ready. It's like seeing the same damn movie over and over again. But tonight Oreste had variations in mind. The fluorescent light cast no shadows and hid no hair or pimple. Oreste joined her on the black and orange rug and thrust his cock between her thighs. (Two thirds of the way up between knee and forested mount of Venus was its natural position.) He moved it up and down with a few knee bends, head back, eyes half shut, mouth open, then thrust her feet and knees apart and dragged it lingeringly up one thigh and down the other, dry, rough, catching and then rolling smoothly. Down on your back, knees in the air, in and out, in, out, in, out, shudders and gasps and then suddenly out and she was flipped over onto her stomach like a pancake; wet and dripping with vaginal lubrication, cock and balls slapped her back, buttocks, thighs, hands seized her buttocks, pried them apart—entrance was being sought up the tight, virginal, and hitherto unconsidered anus. A scream of pain half stifled in the pillow. Huge, oh giantlike. Oreste paused.

—You like it? I stop? Gasp.

—I like it, go on. In, out, yes, definitely pleasure. In, deeper and deeper—there was further to go. Out—oh empty and cold, over again, leave no orifice unexplored, lips, mouth and throat were filled with quivering muscle and the savoury, pungent taste of—was it? yes indeed it was, the natural excretions of her own body, dipped out before their term.

Yet more orifices were suddenly filled; a high wailing cry assaulted their ears. The infant had awakened. Pause. A few more tentative motions. The cries increased in volume and panic. Miranda struggled her head free. She staggered to the basin to rinse her mouth. There was no room to move between the cot and the screen, and as she folded it aside to reach the howling child bangs and cries resounded from either side of the silent, empty hotel.

—*Silenzio.*

—*Piange il bambino!* The thin walls shuddered and creaked to the thumps of disturbed sleepers. The baby's face was puckered and purple. Not rage, but pain and misery contorted her mouth to reveal the pale serrated gums and trembling tongue. Miranda picked the child up and held her close.

—Hush darling, what is it? No need to ask. The sheets were awash with liquid yellow shit. She had a pain in her tum.

Another convulsion, another shriek. Miranda's arms and stomach were streaked with yellow.

—Oh God, what shall I do?

Mother and child whimpered together for a moment. Oreste lay face down on the bed with the pillow over his head. More thumps on the wall. Miranda took a deep breath, stripped the cot and the baby, washed the latter, and put on clean clothes, with a double ration of nappies. Wedged (would she fall out?), clean and dry but unheld into the empty bed, she started to cry again. Miranda quickly washed the crap off her arms, breasts and stomach, and the sperm off her thighs, and putting on her nightdress climbed into bed to hold the child in the warm curve of her body. Out again after a minute to find the brown Boots bottle and dribble a teaspoonful of Kaolin between her daughter's gums, put the bundle of stinking sheets outside the door (corridor still empty, glowing, light, transparent), wrap an extra towel round the baby's uneasy bottom, and turn out the light. No signs of life from Oreste. Was he sleeping? The mother, curled round the eventually sleeping form of her daughter, pushed any thought of him aside. If contact had been made it had already been forgotten except for the ripples of physical sensation that still tingled in her body like tremors of old conversations along telephone wires.

Twice during the night, the window still undefined in the darkness, the baby woke up with cries of pain, shit like golden liquid, and then a thicker, pasty consistency, seeping out of her smooth bottom, uncontrolled, unwilled. Miranda lay awake thinking of death, and emptiness, and judgement, and Oreste slept, or did not move.

At her fourth awakening the window was a rectangle of cold, grey light, acknowledging neither the solidity of objects nor the depth of space, but only the passage of time. No longer a night awakening but an early morning awakening, when there's no more hope of sleep, and consciousness grinds with relentless, chilly slowness. Examined, in the dim light by the window, the latest nappy showed a fairly solid, cake-like turd.

The colour and texture of the light was very much like the colour and texture of the stone ledge outside the window. A car drove out of the city through the beautiful, top-heavy Renaissance gateway, and a slow flourish of carbon monoxide spread its acrid dampness up to the hotel window. The carved ornamentation in the stone of the gateway began to be visible. On the wooden, outside frame of the window, paint was peeling, and the wood underneath was soft and rotten.

The baby still lay on the bed in her mother's warm indentation, knees up, buttocks surprisingly bony and pointed, deep folds in the damp skin of stomach and thighs, cunt smooth and neat like a peeled apple quarter, patiently waiting for things to be done to her. A wipe with Johnson's baby lotion. Looked at more closely the smooth, pale skin was eaten raw in patches. If it can do that to her skin what on earth does it do to her little insides? A thick layer of vaseline, soothing cotton and cellulose; protective plastic (not of the child but the environment), a day romper suit for charm, and a pair of white woollen bootees. When you're sick you've got to wear your woollen bootees. The child was a good child. A calm and placid child. She screamed the bare minimum for survival. She watched her mother dress with round expressionless eyes as if she were a hospital patient staring at a therapeutic light sculpture, except for a flicker of excitement and an effort to raise herself when the nightdress was wriggled over her mother's head to reveal her pre-bottle milk supply.

When they were both dressed, father figure still playing dead, Miranda picked up her sick child, together with a plastic bag full of bottles and thermos flasks, and went out in search of succour and sympathy. It was not yet eight o'clock, but the bundle of stinking sheets had already been taken away. Downstairs the lobby was empty. At the end of a short passage lined with wood and glass cases full of objects for sale, to the right of the reception desk and past the lift was an arched doorway which led to the dining room. Miranda went along it. Twenty or thirty tables in a large, pale room were laid for breakfast. In the far corner, by a window, a solitary man ate rolls and poured coffee. The waitress with the streak of white hair, her uniform still crisp and fresh, her face with the same blank and mysterious beauty, was spreading a heavy white linen tablecloth over a long table which stretched the whole length of one wall. The room was high-ceilinged and pale, but here the plastic barrier had been broken; white linen and white-painted walls and the stained wooden floors belonging to an older civilisation, and the ornate plaster moulding on the ceiling and walls, the ornamental mirrors and heavy marble fireplace to an older still. Did Circe the maid never sleep? Where were the thumpers and complainers of the night? All drugged and bewitched, silent and immoveable behind their closed doors?

—*Buon giorno*, Circe smiled and indicated a table with her head, the tablecloth flapping and billowing, cracking like a whip, and then spread smooth. Miranda's forehead creased.

—*Per favore, non va bene il bambino. Lo stomaco.*

—*Si*, the maid smiled again. Had she removed and washed those stinking sheets? Did she ever have pains in her back and legs? Did she ever complain? Eat? Make love?

—*Per favore, c'è acqua calda? bollita?* Miranda held out the thermos flask. Yes, contact had been made again. With a final pat on the perfect rectangle of the tablecloth Circe flung a napkin over her shoulder and took the thermos. She stroked the baby's cheek.

—*O, la povera.*

Miranda sat at one of the smallest of the tables, laid for four.

—*Caffé?*

—*Si.*

With the brisk grace of a small high-class yacht Circe cut between the tables and swung through the door into the kitchen.

How calm, how orderly, how comforting is the sight of a table laid for breakfast. With what astonishment and relief does the breakfaster wait for his coffee after having traversed by precarious paths the solitary wilderness of the night. Nightmares vanish here; this knife, this spoon, this plate, this cup wait only to be used and discarded, stepping stones for the day. Miranda caressed the thick white china gratefully—picked up a plate and held it against her cheek. Everything was all right. Circe the angel of mercy would bring coffee, water, all that was required and demanded. Everything could be asked of her because she asked for nothing herself. Oh mother! mother! our heroine (in the reality of the imagination only) threw herself down at the perfect marble unchanging feet and worshipped. In her incarnation as a lady sitting at a table she poured her coffee with a shaking hand, created a judicious mixture with milk and sugar and drank; unwrapped a small silver rectangle of butter, spread it and some pale, sweet marmalade on a roll and ate. Had the child remained silent during this interlude? Probably not. But now her turn arrived. Oh no, not milk, you poor little bastard. Sick babies don't get milk until all the nasty germs have gone. Water and sugar is your breakfast. Thirsty and ignorant the infant acquiesced. There was really nothing else for her to do.

The detritus of breakfast by no means has the same comforting effect as the anticipation of it. The whiteness of cloth and china spoiled with crumbs and brownish liquid, marmalade sticky on the knife, crumpled silver paper with an uneaten piece of butter melting in it. All the gifts have been given. The comfort is simply this, a better taste in the mouth, and a heaviness in the stomach. More was required. More, more, more.

—*Per favore.*

Circe, who had been laying the long table for lunch turned round in an elegant pivotal movement on the ball of one foot, back and neck straight and supple. *Si?*

—*Um . . . é possible trovare un dottore? Per la bambina?*

She came over to the table, still holding a handful of cutlery which she was polishing with her napkin before putting it on the table. Her calm eyes gazed at the child who sucked on her disappointing bottle and gazed back. Miranda too gazed up at the maid. Each pair of eyes shifted round. The child to the mother. The mother to the child. The maid to the mother.

—*Il signor dorme?*

—*Si.* Is the child really well now? Does she see that and despise me for wanting expensive words of comfort from a man who should always be occupied with the extremes of human sickness and despair? What would you do, witch, earth mother, for your child?

—*Momento.* Interrupting the perfect completeness of her actions she laid the cutlery down on the table with a napkin on top of it and swung unhurried, purposeful, out into the lobby. A hollow bubbling and hiss of air. The bottle was empty. The child experimentally blew, sucked, lipped the teat until her mother took it away, and looked round, unsatisfied, for something better. Miranda packed thermos, still half full, and bottle back into her plastic bag and followed Circe. The maid stood in respectful silence by the desk, waiting to speak to the manager. An elderly man with a raincoat over his arm was taking his time paying the bill. When the bill was paid and the guest departed she introduced Miranda and her needs like a hostess at a ball, and withdrew with a graceful gesture of the head.

—*Buon giorno signora.* The manager gazed at them. *Un medico.*

—*Si, un medico.*

He looked exactly the same as on the previous day. Nothing changed in this hotel. Nothing aged, rotted or grew dirty. His suit, his shirt, his hair, showed no signs of having been in bed, or thrust under a shower, or tossed on a chair. He reached for a telephone directory under the desk, found a page, and slowly moved his finger down it. Changing hands, but keeping the place marked as if it would fly away if he let go for a moment, he found a pencil and paper and copied down the name of the doctor in a large, tortured italic hand, each letter struggling wildly to dash itself down with a casual stroke of the pen, and being prevented, held back, forced into clarity, precision and elegance. The tension of watching him was so extreme that Miranda had to force herself to let her breath out and relax her grip on the baby which had become almost stiflingly tight, and was astonished, when he handed her the paper, to see that recognisable words had been formed. *Dottor Luigi Malatesta, viale Giacomo Matteotti 7.*

Dottor Luigi Malatesta. He would cure the sick child. He at least would see that a mother with a sick child should be respected and cared for. Tears came into Miranda's eyes.

—*Grazie.* Clutching her talisman she went up to the room. Oreste was still sleeping. Miranda cried noisily, determined that her tears should not be ignored.

—Mummy's poor little angel. You might have died in the night and he wouldn't care. He wouldn't even have noticed. She banged the wardrobe door, and then turned on the taps full blast, and bumped into his bed. Oreste turned over with a sleepy groan, then opened one eye and stretched luxuriously.

—Oh I am so sleepy.

—You're sleepy! Miranda picked up her cue and turned on him like a bird of prey. You're sleepy! What about me? I didn't sleep all night. And what about the baby? Don't you care that she's sick? It might be dangerous. I'm taking her to see the doctor.

Oreste sat up and rubbed his eyes. Yes, he had noticed the tears. He stood up, naked, relaxed, smelling warm and musky. He looked at the baby, then put his arm round Miranda and wiped away the tears with one finger.

—We take the child to see Leone.

—But I've got the name of a doctor.

—Leone knows who is the best. A friend. Not too much money. He started to put on his jeans. We go all together.

The image of Dottor Luigi Malatesta bloomed into a grand, beneficent godlike figure, blue and yellow, ornately framed; but godlike, he withdrew at the same time, out of reach. Miranda crumpled the paper and shoved it into her pocket. They traipsed downstairs again, infant cradled in her mother's arms, mother's tears wiped dry, father figure unshaven, but a rock and tower of strength, his hand on the waist of his tall wife. He did not even pause for coffee, but led them through the lobby and out into the hot, blinding, dusty, bustling, sunshiny day. Up the steep, tunnel-like street, along the Corso

Garibaldi towards the Piazza della Repubblica, stepped the urgent procession. Round the corner, across another street, and there was the green cross of a *Farmacia*. Between them surged crowds of slow-moving cars, buses, and people walking on the pavement. Across the woman and her burden were led, frightened, pulling back, held by an irresistible grip on her upper arm (a new soul unwilling to cross the underground river) horrified and affronted by this daytime life which so mysteriously vanished at night. But her guide was strong and firm and knew the secret ways, and led them into the cool, dark interior with its carved altar and white-coated priests and smell of medicaments.

An urgent conversation began, spoken fast, so that a foreigner could understand nothing. There was much gesturing, and at one point Leone snapped a few words at an acolyte, who disappeared into the street. Had he gone to fetch a doctor? Miranda clutched the child, her passport, to her motherly bosom, and stared from one man to the other trying to squeeze some sense out of their words. After a few moments the acolyte reappeared with a tray on which were two small cups of black coffee, and two glasses of water. Oreste took one of the cups of coffee and sipped it as he continued to talk, without looking at Miranda. There was one chair by the counter, its seat covered in green leather. When she sat down she could no longer see over the top of the counter, and Leone became invisible. She stared instead out of the door at the blinding pattern of light and shade, the flash of sun on metal, clatter of feet, voices, engines, smell of dust and exhaust fumes.

—Let me look please? Please may I have a look? Leone leaned over the English woman; spoke to her; took the child out of her arms. The child hiccoughed and whimpered as her tender, flabby stomach was poked and pressed, and her head turned this way and that. Back in mother's arms. Leone said,

—There must be, I think, a small infection.

Miranda asked, —Is it dangerous?

—Nothing important, but we go to see the doctor. Another

staccato burst of instructions and then Leone and Oreste swung through the side door and out into the alley. Oreste looked back over his shoulder and called,

—Come. Stumbling in her haste to get off the chair and out through the door the Englishwoman picked up her bag and ran outside. They had vanished; no, there they were, behind three plump matrons, shopping bags over their arms, who took up the whole width of the alley as they stepped delicately among the cobbles. Squeezing past the placid ladies Miranda found the two men again earnestly in conversation, and as she reached them they turned and led the way through the side door of another house. A long dark passage. Through a half-open door on the left could be glimpsed a waiting-room painted cream, chairs around the walls, a stack of tattered magazines on a small table, and people staring blankly in front of them imagining, perhaps, hospitals and funerals. Leone tapped at another door, and after a moment a nurse dressed in white opened it. They conferred, she withdrew, Leone followed; after another few minutes a workman in blue overalls came out and disappeared into the street through a side door, and the nurse beckoned Oreste and Miranda into the doctor's office. The faces in the waiting-room remained unchanged. The doctor's office was brownish wood and leather, screen, desk, papers, white overalls, soft voices. The doctor himself was large and white, with a soft, freckled face, bald head, glasses. He was a generation older than Oreste and Leone. The father of one of their friends? He bowed and shook Miranda's hand.

—*Buon giorno, signora.* Would you be so good, to undress the child?

A slow fumbling with safety pins, buttons; in her nappy was a small example of her condition. Pale yellow, slightly bubbly, not as liquid as it had been the previous night, but still definitely of medical interest. The doctor examined it, and passed the precious sample to the nurse, who threw it away and handed Miranda a tissue to wipe the infant bottom. Now completely naked the baby lay with her thin soft arms and legs bent at odd angles like the limbs of insects when they are helpless on their backs. She gazed up at the ring of faces gazing down at her. The doctor picked her up gently, her entire body almost fitting into his large hand, and felt her stomach. He turned her over so that she lay curved like a Viking ship, head up, staring round in astonishment from her new vantage point at the faces now so close. Suddenly she started to laugh. With intelligence, humour and wit she looked from one to the other of the anxious surrounding faces and laughed. The doctor passed his hand over her wispy head with love.

—She is not very sick, this baby.

They all laughed, delighted with the child. She was not very sick, but still, to be safe she should have pills, and drink nothing but weak tea with sugar for a day, and then, (already her plumpness had shrunk a little) plenty of body building tonic and apple puree, and no milk until the end of the week. Miranda kissed her baby, proud and happy. Prescriptions were scribbled out by the doctor and the bill by the nurse—the latter paid by Leone. Relieved, relaxed, a course mapped out for them they trooped out into the street and back to the *Farmacia*.

Oreste nudged Miranda.

—You have cheques? She looked at him uncomprehendingly. —For the medicines; the doctor. Money.

Her hand shook as she took out her folder of travellers cheques. Only £15 were left. Louis had brought most of the money in his name. No comfort is given for free. She signed a £5 cheque and gave it to Oreste.

—I hope there is enough for the hotel. He ignored her, and a new version slotted into her mind of the scene she had described to him at the Consul's office, in which she was brisk and reasonable. She had come on a trip, the child had become sick, and she had spent all her money on medicines. The Consul's attitude changed immediately, instead of being impatient he was friendly and concerned; his wife took Miranda and the baby in for the night, and the Consul gave her enough money to get back to Volterra, and to see her through until the expected date of Louis's return. Dark clouds billowing in from the sides of her vision obscured this dream before it could suggest a practical course of behaviour: get into the car now and drive back to Volterra. I'm tied hand and foot. I'm expiating some vast and monstrous crime. I can take no action; make no move, no protest. Stubbornly she shut her mouth and turned off the anguished internal weeping and groaning. Nothing must appear. Nothing. I am dead. Silently, with clamped teeth she picked up her parcels and walked back to the hotel, turning her head stiffly through 180 degrees to see whether it was safe to cross the road. Dead. Immobile. Unfeeling. 'Never explain, never complain'—a very good motto for the dead. I shall make it my own. Why the hell are you feeding the baby on the shit this stupid wog doctor gave (gave!) you? Who knows what the hell it is? It could kill her. She gets slowly thinner. Curling up with that same blank expression she turns into a skeleton because a wog doctor said give her no milk. Her life is in my hands and my bloody hands are shaking and incompetent and yes, bloody. Never explain never complain. Never complain never explain. Why? What? Dismal Disraeli. Bodies thrown, scattered; casually smashing against the wall, bouncing off the merry-go-round. There goes a woman with no nose, rolling over with her legs in the air, a young man is caught up in the machinery, one, two, three, off come his fingers, and his leg is ground up, minced and mashed. By a river bodies are dangling in the sun—flayed, blue and purple, blood still dripping to the ground. Were they intelligent beings or furry and delicate beasts? A young man jerks on the floor as bullets smack into his body. It's all a game, a carnival, full of noise and colour, dust and screams and the grinding of machinery; a little music, bright colours, lozenges of red and yellow bordered by black. Red, yellow and white, and the wooden horses painted like toys, pink and blue with golden manes, frozen in playful movement. There are always more of us to scramble on, if I lose or forget this child, or kill her inadvertently or intentionally. What's a life here or there in the endless procession of millions of dead and nearly dead? Millions and millions and endless weight of millions pullulating like worms and then ground back into the earth.

Another day and a night passed in the hotel and the child was not dead. There was good will in this town. Not enough, perhaps, for the foreigner, the helpless babe, babbling words half understood, hoping to find refuge in the motherly arms of strangers; but still, the wife of Leone sent round to the hotel, to ease the childbound vigil, a sweet cake, with almonds on top, and a bottle of white wine. Oreste brought it, and he also brought an English newspaper, *The Observer*, five days old.

—Last night I have a dream. I read a newspaper, and I think, 'poor Miranda, she have nothing to read in the lavatory'. I know you like to read in there.

They ate and drank in companionable silence, one on each bed, with the cake and wine on the teak table, and their feet facing each other on the orange rug. The baby slept. After they had eaten they too dozed, fuzzy with wine. In the middle of the afternoon Oreste got up. He stood by the woman's bed with his hand on her shoulder.

—Tomorrow we go to my house. My mother, she will know what to do for the child.

VII

Down by the sea, among the dunes and lagoons, the old parents.

They passed towns and villages, fields and vineyards and factories. The hills rose up behind them to join the opalescent and insubstantial clouds, and their Fiat, tiny, rounded, soft olive green, remained the moving centre of a bubble, a sphere, tawny and blue behind, pale and bright ahead.

They arrived soon after midday, at siesta time. The country stretched away, flat in all directions. Ahead there were the marshes and the sea; to the right salt pans, now disused; to the left sand dunes, and then smoke and haze of the town. Behind them the road, scattered farms, a countryside like any other. But they had their backs to that. The only other buildings in sight were a collection of concrete huts at the edge of the salt pans, and half a mile closer to the sea, one other farmhouse. In spite of the flatness of the land the air was close, and the sky pressed down heavily. Everything was grey. Modulations of grey and brown and white, but burning with light, a colourless film of light that existed for its own purposes, not to reveal objects to the human eye. Chickens scattered from under the wheels as the car pulled up. Squawking with wings half raised and dusty purple cockscombs flapping, their yellow feet splayed and then neatly pointed as they raised them to run, like old ladies surprisingly agile in their high-heeled shoes.

The visitors sat in the car as the silence settled again. Nothing moved but the chickens.

The house was square, whitewashed, though the stone was showing through and even crumbling in places. Behind it was a lean-to shed, and three more sides of a courtyard were formed by a low stone wall. Two barns stood roofless, the wood so soft and rotten and silver grey with age that it looked as if a child might easily have broken the fallen beams with his bare hands. In front of the house, where the car had stopped, and the chickens now pecked and scratched peacefully once more, was a patch of gravel half buried in the sand, with scattered clumps of rough, yellowish grass; and then there was the dirt road, and the dunes, with pools of stagnant water.

Oreste sat slumped in the front seat—his chin on his chest. The front door was half open. Baking in the heat, colour and form sucked out of them so that they were barely visible, a wooden table and two benches leaned against the wall. The windows were shuttered. The house looked as if it could have been empty for months, chickens scratching a livelihood from the debris of an old life, and the door swinging and banging in the wind.

An old woman appeared in the doorway. Plump, wearing a long, white cotton nightgown, low necked, sleeveless. As she raised her arms to find out what had become of the wispy coil of grey hair the flesh of her upper arms drooped and shook. She peered round, wakened from her midday sleep, old, half blind, uncertain what had awakened her, her mind registering but not taking in immediately the dark shape which had appeared suddenly in front of the house, the banging of a car door, the figure walking towards her.

—*Mamma.*
—*Mio figlio? Oreste?*
—*Si mamma.*

Soft, soft, how infinitely wrinkled and soft those sagging cheeks. He was hardly taller than she was. Perhaps an inch. A hairpin fell to the ground. She peered into his face, felt his rough, young, healthy, masculine chin, her fingers, hard bones, soft skin, the freckles of age, nails so dry it seemed they could hardly continue to grow, pressed into his back.

—*Mio figlio.*

His hair was thinner. There were flecks of saliva stained with nicotine at the corners of his mouth. His clothes were not clean. But the lines round his eyes and at the corners of his mouth were the pressure of living on healthy flesh, still young, and his eyes shone dark and clear. The car door banged again. Another figure, shimmering in the heat, crossed the gravel, A young woman, holding a child. The old woman peered uncertainly at this apparition, and then back at her son. Had he chosen this moment to arrive so unexpectedly with the longed-for wife and grandchild?

With one finger he lifted the heavy tail of her hair, escaping in wispy, brittle ends. The neck of the nightdress, colour of stones, bones, was pulled aside to show the straps of underclothes and the flabby beginnings of one shoulder. Flesh so old that it had lost all its rubbery vitality, all indentations, rises and falls; gravity now was the only law it obeyed.

—*La tua moglie?*

—No, said the woman shrilly in a strange accent. A foreigner. The old woman looked at her son. He said nothing. They stood in front of her, suddenly immense dark figures confusing in her familiar landscape. The old woman turned round, pushed the door. It grated on sand, caught between the wood and the stone.

—*Dov'è Papà?*

She beckoned with her head for them to follow.

—*Scusi.*

Inside there was a low, narrow passage, with a stone-flagged floor. Reflections of light on the stones from another door open at the back of the house. On the right a small dark room, half-open door. A muffled scream.

—*O Signor Oreste, Signor Oreste.* A tiny creature, wrinkled and brown with a mat of frizzy hair hurled herself out of the shadows and into Oreste's arms. He kissed her on both cheeks and held her away from him at arm's length.

—*Immacolata! Sempre bella!*

—*O Signor Oreste, Signor Oreste.* Tears rolled down her cheeks, wavering and turning among the many paths which offered themselves, and she turned her head to one side and pressed her face against one of Oreste's hands as it held her arm. He embraced her again, and patted her shoulder. From inside a room further up the passage the old woman's voice called,

—*Immacolata!* She appeared in a doorway tying a wrap round her, and motioning to Oreste and the woman to wait, she went in again. The maid, looking backwards, nodding and smiling, followed.

The narrow, stone-flagged passage divided the house in two, with three doors opening off it on either side. Next to the maid's room was the kitchen, dark behind closed shutters, stone floor, cupboards unpainted wood like the table. A kitchen for infusions of tea in the cold dawn as another night drags to its close. Oreste led the woman and child into the room next to the kitchen which was furnished as a dining room and parlour. They sat on two hard mahogany chairs at the oval polished table in the middle. Light and heat were kept at bay by shutters, a wire screen, lace curtains. It was just possible to make out a daybed against one wall, a few more straight-backed chairs, a sideboard and china cabinet, and many pictures. On top of the sideboard were two photographs of Oreste as a schoolboy, sombre and dark-suited for his first communion, and impossibly, perfectly, handsome, as a young man at his sister's wedding.

The visitor got up to look closer, shifted the child to the other arm, sat down again. She opened her mouth to speak but Oreste stopped her.

—Sh, hand lifted, head cocked to the muffled whispers and heavings from his parents' room opposite. No cry for help. These three people had worked out their lives together.

—What you say?

Would there be a place for me here if I was really his wife and had really borne his child?

—How old is Immacolata?

Oreste tapped a cigarette packet from one hand to the other, turning it over and over.

—Thirty, thirty-five, I don't know.

—What! She looks more like seventy. It was wrong, wrong. She was the young plant off whom the old were feeding.

—Maybe forty.

As they got older the paths that they trod around the house became smaller. The rooms upstairs had been unvisited for years. No need to go more than a few steps outside to throw grain to the chickens, and buy from the grocery van when it came to the door. Perhaps his mother had not stepped round the far side of the table in years, feeling her way always by the familiar, shortest route to the kitchen.

—My parents take her in when she is ten, twelve. She is orphan.

—I thought she was the maid.

He stared at his parents' room. How many times a day did those two women struggle and pant to lift his father from one necessity to another?

—My father is very good for her. She never learn to read or write, he send her to school. She want to marry, but the man no take her without money.

—A dowry?

—Yes, so my father, he give. But she is stupid girl. The man take the money and leave her.

—Poor girl.

—She is poor and stupid. There are many like that.

The door of his parents' room opened. Oreste jumped to his feet. There was a bump, Immacolata rushed out to hold the door open, kneeling down with her back to the watchers in the dining room to push the right front wheel of the invalid chair free of the door. In the chair sat Oreste's father, statuesque, immobile, his white hair brushed smooth. His skin was white too, and his flesh had something of the greasy smoothness of old marble. The features were less classically beautiful, more distinguished than his son's—forehead higher, nose more aquiline. He wore white pyjamas and a cotton robe, printed in pale blue and brown to look like plaid, with a plain blue collar. His hands rested, empty, on his knees. A good child who had nothing to hide. His wife, wearing now a grey housedress, with her hair pinned up at the back, pushed the chair, and Immacolata, like a small tug or terrier, guided it from in front, pushing the dining-room door open as far as it would go, moving one of the straight-backed chairs, smoothing the old man's dressing gown over his knees. She stepped aside, mission accomplished, hands clasped proudly in front of her.

Oreste knelt down beside his father's chair, kissed him on both cheeks, took up one of the limp hands in his own. The old man did not move or react.

—*Papà*. It is I, your son. Your son is beside you, and holds your hand in his.

One profile was still impassive, waxy, but on the other side the flesh sagged and twisted slightly, and now trembled, as an unformed grunting came from the old man's throat, and a tear—not round and full like the tears of the orphan maid, but a glint, a snail trace of wetness appeared on his left cheek.

The foreigner made an act of will to reconstitute herself either as some inanimate part of this room, like the wall, or the daybed, or any other incarnation that would have her, even herself in another place.

—*Papà, ecco, io.*

—He understands, said the mother, but he cannot speak.

—Hullo father dear, you look well. No, not well, since you can neither move nor speak, But you are here, you are present, your face is still the same, and you can know that your son has come back, you can feel his love. Love silent, unspoken, fruitless. What can I do for you that a son should do for his father, and what can you do for me that a father should do for his son? Another tremor in the cheek and gurgle in the throat. The mother leaned forward and whispered to Oreste,

—He asks if he can see the child?

Oreste gestured to Miranda with his head. She got up and awkwardly held out the child, half offering, half protecting this tiny symbol of the continuity of the generations. The infant reached and waved with her hands and feet, twisting her head and opening and shutting her mouth like a creature out of her element, searching for the familiar pressure of liquid, or flesh. The blood that runs in these veins is not yours, old man. The genes that formed the splitting cells of this small body came from some Jewish doctor in New York, and of course an old faggot living out his shame in Cairo.

—*Maschio?* For the first time the old woman looked directly at Miranda. Saw? Probably not, but peered in her general direction.

—No, *femmina*.

And yet the child is wearing a blue suit. Who can tell, under the little nappy. Poor thing, she is foreign, perhaps she doesn't understand.

—*Immacolata, caffè.*

—*Si.*

The maid bobbed and ran into the kitchen, giving the visitor a smile of secret fellowship as she passed. She, too, had almost been married once. The old woman felt her way to the sideboard, bent slowly down, and opened one of the sliding glass doors. How long since they had been opened, and the tray with the tiny glasses, the size of thimbles, brought out, with the cut-glass decanter of liqueur? Oreste knelt, holding the limp hand of his father. He made no move to help his mother, but stared grimly, heavily, at her slow and shaky progress from sideboard to table. After the liqueur glasses the coffee cups, equally tiny, on a china tray. Knees creaking, hips spreading, slowly, slowly, infinitely slowly the grey back and rump rose and descended and rose, riveting the attention like a climber inching his way across a sheer rock face. Oreste transferred his gaze to Miranda, but she ignored him, rigid in her chair, the baby on her lap. Coldly she watched the old woman. I want none of this family. I want none of their age, their poverty, their sagging flesh and creaking bones. I have nothing to do with them. She turned her head towards Immacolata in the kitchen.

With bustle and flourish in every movement she scurried from cupboard to table to sink to stove. She had taken the opportunity to get dressed, and was wearing a faded cotton frock decorated with a red and black abstract design of the kind that was known as contemporary after the second world war, which reached almost to her ankles. The small aluminium filter coffee pot, the tin of coffee, the spoon, all played their role in the life of the house. There was no choice of spoons, there was only one spoon for each purpose. There was no possibility of waste in this kitchen, of things half used and then forgotten. Immacolata filled the pot with water and spooned in the coffee with concentration as absolute as a child playing in a sandpit. She lit the flame on the tiny calor gas stove with a large match, waved it out, and placed the remains of the match carefully in a saucer kept for that purpose. While the water boiled she stood in the doorway smiling at the assembled family.

The old woman, breathing heavily, sat down, closed her eyes for a moment, put her hand on her heart. She eased the cork out of the liqueur bottle and poured a tiny drop into three glasses, then, after hesitating for a moment, a fourth. Oreste got up and handed a glass to his mother, one to Miranda—he looked towards his father, but the old woman shook her head—and one to Immacolata, who gave a high-pitched giggle and blushed and hid her face behind the door. The liqueur was golden and tasted of herbs and was very strong. The old woman looked at her son and said something in Italian.

Miranda felt that the silence of the old man had infected her vocal chords. His silence and her own silence began to scream in her ears. Isolated words ran through her brain: I say, jolly good, what ho! O.K. Oh P. G. Wodehouse, Bertie Wooster and Jeeves, rescue me from these foreigners, this silence. Dumb show is useless. If people don't understand words how can they understand gestures, since one must be translated into the other?

She stumbled to her feet, pointing to the child.

—Thirsty.

Did she once imagine she knew a little Italian? and ran out of the room, down the cool stone passage where there was even the suggestion of air moving, out into the blinding white blanket of heat. The sand under her feet crept burning into her sandals. Heat, emptiness, freedom, pressed in and pushed her out of shape like giant hands playing with a half-filled balloon. She shut her eyes, gave herself up to the heat, tried for mouthfuls of the unbreathable air. The child screamed when her mother put her onto the car seat, soft flesh on the burning leather, stifling, burning up, in an oven, while she fumbled for bottle and thermos; her hands are shaking, her body shrinks and rejects that house. But like a good daughter-in-law back she goes. Is it possible to become so small, to haul in all those screaming flapping rags of despair that are trying to tug her away over the roof, the mountains, out to sea, back to London and a pillow stained with Guinness and the Drones Club and Agatha Christie? In, in they come, to this harsh corner of the world from which, for some, there is no escape. Enter that rectangle of dark coolness, plunge into icy water, water as hard as concrete, skin rubbed and scraped off, bouncing, bumping, dragged at great speed, a loathsome somersault of sensation into some deeper layer of untortured flesh.

Back again with the chair, the child on her lap, the cup, now full of coffee, the glass, empty, the family—no change there. O.K. humourless bitch. Play some sort of role, do something, don't just sit there like an arsehole. You, an English woman, are sitting in this Italian house. Make a contribution. Let them see that their lives have been brightened, if not by a wife and grandchild at least by an interesting foreign lady. Part of that outer world in which their beloved son is swimming about.

She smiled brightly at Oreste, and said in English,

—What a beautiful face your father has. I should like to draw it.

Oreste translated, and the old woman smiled, nodded, and asked Oreste if his wife was a painter?

—*Si*, replied Miranda.

I shall be a painter. Why the hell shouldn't I be a painter? I was extremely talented as a child. She said, gesturing with her eyes since her hands were occupied with giving the child her bottle, *bel' uomo*.

Ah she speaks Italian, isn't she clever, what a surprise. Noddings and cluckings from Immacolata. The old lady rose to her feet, moving with the same hallucinating slowness, and fetching a photograph from the top of the sideboard handed it to the foreign visitor. Yes, of course, hiding behind the wedding of the sister, in an ornate silver frame, was the wedding of the parents, also in a silver frame. There they stood, a thousand years ago, all dressed up, with the rest of their lives in front of them.

—*Tutti e due belli (belli?)*

Smiling and nodding she handed it back. And now comes the moment when I should produce our wedding picture. Quite. What am I doing here? What on earth am I doing here sowing confusion in the minds of this harmless old couple? If I wanted to be a daughter-in-law it's all laid on. I am a daughter-in-law. I just have to go to New York and there they would be, David and Miriam. Mum and Dad. They sent five hundred dollars as a wedding present, and several little woollen garments when the baby was born. Poor old Louis, he just had to let me go for a moment and I slipped right out of his hands.

Oreste and his mother were having a low, rapid argument with much shoulder shrugging on the part of Oreste. Immacolata fingered the visitor's dress, the blue one today, and proudly, as if she herself was speaking a foreign language, repeated the one word that had already been established as familiar to them both.

—*Bella, bella.*

The young man, the son, the lover, stood up and nodded to his woman. (His version of a nod was in fact the direct opposite, a sharp upward jerk of the head.)

—Come. My mother she show you the room. She want that we sleep in her bed.

What? The old woman wants me to sleep in her bed? Me? Not the hard anonymity of a hotel mattress (where rapes, murders, suicides may have taken place the previous night but all is hidden under the changed sheets), but the very humps and indentations, geological formations created by the pallid solidity of your flesh? Oh, no, old woman, you're not going to win me so easily. I'll sleep on the floor.

—We can't do that!
—She want.
Oreste went out to the car to fetch the suitcase, and running to keep up, her feet echoing on the stone floor and then silent on the sand, Miranda followed him.
—We can't turn them out of their bed; I absolutely refuse. Haven't you told her we're not married?
—They no understand. They too old. They think, my woman, my child.
—Why did you bring me here? You're crazy. She put her hand on the car bonnet and then snatched it away again. The metal was too hot to touch.
—What are you going to tell them when you see them again and I'm not there? What are you going to tell them about the child?
—They are old. Soon they will die.
—But what happens if they don't die, Oreste? Do you mean that you will never come and see them again while they are alive? If you wanted someone to come with you why didn't you bring one of your girl friends from Rome? She rocked to and fro, hugging the child and shaking her head. Oreste heaped sand into pyramids with his foot.
—I could not bring the women I know in Rome to my house.
—But Oreste, why did you bring me? I'm somebody else's wife. There must be thousands of girls you could marry. Nice girls. Even nice girls with money.

—Not in Italy. He snapped his fingers. A woman with money I could marry like that. But I despise to do it. Did Louis marry me for money? or if not for money, for a work permit?

—They are not good people the bourgeois in this country. They are ugly people. Stupid, ignorant, greedy.

—But what about Leone's wife, isn't she nice?

—She a good girl, yes. He know her since a child. But I cannot marry like that.

They stood side by side leaning against the car, their shadows beneath their feet.

—But I can't even talk to your parents.

—Make pantomime. You know to speak some Italian words.

Silence. Inside the house the women put clean sheets on the double bed, and the old man sat unmoving.

—Be nice to Immacolata. She have nothing in her life. Show her your clothes.

—All right. I'll give her a dress. Another pause. The sun was beginning to make Miranda feel dizzy, but she wanted to prolong this moment of quiet and conversation.

—How long has your father been paralysed?

—Three years ago he have a stroke, and then last year another. I do not want to see him like this. For three years I think every day of him, and I cannot come. He brushed his pyramid of sand flat with one foot, and turned his face towards Miranda. She put her hand on his shoulder,

—They must be very happy to see you now.

—Yes, they are happy.

The old woman appeared in the doorway and beckoned.

Oreste opened the back of the car and got out the suitcase and the baby's carrycot which he held awkwardly under one arm. He had never before touched anything belonging to the baby (except once, her cot) and the domestic nature of the object immediately reduced him to a small, poor, anxious man. Yes, thought Miranda, I do see why a man with his ambition and his background cannot marry and have children, at least until the ambition is finally dead, and the man has changed.

High bed; heavy carved wooden ends. How is it possible to manoeuvre the old man on and off it twice a day? Pervasive, yellow, dull smell of rubber undersheets and the old man's commode. I can't sleep here! I can't sleep in this coffin, this morgue! On the dressing table crocheted mats, empty cut-glass jars, a few forgotten morsels of cotton wool, an ornate silver hairbrush with hardly any bristles left in it. An oval mirror on a wooden stand propped with newspaper to prevent it from drooping to reflect only the torso of the observer. A cavernous mahogany wardrobe, a pair of ladies' black suede shoes wrapped in a plastic bag, two more housedresses, faded blue flowers and a grey check, and far in a corner, preserved in cellophane, two dark suits never again to be worn by their owner. Where were his shoes? Hidden in some other corner, or had they already been given away? Shutters closed to prevent the smell from escaping. As my flesh touches these sheets it will become flaccid, old and grey, my bladder will cease its social routine, my muscles seize up and forget their functions, my body change its quality and stick like meat to a hot ungreased pan.

Immacolata, prompted by Oreste, plucked up courage to hold out her arms for the child, who, staring through the gloom at this unaccustomed wizened face and fuzzy aureole of hair started to pant with anxiety, but the brisk rocking of the skinny brown arms and marching up and down the confined space of the room soothed her almost immediately, in spite of her astonishment. A wrinkled brown hand felt its way along six inches of soft, pale, malleable leg until they reached the feet. Soft, flat, their use as yet undiscovered. Toes turned in, overlapping. Bare.

—*La povera, a freddo nei piedi.* The newly appointed nurse laid her down on the bed and seized a pair of bootees, that the careless mother had unpacked. The child stared intently, eyes swivelling from side to side, following every movement of the hands. She allowed herself to be turned into an Italian baby, with bootees and a little cardigan. Immacolata picked the properly dressed grandchild up again, and stood, bowlegs planted wide apart, herself watching with eagle-eyed fascination as the foreigner unpacked.

The Englishwoman emptied her cornucopia and laid her princely treasures out on the bed. Four dresses; the red one, the green and brown one, the mauve one with the gay white braid, and another blue one. Two transparent nylon nightdresses, trimmed with lace, and the matching négligé, lacy bras, coloured Marks and Spencer underpants lay piled on the bed, glowing and shimmering like the Arabian nights. Into one heap went the red dress, some underclothes, a nightdress.

—Um—What the hell's dirty in Italian?—um, *a bisogno di*. She made energetic rubbing motions.

—*Si, si*. Immacolata nodded so eagerly her head looked as if it might fall off, and would have tapped herself on the bosom had the child not been pressed against it, instead she tapped the child on the thigh. What, out of this superabundance should be offered to the orphan, the starveling, the non-consumer? The red dress was a little too smart, too citified, for a woman who spent her life among the dunes and marshes. The mauve one? No, in spite of everything Miranda still had a residue of hope invested in those white braid trimmings and the triangular headscarf. The blue one could probably be parted with most easily, and here, why not? a cheap bead necklace to go with it. The visitor's hand wavered for another moment over the heap on the bed, and then she held out the chosen gifts.

—*Per lei*.

—*Si, si, grazie*.

Immacolata put the child down carefully in the carrycot, which had been set down in the corner of the room by Oreste. How odd, he was becoming almost fatherly. Seizing the dress and necklace Immacolata scurried off to her room.

The Englishwoman took the opportunity of her momentary freedom from that avid stare to change her underclothes and put the dirty ones into the heap for washing. Oreste came in and said,

—Tomorrow my mother want make a big dinner. They kill a chicken.

He too had changed, into clothes that had been neatly folded, waiting for him for four years. He went to shave with his father's razor. The bathroom was modern, white tiled, with a hip bath and shower in one. His father had had it installed when he retired, and gave up the flat in the city. For the carefree summers of his youth there had been an outhouse and a pail of water. He stared in the mirror into his own melancholy eyes. Where had they gone, those golden years? Where was the hope and certainty of his youth? Years ago the sheer vitality of his presence had filled that house. He had struggled with such casual violence to free himself from the strong father slowly losing his authority, and the black-haired busy mother becoming grey and slow. Now he was free. The struggle that remained in his house had nothing to do with him, but was concerned with the day to day mechanics of living and aging.

The medicine cabinet was full. An enema bag lay coiled on the edge of the bath. He had succeeded in stepping outside the pattern he so bitterly hated. As his father became incapable he had not taken on the mantle of paternal authority. His voice made no one quail, or shriek with joy. The bundle curled, dozing, in the carrycot, would never run, hot, sticky and disobedient over the dunes to the distant sea. The pattern was broken. There might still be time to patch it up, but the desire was not really there. Only nostalgia and emptiness. It's a cheap way to get through life, to identify with your father and then with your son. A soothing poultice against the dread of death, the pain of loss, the passing of time. Oreste splashed his face with cold water, holding his hands over his eyes for a moment to soothe them. The strong do not need such props. For an artist, who wants to do something with his life, even if it is only to see life truly, for what it is, they get in the way. He dried his face with a small, rough towel and put on his shirt, thick white cotton with a pink stripe almost faded into invisibility, soft and smooth against his skin, and went to sit in silence beside his silent father.

The old woman was arranging the other bedroom, opposite Immacolata's between the bathroom and the front door, for her husband.

Immacolata crept out of her room, wearing the new dress and necklace. She scratched on the door of the double bedroom, now inhabited by the strange woman, and sidled in. No fervid expressions of thanks—how kind, isn't it lovely, I am grateful. She preened at her image in the wardrobe mirror from the far side of the bed, and looked round expectantly. The dress drooped low to reveal her skinny chest, and the skirt hung down to her ankles.

—*Un po' grande*, said Miranda.

—*Bella*, replied Immacolata, smoothing down the skirt. Everything else had been put away now except for the neat pile of washing, wrapped in a nightdress.

Pause. The Englishwoman was disconcerted by this lack of effusive gratitude. Immacolata's eyes were still expectant. Perhaps she would like to try on my other dresses, thought the Englishwoman, partly because she could remember the word for try. She picked a verb ending at random, rather as Oreste drove the car, by imitation and instinct, ignorant of the underlying mechanics.

—*Vorebbe provare?* That sounds bloody good. She took the mauve dress out of the cupboard again, and its headscarf from a drawer. Utterly unsuitable, of course. Without even a belt to hide the difference between our sizes and figures. But it might give her a moment or two of enjoyable fantasy.

—*Non per lei, prova sola.* That ought to make things clear. The maid took the dress, and scooped up the bundle of washing under the other arm.

—*Per lavare.*

—*Si.*

The Englishwoman sat down on the edge of the bed. She thought, I came here expecting to be looked after and cherished. Did I? Vaguely expecting, which is the way I always expect things. And here I am with many problems which I can't cope with and don't want don't want to cope with being thrust upon my shoulders. I thought Immacolata and the old woman were going to look after the baby. I'm surprised they can look after themselves, let alone the poor old man. And here I am bringing them hope. My role is to give them enough illusions to see them through the next few months or years, until they die.

The afternoon brooded over the house. Even the baby had fallen asleep and offered no distraction. It seemed a shame to be wasting one's holiday in Italy lying in this stuffy room, but what could she do outside, on that burning and uninviting expanse of sand? There was nowhere to sit, except the dining room, and there the old man waited. Oreste had vanished. The Englishwoman got off the bed, pushed at the shutters, forced them open a few inches, was rewarded by a stripe of fresh blue sky, grey mountains, green plain. Sunlight shone on her hands. She walked over to the door, opened it a few inches. No, the old man was not waiting, alone in the dining room. He had been wheeled into the kitchen, and there, slowly, methodically, his wife was feeding him, a napkin in her hand. Through the half-open door, across the dark passage, the Englishwoman stared into the old man's eye. He stared back, fishy, blank. Was his concentration on the food so intense that he did not even see her standing there, in the door of his room? Or did his eyes glint with malevolence, one open, and one half hidden under a hooded lid? What sort of woman would have played this part better? Someone who could have sat in the kitchen as the heat faded outside, and chatted to the old woman as she spooned bread softened with water between her husband's slack jaws? Shame made the Englishwoman shrink from them as if she had caught them making love. How does he eat? How does he pee? Obscene curiosity. Bluish silhouettes, the old woman slowly mashing and spooning and wiping, and the old man in his chair. A stray circle of sunlight fell onto the chrome of a tap and was reflected in their shadows on the floor. Gently, so as not to alert the attention of the old woman whose back was towards her, the Englishwoman closed the door. Went back to lie on the bed.

After five minutes she got up again. Woke the child. Changed her nappy; no more diarrhoea. Her diet was now sugar water, apple sauce, plus beef. Tomorrow she would be allowed diluted milk. There was enough water in the thermos for them to be self contained. No need to challenge that other couple in the kitchen. It was now five o'clock in the afternoon. They had had no lunch. What was the routine of life in this household? When did the women eat? Oreste had said that they would cook a chicken tomorrow—what would they eat tonight? Could they all share in the old man's bowl of bread and water? Inertia lay over the house. Everyone had shrunk back into their own private concerns. They were hardly aware that the stranger among them existed.

VIII

Outside there was a sudden wild squawking and flapping of wings. The Englishwoman picked up her child, ran out of her room, to the front door. The silence had been broken! Something was going to happen. The dun-coloured light had become thick and golden as the sun sank lower, and the shadows were brilliant and black. Immacolata, once again wearing her old red and black dress, was trying to catch a hen. Hair flying like a clown's, angular elbows and knees, she darted and pounced. Intent. Frustrated. Stalking like a cat around the green Fiat. The hens evading her with a squawk and a flutter, then reappearing round the other side of the car, slowing down in mid-step, unhurried, unafraid, smoothing their ruffled feathers with their beaks. A game, but an irritating one. Not too bright, these birds. They hadn't succeeded in putting two and two together. Or perhaps it didn't happen often enough to give them the opportunity. Now, it happened. Immacolata emerged from behind the car with a skinny white hen clutched firmly in her hands. She tucked it under one arm, came towards the house, grinning broadly.

—*Per domani.*

The Englishwoman grinned back,

—*Bene.*

What about today? Forget about today, you spoilt product of a greedy and materialistic society, be grateful for a chicken tomorrow. The bird stared at her curiously, and twitched its neck from side to side. Its fluffed out feathers made it look quite plump and bonny. Immacolata switched it in a neat movement from under her arm to between her knees, and twisted the neck sharply. The body twitched, scaly yellow feet in their cotton cradle scrabbled, bright curious eyes became dead. Immacolata hadn't taken her eyes from the foreigner's face, and hadn't stopped smiling. Once, long ago, a visitor from the town had screamed and covered her face with her hands at the strangling of a chicken. This one continued to smile and nod. How easy, she thought, and how quick. Click, and the neck is broken. Finito. Down, creeping horrors. Down, black clouds, screams and shouts reverberating from the flat sky, clanging and banging together like cymbals.

Oreste appeared round the corner of the house, rubbing his hands together.

—I am in the loft. There are many things there from the past. I think when I was a boy.

They sat down on one of the wooden benches, which had gained substance in the evening light. Immacolata fetched a bowl and a cloth and a knife, and started to pluck the chicken. With a strong flick of the wrist she pulled out the white feathers, a few at a time. It was hard, because there was very little flesh, and with the feathers the entire subsance of the bird seemed to vanish. The other hens clucked and pecked, unconcerned with their slaughtered sister.

The old man had finished his meal, and was wheeled out to be social, and enjoy the sunshine. His wife had removed the dressing gown and put a grey linen jacket on him, and tied a scarf round his neck. Over his knees was an embroidered cotton rug, and underneath, his feet, still in their red leather bedroom slippers, peeped out. Oreste helped his mother manoeuvre the old man's chair into a comfortable position, and then she too sat down on the bench. The visitor took a mental jump and studied the scene from twenty yards away. The farmhouse no longer looked abandoned, dead, decaying. Instead it made a charming scene; colourful, picturesque; one might almost stop to photograph it. Colour and tone, instead of making objects indistinguishable, were now embarrassing in their variety. An entirely new palette was required. The dunes were golden brown, with much use of purple in the shadows, and pink in the light. The house glowed in its whiteness. The figures sitting outside the door symbolised all that was most warm and human in Italian family life. When you want a chicken, kill it, pluck it, cook it and eat it. None of these frozen, battery-bred, plastic-wrapped obscenities for us. And none of this shoving of the old folk off to Homes and hospitals as soon as they get a bit doddery. No, we simple, Catholic peasant families believe in loving each other and staying together. And think what a rich social organisation this child is going to grow up into, by the time he's got a few brothers and sisters of course. He won't be isolated from everyone except his contemporaries and his parents, like the unfortunate products of more highly industrialised societies.

The visitor returned to the bench. Whatever the realities of the situation might be, things were definitely improving as the sun sank over the hills, and the evening got under way. Of all the hours of the day, the Englishwoman was most frightened of noon, shadowless noon, where time itself might easily stick—a chance piece of dust or fluff on a gramophone needle—and the day never lurch into gear again.

Immacolata had finished plucking the chicken, whose body was now about the size of her clenched fist. She wrapped the feathers up in the cloth which had been spread on her lap, put the chicken and the knife into the bowl, and went into the kitchen. What do they do with the feathers? wondered the foreigner. Stuff mattresses?

—*Che cosa . . . ?* Oh hell, it's too difficult. She stopped and smiled inanely. The old woman said,

—*Per domani.*

—*Si. Benissimo.* For a change.

The old woman nodded, then turned to her son, and slipped a note folded very small into his hand. They talked for a few moments, and she gestured with her head towards the car.

Oreste said to Miranda,

—We go with Immacolata to the village for shopping. You want come?

Do I want to come? Oh sure. That would be an unexpected bonus. A whole slice of the evening could be occupied by shopping.

Immacolata came out wearing the new blue dress and necklace, coy and shy, like a bride. The old woman nodded and smiled. *Bella?*

—*Bella*, she said. Again no exclamations of astonishment and delight at the staggering generosity of the visitor. She began to feel rather paranoid. Thank God there are no other children here, or they'd strip the baby. And what about my mauve dress that she hasn't given back yet? Is she going to wash it?

The old woman thought, perhaps the wife has money. Why else should he marry a woman so thin, and a foreigner?

As they got into the car Oreste said,

—They are disappoint the child is not a boy.

Well it doesn't really matter much, does it? The Englishwoman settled herself behind the wheel and placed the child in his lap. He held her, not looking, stiff with astonishment. The baby began to whimper. He handed her over to Immacolata in the back. Disappointed are they, the old bastards. They've got something more to be disappointed about, if they only knew it. The Englishwoman made a wide U-turn, avoiding a soggy looking patch of sand, and waved to the old couple as they went by.

—Where to now, your Honour?

The village consisted of a small square with a tree, a bench, and a café, a few streets of old houses, and a new hotel and row of villas that had sprung up in the last few years to create a seaside resort, although any sea worthy of the name was a good twenty minutes drive away. So the maid's life was not as isolated and empty as it had seemed.

—Immacolata she come here once every month, to get the money for my father's pension.

—How does she get here without a car?

—She walk, and then she take the bus.

In the back of the car Immacolata was nodding and smiling like a queen, although not many of her subjects in the street noticed. They bought a pound of loose pasta, a pound of rice in brownish, soft paper bags; a bag of eggs, a lump of hard cheese, a round, flat loaf of bread, a bunch of grapes (black), tomatoes (red), and filled Immacolata's plastic shopping bag with dark green leaves. Were they salad? Spinach?

—*Spinaci.*

—*Ah si.*

It was now dusk. In the café a group of people sat round a very small television set with a flickering image, perched in the branches of a tree. One solitary man sat at a table with a white cloth on it, eating spaghetti.

—Shall we have a cup of coffee? said the Englishwoman hopefully. The baby was unbathed, and probably in need of a clean nappy, but sleeping peacefully. Perhaps by the time they got back the parents would have retired to their temporary beds.

Oreste shrugged his shoulders and shook his head, the corners of his mouth turned right down and his eyes shut. He indulged in gestures and expressions with as much sensual satisfaction as the baby did, and they were almost as central to his ability to communicate. Who the hell needs words anyway? You need not bother to learn to speak, my child. Oreste and I have no need of words. Words would not help me with his parents. It's not words that could bring us together.

—Immacolata, said Oreste, jerking his head sideways towards the maid, whose arms were piled with the shopping (he himself carried nothing), and leading the way to the car.

—I have just made a great discovery, said Miranda. Words are quite unnecessary. We can get on better without them.

Oreste ignored her, proving her point. Was it not done, by the way, to sit in a café with your orphan maid, or would the excitement of it be so extreme that she would faint dead away?

Night had fallen completely when they got back to the house. A thin film of cloud covered the stars. Far in the east, over the sea, a glimmer of paleness from the rising moon smudged the undersides of a scattering of cirrus clouds. The dramas of the night, as secret and silent as the dramas of the day, had begun.

The light bulb in the kitchen was as dim as the lights in the house at Volterra. One standard lamp burned in the dining room, and there was a glow behind the closed doors of the old man's room. Immacolata left the shopping piled on the kitchen table. No milk, no butter, no animal fats. The old man shouldn't have had a stroke.

Immacolata went to help put her master to bed. Oreste found a book in the dining room, and sat at the table to read. The Englishwoman saw over his shoulder that it was a volume of Dante. It looked like his old school copy, abridged, with a red binding and inky underlinings. He read with elbows spread wide, both hands holding the book. He said,

—Is a difficult life for those women, with my father sick.

—Well why don't you go and help them, since you're here for once?

He turned back to his book.

—You understand nothing.

She drew her finger backwards and forwards across the table, making an unpleasant squeaking sound.

—I understand perfectly well; it's masculine pride. Yours and your father's. And I hate it.

He didn't answer. She sniffed and took her child into the bedroom. As she undressed, wiped and changed the baby—too late to bother about a bath today—she thought that they seemed remarkably uninterested in this famous grandchild that they had wanted so badly. The baby half woke to drink her bottle of sugar water, and then rolled over into sleep again, in another strange room, in another strange house, without a murmur.

The visitor lay on her back on the bed. She was as passive as the child, waiting to be served by the routine of the house. She was miserably hungry. It was days since they had had a proper meal. Not since Oreste had cooked spaghetti and veal in Volterra had they sat down at a table with steaming plates of food in front of them. No wonder Oreste was so slim. Or had he been secretly eating in the last hill town before the Adriatic, while she lay alone in the hotel room with the sick child? Tears came into her eyes. Her destiny was to lie alone, unfed, uncared for, in strange rooms. The thought entered her mind that had she been a true daughter-in-law and not here under false pretences she would have gone into the kitchen and cooked a little supper for herself and Oreste, but then on the other hand, perhaps not, in a strange house, in a strange country, on the first day of meeting.

She shut her eyes, and immediately the dimness of the bedroom was replaced by a clear image of the dining room, dark, except for one pool of light from the standard lamp with a frilly shade that fell obliquely across the figure of the man and his book, his dark head bent close to the page, waiting, but quietly and patiently, part of a ritual he understood. Then the vegetables on the kitchen table, waiting, the dark green of the spinach leaves (writhing and unfolding inside the bag?), the tomatoes, huge, round, yellowish red, flat on top, and the grapes black, a patch of shadow, a hole in the composition, waiting. The old man was being laid out on his bed, staring blankly at the ceiling or into his closed lids. Was it the impossibility of saying *buon giorno* and *buona sera* that hurt him most, the simple signals by which people can show their goodwill? Or did he now suddenly want people, anyone, to understand him and his life and his courage and his lack of it and his love and his evasions? Did those motionless lips indulge endlessly, in the existence they still must have in his mind as eager and elastic servants of his will, in conversations with friends or enemies or people remembered by chance, in which truths and understandings were pursued as they had never been when there was a voice between them? Or was his silence and his helplessness a blessed relief, an end to the unrelenting struggle, a free gift of the passive and uncommunicated joys of infancy again, before his consciousness was extinguished?

The quality of the waiting had changed. There was a smell of food. The Englishwoman opened her eyes, sat up, swung her legs over the side of the bed, stuffed her feet into her shoes.

In the dining room the old woman now sat beside her son, who had pushed his book to one side—though his hand still lay on the open page.

My son is sensitive, he is an artist, he always liked to read, even when he was a little boy. He is not like the others. She had taken off her housedress and was wearing her nightgown and wrap again. She sat sideways on to the table, leaning one elbow on it, her feet in leather slippers like her husband's, perhaps an old, discarded pair of his, flat to the floor. No spring in them. Many years since she had risen onto the balls of her feet, toes spread to keep her balance, or stretched and rolled her ankles. Sad black suede shoes in the wardrobe, with their inch and a half of heel.

Mother and son were talking in slow, quiet voices, discussing probably, family news—births, deaths, marriages, the progress of his nephews and nieces at school. The old couple's lives did have substance, after all, apart from Oreste. He was not their only child. If they did not have a daughter-in-law they had a son-in-law, an upstanding young man he was too, from his wedding photograph. They had grandchildren. Their blood continued to flow.

But not our souls. Our souls and our justifications are in the hands of the child who escaped.

In the kitchen Immacolata had remade the still life. Some of the tomatoes were now chopped and sizzled in a pan, and two eggs lay on the table, next to a bottle of oil.

A meal, a meal! She was preparing a meal! The visitor looked round for plates, knives, forks. In England, the first thing to be done when preparing a meal is to lay the table. Into the pan of tomatoes Immacolata broke the eggs, one by one, and stirred briskly. *Oeufs brouillés aux tomates.* Very nice. Is that for all four of us? Immacolata nodded and smiled, first towards the pan of food and then to the Englishwoman. Oreste looked round and called,

—You want eat?

—Yes, I'm starving.

She went through the kitchen door into the dining room. The old woman made a gesture with her head that conveyed in the most gracious manner, Do come in and sit down. I would get up, but my muscles are too old for politeness. Excuse me.

Relaxed and still, now that the first shocks of meeting were over, with her hair combed and pinned up and her husband in bed it was possible to see that her features were fine, and her manner had, or had once had, authority as well as charm. She was no simple peasant, but a bourgeois lady. The Englishwoman wondered who had created that other image, Oreste or herself.

—*Si accomodi.*

—*Grazie.* She sat down, in front of the shuttered window, next to Oreste, opposite the old lady.

—*La bambina dorme?*

—*Si.* Pause. *Stanca.* The word had an unsuitable, brash sound in this room. The old woman shook her head and sighed.

—*La povera.*

—*Troppo sole.*

—*Ah.*

—*In Inghilterra non ha basta de sole.*

—*Ah?* Try as she might the old woman's interest in the climatic conditions of England was minimal. Politeness, however, forced her to try.

—*Piove?*

—*Si.*

How much better it would be if custom did not dictate that we make an effort to talk. If we could only sit at the same table and observe one another, how much deeper our understanding, our sympathy, would be.

Immacolata brought in the dish of eggs and tomatoes, two plates, and two forks, and put them down in front of the visitors. The foreigner looked enquiringly at the old woman, but she shook her head. Oreste said,

—She eat already.

Immacolata came back with the flat loaf of bread and a knife. That was all. Oreste cut two slices of bread, and slid half of the eggs onto Miranda's plate and half onto his own. It was good. Through the doorway into the kitchen the Englishwoman caught a glimpse of Immacolata eating bread dipped into a cup of coffee.

She wanted to convey, herself, not through Oreste, I am sorry to have turned you out of your bed. It was very kind of you.

—*Er, scusi per il letto.*

The old woman's face wrinkled with incomprehension. There is nothing more aggressive than a failure to understand. She doesn't want to understand me. She's doing it on purpose. How do you mime: I'm sorry? Me, tap the chest, and him, point to her son, in your—yes, I'm talking to you, bed—head leaning sideways on hands, eyes shut, you over there, point to the daybed. Now what? Shrug the shoulders, shake the head? They stared at each other. I give up, thought the Englishwoman.

—*Si*, said the old woman, nodding. Oreste translated rapidly, bored and irritated. The old woman, understanding, spread her hands gracefully.

—*Niente.*

That was that. The food was eaten, the conversation over, now it was time to go to bed. Immacolata piled up the dishes with the bread on top, and took them into the kitchen to wash up.

—*Buona notte.*

—*Buona notte.*

The Englishwoman retired to the bathroom and then to bed, followed soon by her lover. The mattress was very hard. They lay side by side, not touching, the usual habits of the room pressing down on them. It was as if the force field of their bodies, which protected them from being swallowed up by this room, was very weak.

Oreste muttered in a low voice, —Tonight I need make love.

The Englishwoman put her arms round him, but he whispered,

—In my mother's bed I cannot. We wait till they are asleep.

They waited. Many trips to the lavatory by Immacolata and the old woman. Opening and shutting of doors. Pushing of furniture from place to place. Whispering. What happens if the old man wants to pee in the middle of the night? The wardrobe, the dressing table, the carved bedfoot made their presence felt in the darkness. The Englishwoman was half asleep when Oreste shook her gently by the arm.

—Come. He slipped out of bed. He was naked. He put on an old dressing gown of his father's. The Englishwoman was wearing a pale green nylon nightdress.

—Where are you going?

He motioned her to be quiet, opened the door, listened, holding her tightly by the arm. Silence. Darkness. The stone floor was cold to their bare feet. They crept down the passage. There was no light at all. The front door was shut. The Englishwoman stood, sick with nervousness, between the maid and the old man, while Oreste fiddled with the bolt. Did the old man hear the grinding of the bolt, the clicking of the latch? Did he sleep deep and drugged, or was his sleep so light that there was hardly any difference between sleeping and waking? Was he lying there now with his remaining senses tense and alert wondering if some stranger was creeping into the house to batter his helpless body in a search for imaginary gold?

—Hush . . . your father, she whispered, so quietly that even Oreste didn't hear. The hinges groaned and the door swung open. They ran outside and pushed it shut again. How large the outside world was. The air was still warm; it was not much past ten o'clock. They moved off the gravel patch onto the dunes. It was damp and rough under their feet. Oreste looked round carefully.

—Here. He knelt down, pulling at her hand.

—What? right out here in the open? The Englishwoman stood pulling her nightdress round her, refusing the ground.

—Is no one here.

—What happens if someone comes?

—No one live here. No one come here. He stood up and kissed her, letting his dressing gown fall off, and putting his hand up under her nightgown. Awkwardly, clasped together, bottom, knees, back, elbows, like a camel or an elephant, they got down. Oreste was so horny that his cock seemed to have grown as big as an elephant's, or maybe it was that the Englishwoman, in her fear, was tight and dry. She tried to hitch the discarded dressing gown under her buttocks to protect them from the sand, but Oreste was on her and in her, and she couldn't move. In his orgasm he tried to push her breasts off the rib cage up into her neck. She stared up at the moon, rigid, exposed to the air. Experiencing no pleasure. Oreste groaned, sighed with release. He whispered,

—You did not come?

She shook her head. He paused, rested his head on her shoulder, then tried again. A hen, still awake, stepped—paused, stepped—paused, like a guardsman slow marching into his line of vision. She clucked quietly. Intimate. Friendly. He said,

—Shoo!

She came closer. He balanced himself on one elbow. Threw a stone. She ran off a few yards with raised wings, feelings ruffled, scattering sand, with louder cluckings, and continued to peck and bubble to herself, a soft sound, somewhere between a cat and a pigeon. The Englishwoman made a few half-hearted movements of the hips, shut her eyes, opened her mouth. When Oreste said,

—You are ready? you come now?

She nodded, grimaced and squeezed in on him. But nothing could make her come that night. She was as dead as the old man.

She stared at the moon. The moon sailed free from a veil of light cloud. It seemed to be coming closer. The vast blackness of the sky edged closer. Dampness breathed up from the rough sand. The crystalline structure of each grain could be seen and felt. Far away, in the lagoon, tiny waves shushed and lapped, and on the other side the occasional distant, parabolic whine of a passing car.

Oreste pulled himself free, picked up the dressing gown, wiped himself with it, put it on. The Englishwoman sat up, tried to shake the sand out of her hair. Stood up, itched sand from between the cheeks of her buttocks. Oreste put his arm round her waist. She put her arm round his shoulders. Cold, empty, satisfied, they walked back to the house, two Magi, barefoot over the sand, in flowing robes, under a starry sky.

Enclosed in the heavy breathing darkness of the house once more, they became aware of its night existence. This was not a house where people slept solidly for eight hours and went about their business for the other twelve, but a house of the old, where to sleep means to doze, half conscious, in a blue grey twilight. Immacolata, perhaps, slept heavy and loglike, waking only when called to some midnight necessity of her master's, but the old woman was a night wanderer. Her deepest fear was that her husband might die while she slept beside him. Tonight, since she was not sharing his bed she got up, slowly, awkwardly, at least once an hour to peer into his room, listen at the door. Her bladder was weak, too. The house was never free for long of movement, muttering, the opening of doors, gurgling of water. After dawn, when Immacolata was up and started on her day's work, then the old woman might sleep for a few hours.

A light was on in the dining room. As they paused outside the door the daybed creaked. The daughter-in-law fled into her room, but Oreste, guilt reduced now that his desire was satisfied—it hadn't disappeared though, he was careful to go into the bathroom and flush the lavatory noisily to produce an alibi for his own wanderings, knocked on his mother's door.

The addition of sheets, pillow and quilt made a touching oasis of rest and privacy in this daytime room. The central light, a small cut-glass chandelier hanging over the table, was turned off. Light came from the standard lamp by the bed. Beside it one of the hard chairs was pulled up, a glass of water, several bottles of pills, a handkerchief, some pieces of cotton wool on it. The old woman was sitting on the side of the bed. Her son helped her to lie down, arranged the pillows comfortably behind her back, pulled up another chair, sat down beside her. Mother. He sat in silence for a few minutes. Neither of them mentioned the Englishwoman or the child. Oreste began to talk, as he had talked when he was a child about his school, about his life in Rome. Not too many details. He talked with passion about corruption and stupidity and lack of talent and how thwarted ambition can degenerate into bitterness. He sat, knees apart, elbows on his knees, cleaning his nails with the nails of the other hand, absorbing strength from this old, worn out woman. She, who all her life had been involved in a different struggle, listened to the story of her son's struggle, and sighed, and shook her head, and wondered why the world had become so harsh and difficult.

Not long after dawn the Englishwoman was awakened by the babbling of her child. Half-formed syllables—Da—da—ba—ba—a soft, continuous, contented sound. She smiled when she was picked up, full of life and charm. She had definitely recovered. She opened her mouth and blinked, hungry for a new life, a new day. The room was dark and stuffy. The smell of their own bodies had superceded the old people's smell. The mother, clutching her daughter, crept out of the room. The house was still full of sleep. Light came through the door at the back of the house, leading to the courtyard. The visitor had not been through it before. She tiptoed down the passage, and saw Immacolata in the bright morning sun, slapping and scrubbing clothes on a ridged wooden board balanced on an old horse trough in a corner of the yard. The Englishwoman's clothes.
—*Buon giorno.*

Immacolata looked up and waved.

—*Buon giorno.*

The broken down barns, silvery in the sunlight, were shaped like small ruined chapels. It was quiet, hot, fresh. The Englishwoman felt light-hearted. As long as the old people were asleep she could be more at ease in this house.

In the kitchen, she started to prepare food for the baby, moving quietly to prolong her solitude. The baby sat up in her chair on the table as she had done in the kitchen in Volterra, watching with alert concentration as Mummy prepared her breakfast. There was not very much milk left in the tin. Even diluted it would not last longer than another day, and there were only a few tins of apple and one of meat. The baby devoured her apple, and some cereal, and then as she drank her bottle, they went to sit on the wall in the sunshine and watch Immacolata. Up at dawn to wash my clothes, poor wretch. Ah well, she didn't have to. It was her own suggestion. Oh yes, and what about my dress?

—*Immacolata, dov'è la mia vestita?*

—*Come?* Immacolata wrinkled her brow, wrinkled in fact her whole face, as she squeezed and wrung the clothes. Not really the best way to treat nylon, but still.

—*La mia vestita.* Oh Lord, how do I say this? *Provare. Provare solo.* I'm fine with the infinitive, but when it comes to changing tense or person I come unstuck. Heaping the pale, multi-coloured sausages of cloth onto her board Immacolata asked with a sullen expression,

—*Non è per me?*

The Englishwoman shrugged her shoulders apologetically.

—*Uno, bello.* Dammit, she wants to strip me naked. That's probably why she suggested doing my washing, she thought she could take her pick. Immacolata hung the clothes on a line that stretched from the house to one of the barns, and walked past the Englishwoman and the baby, hugging her board to her hip, smouldering with childish rage and disappointment. But no one needed to fear the rage of Immacolata. The orphanage in which she lived before she was taken in by the Miras had been run by nuns, and they had done their work well. Her rage was weak and impotent, her disappointment a habit.

When she got back to the room the Englishwoman found the dress on the bed, draped over the still sleeping form of Oreste. She put the baby back in the cot, and tried the dress on again, turning and posing in front of the wardrobe mirror. Yes, it was becoming, gay, charming; and with the headscarf made her look like a Hollywood or travel brochure version of a peasant. Perhaps she would wear it for dinner tonight. What did Immacolata want with phoney peasant dresses? She was the real thing.

When Oreste awoke, Immacolata brought some coffee into the dining room. The old woman had woken and gone to her husband. The sheets were folded and put away. Only the bottle of pills, the cotton wool and the handkerchief remained on the chair by the daybed. The grapes had been put into a cut-glass bowl in the middle of the table. They drank the black coffee and ate the black grapes, same colour but different sensations, hot and bitter, fresh and cool, with the unexpected translucent green under the thick skin.

The Englishwoman said,

—Can we go to the beach today?

Oreste shrugged his shoulders. —Is no good beach here.

—But the sea can't be far away.

—We must drive, and then walk.

Oreste went into the bathroom to shave. The Englishwoman moved the car into the shade, changed into her bathing suit, put her dress back on top, filled up the thermos with boiled water, lay down on the bed. It was too hot to walk around outside. When he had finished shaving, Oreste went into his father's room. The Englishwoman waited. It was absurd not to visit the beach when it was so close; in summer, in Italy, on holiday. But it was equally absurd to anoint herself with Ambre Solaire Mousse and drag an unwilling Oreste from one patch of sand to another for the sake of—what? A swim in the shallow, brackish water of the lagoon? A tan? Better perhaps to lie on the bed all day, in the dark room, in her bathing suit, covered with suntan lotion. If only I was very tired, or ill, then I would have a reason to lie here all day. I could easily repress my childish, Northern excitement at the idea of a sunny beach.

But by noon Oreste was ready. In spite of the shade the plastic seats of the car were almost too hot to touch, even through their clothes. The best hours of the day had been wasted. The baby was protected by a sunhat, Nivea cream, and a special canopy that fitted over the carrycot, but she still whimpered and panted with the heat and demanded a bottle every few minutes.

—This is the first time I've been to the beach this summer. It's over an hour's drive to the sea from Volterra.

Oreste grunted. They drove along the main road away from the village, and then out towards the sea along a dirt road, past patches of green, reclaimed land, an occasional house, canals and ditches. The road became a dike, with mudflats on either side, and occasional seabirds lumbering into the sky. The mud was brown and silver, the sky grey, not with cloud, but with haze. They turned onto another dike, running at right angles to the first. Oreste said,

—We stop here.

The dike ended on a concrete embankment. Below it was a narrow strip of dark brown sand, glistening with particles of quartz. The water was so shallow that it was brownish yellow for a hundred yards, until the long arm of a sand dune lifted itself up, and beyond that was a tantalising strip of sparkling, azure sea. The Englishwoman stared round blankly.

—Can't we go over there?

—You must walk. When I was a child we go there.

There were no gay striped umbrellas, no comfortable mattresses, no juke box or Coca-Cola stands. They got out of the car. The heat settled down on top of them like hot irons clamped around their heads. The young man took off his shirt and tied it around his head like a turban. He smoothed some of his companion's Ambre Solaire Mousse on his shoulders and the bridge of his nose. The woman put on a sunhat, wiped the sweat off her sunglasses, took off her dress. Looked at the baby who was crying fretfully, and the concrete embankment which was six foot high and sloped at an angle of seventy-five degrees. There were no steps.

—I'd better take her out of the carrycot. You go down first, then I'll hand the carrycot to you, and then the baby.

She piled towels, nappies, bottles of juice into the carrycot, she paused, hands on hips, surveying the pile.

—Isn't there a better beach somewhere near?

Oreste jumped down the embankment, staggered to keep his balance, adjusted his turban; called up,

—Is too much people, and the water very dirty. He made a grimace of disgust. —From the town, the factories.

—You mean sewage?

He held up his hands for the laden carrycot. She tucked the baby under one arm, crouched down, squeezing droplets of sweat from between calves and thighs, tipped the carrycot over the edge and slid it down, the rough concrete making tearing noises on its canvas bottom. The baby too was passed down, wriggling and arching her back in sudden terror as her mother lay down on the dike and pushed her over the edge.

—Don't drop her!

The child screamed in ear-piercing despair, rigid and trembling, only giving herself time at each breath to take in enough air to start screaming again. The young man held her naturally this time, rocking her in the crook of his arm. He said soothingly,

—Hush baby, your Mummy she come, as the young mother scrambled down the embankment, ran to her child, held her in familiar arms. A pause, the eyes opened slightly, the rectangle of the mouth softened, the shrieks tapered off. She gulped at a bottle of juice, stomach rising and falling, with a quiver in each breath, lashes stuck together with tears, eyes fixed accusingly on the woman's face.

Her bed was prepared, a hot little refuge from the sand. A towel to protect her from the burning plastic mattress, and another draped between the hood and the parasol to protect her chubby knees from a stray ray of sun. Shirt off, rattle for amusement, and there she was in a cocoon of green and orange light reflected from the towels, with a narrow gap through which she could peer to make sure that Mama was still there. This left no towels for the adults. Oreste took off his jeans and used them to lie on, and the Englishwoman scrambled up to the car again to fetch her dress.

Large, glittering grains of sand stuck to their greased bodies. Moving carefully the woman tried to wipe her body free of it, but the Ambre Solaire came too, and when she smoothed on more, gritty particles of sand scratched trails along her skin.

—I give up. I shall have a dappled tan.

Oreste was lying on his stomach with his head pillowed on his arms in the six-inch shade of the carrycot. He opened one eye.

—You want walk to the sea? The water she is good there.

—You mean right out beyond the sandbank?

—Yes.

—What do you suggest I do with the baby? Leave her by herself, or will you carry her?

He shrugged.

—You should have give her to Immacolata. I tell you Immacolata will take care of the child.

The woman turned her head the other way in silence. The heat was heavy, dark, dazzling. The woman thought, noons like this, one can see that space is black. After a few minutes she could no longer bear the heat, and waded into the sea. The water did not come as high as her knees, even after she had waded for several minutes. She stood, gigantic in the flatness. She half turned to see Oreste and the carrycot. They lay small, foreshortened, almost invisible in the shimmering air. Beyond the sandbank and clearly unattainable a small patch of sea took on a normal turquoise and the strip of sand shone white. At the edges of her vision were fibrillations of blackness. She lay down in the tepid, salty water, and allowed water and mud and sand to wash over her body. No protection for the head and eyes, little refreshment for the body. Her back and legs prickled with heat after only ten minutes exposure. Strange sensation to pull your body free of the buoyancy of water and stand up, unexpectedly topheavy. Stiff legged, sending a plume of disturbed yellow murk ahead of each foot to cloud the transparent water, she waded back to shore.

Hot. Hot. Hot. On her back this time, hat pulled down over her eyes, conscious of the trickling of sea water and sweat, rivulets soon dry, and the white incrustations of salt on her skin. The baby should have some lunch. Or was it too hot? Perhaps she could wait till they got back to the house. There was only one tin of beef anyway, so the later she had it the less hungry she would be for supper. They couldn't get any more until tomorrow, because it was Sunday. Sunday. Louis had taken a plane from Pisa to London on Sunday. He had said he'd be gone—how long? A week or ten days? The woman sat up with a dull gasp as if someone had hit her in the stomach.

—I have to get back.

—We just come.

—I have to get back to Volterra, now, today.

—My mother she make a dinner for us tonight.

She leaned towards him and enunciated clearly, through her teeth,

—My husband may be coming back at any minute. He may be there now.

Oreste turned over, leaning on one elbow, his expression became harsh. —You are with me now. I am your husband.

The Englishwoman stared at him blankly. She took refuge in being an Englishwoman and staring at him blankly. She gave an affected laugh. My God, the poor bastard doesn't think I'd ever actually marry him, does he? The Englishwoman stared at him blankly. She said,

—And who do you think is going to feed the baby? You couldn't keep a mouse, let alone a wife and child. The Englishwoman stared at him blankly. She repeated,

—He's my husband. I've got to go back.

—You no go back to him.

Impasse. The woman's head began to ache.

—I'll stay for dinner and go back tomorrow.

—You no go back to him.

Oreste's face had become suddenly thin and pale. A muscle in his jaw twitched. He looked like a skinned rabbit, useful nursery term, every addition that experience or society makes—clothes, haircut, expression, manners, had been stripped away. His ears stick out. The woman stared at him with hysterical dislike; but she became afraid of hurting him.

—I have no more money.

—Money is nothing, he said with a curl of the lip.

—I can get money. Back on familiar ground he began to look better. The child started to cry again. The heat, the brown sand, the salt and sweat suddenly became intolerable. The woman stood up.

—Let's go.

—I tell you the beach is no good.

Just because we're having an argument doesn't mean we can't co-operate on practical things. The Englishwoman started to dismantle the baby's hideout; she methodically folded and stowed. Oreste did not move. I can manage perfectly well without you. She had worked out a way of getting carrycot and baby up to the car. Easier up than down. Tuck the baby (protesting, but never mind) into the carrycot beside the towels, attach her harness, push the carrycot up the embankment until it tipped over, found solid ground, one end sticking over the edge, was pushed all the way to safety. Cries of rage and astonishment echoed down from above their heads. The young man remained supine, looking out to sea. She thought this must be the nastiest beach in Italy. She said,

—Are you coming? He said,

—I no recognise you. You are different woman.

She shrugged her shoulders, scrambled up the embankment, picked up the carrycot and child, staggered over to the car. No longer a car, but an oven, a fiery furnace, an outpost of hell. She heaved the cot into the back seat, uncovered the child, stuffed a dummy into its mouth, slipped on her dress. The young man had not appeared. She called,

—I'm going now, it's too hot to wait here.

Silence. Not even the sound of a seabird. They were few and far between. Not even the sound of another car, in the distance, or the earth cracking, the sea steaming in the heat. She started the engine, rolled forward, slowly. Blessed relief of moving air through the windows. No figure behind her, running, calling, waving. She gathered speed, turned left, back the way they had come; pressed her foot on the accelerator; oh, beautiful coolness. Past a few farm buildings and patches of green.

When she reached the main road the Englishwoman turned left, away from the mother-in-law, and the old man, and Immacolata, and the celebration dinner. She was free, and alone except for the complaining child in the back. Why don't I drive straight to Volterra now, leaving Oreste lying on the beach, and all my possessions for Immacolata? Last Will and Testament. At the first village she stopped for petrol, gave the child the last prepared bottle of fruit juice, and made a U-turn.

When she got back Oreste was sitting on the edge of the embankment, his feet dangling over the edge, wearing his jeans and shirt. As he got into the car he said,

—I know you will come back to me.

IX

No siesta today at the house. Preparations for the feast are going forward. Immacolata is busy in the kitchen, her hair sticky with sweat. The old man sits in his wheel chair in the dining room, dressed, with a clean white shirt and spotted bow tie under his linen jacket. He sits to the left of the door that leads in from the passage, and his wife is sitting opposite him, by the door leading into the kitchen, where she can polish the silver and keep an eye on Immacolata at the same time. Oreste and the Englishwoman come in, gentle with the sweet relief of a reconciliation, though the woman knows quite well that no reconciliation has taken place.

—*Buon giorno.*

—*Buon giorno.* The old lady inclined her head politely. *Va bene la bambina?* The child was whimpering.

—*A fame.*

—*Ah, poverina.*

Oreste went into the kitchen and poured himself a glass of water. He handed it to the woman.

—You want.

—Thanks. She drank, and handed it back. Immacolata said nothing, but turned her skinny shoulders and snub profile away. The foreigner retired to the bedroom. A change of nappy, change of clothes, cool sponge over the face and hands, slowly the child's whimpering died down. Her mother filled the bottle, thrust it into the avid mouth, and was nerving herself to join the family circle round the dining room table and feed the baby on her knee (charming maternal picture) when Oreste came in.

—What you do with Immacolata? You give her the dress, then you take it back?

Oho, so she's trying a bit of blackmail is she, the bastard orphan bitch.

—I gave her one dress, and some beads, and let her try on another one. I told her so very clearly. *Provare* means to try, doesn't it?

—She no understand.

—She didn't want to understand. You told me to show her my clothes. Does that mean everything I show her I've got to give her?

—Immacolata is poor girl, not clever. What you need with that dress?

What do I need with that damn dress? I hate it.

—O.K., O.K., she can have it. I don't care. Take it away. The Englishwoman picked up the dress and threw it at him. Here, this too. Don't forget the headscarf. A cancerous lump of pain had grown in her throat. Sometimes it moved to the top of her stomach. She's a damn sight cleverer than I am. Her husband isn't returning to an empty house on the far side of these mountains, now, at this very minute.

Slowly and heavily she picked up the child, with her bottle, the jars of beef and apple, the bib, the spoon. The child sucked up the last of her juice, was heaved up against Mum's shoulder. The visitor, the stranger, moved into the dining room, smiled at the old man, squeezed past his immoveable legs, sat down. Patted the baby's back to bring up her wind. The baby stared from one to the other of the photographs on the sideboard. A bubble of air worked its way up from her tum and popped out between her lips. All right, now let's give the old man a treat. He can watch the baby being fed. Immacolata appeared at the kitchen door, wreathed in smiles, nodding and bobbing.

—*Grazie, grazie.*

The Englishwoman shrugged her shoulders and smiled unwillingly.

—*Niente.* How absurd.

The old woman was making a gesture which seemed to mean: poor Immacolata, such little things give her so much pleasure.

The visitor repeated her shrug and smile, and thrust in the next mouthful of food in answer to an outraged cry.

—*Mangia bene.*

—*Si.*

The old woman gave each piece of silver cutlery a final wipe with her chamois leather cloth.

—*È magra, la bambina.*

—*Si. Mala a l'estomaco. Ma adesso va bene.*

—*A bisogno di mangiare.*

—*Si.*

The cloth was slowly, neatly, folded up. Rectangle, square, rectangle, square. The top screwed onto the bottle of polish. The silver wrapped in a piece of green baize cloth. The jar of meat was already empty. Miranda unscrewed a jar of apple and didn't even wait to wipe the spoon before loading it again, and thrusting it into the open, anxious mouth, Was the old man watching, appreciating this tableau of family life? No, his eyes were fixed on the open door of the kitchen. They don't want me here. I'm doing nothing for them. Louis entering the dark hallway of the house in Volterra, arms full of books and toys, bursting with news. Her forearm lay on this dark, polished table, in this small, stuffy room, where the dust on the floor was a fine drift of sand. Reflected in the far side of the table were the bottle of polish, the knives and forks wrapped in their green baize cloth, the old woman's arthritic hand, the fingers never quite still, imperceptibly changing their pressure on the table from moment to moment. The silence of the old couple, the smells of food drifting in from the kitchen, the stupid gratitude (at last) of Immacolata, wound round her like a cocoon, a spiral of lassitude. From the bathroom came the rushing of water as Oreste took a shower. The Englishwoman could still feel the salt contracting the surface of her skin. Louis put down his books, his parcels, puzzled by the silence, the unaccustomed neatness of the house. Why had the door been shut? Where was the car? Ah yes, they had gone for a drive, they'd be back soon. The child, having finished her juice, beef and apple, drank greedily from her bottle of diluted milk. Only enough for one more this evening. Her lashes drooped with sleep, eyes rolled in an effort to keep the lids open. She could no longer summon the energy to do more than give an occasional suck at the half-empty bottle. The mother eased the rubber nipple from between her daughter's lips, put it down to add its inverted reflection to the images on the table, and leaned the baby over one shoulder again, head lolling, to pat her until the wind came. It was six o'clock. No sign of them yet. Louis had unpacked, been surprised to discover the twin beds in their room, wondered—went up to the bathroom and could not find his wife's washing things. Some of her clothes were missing, and a suitcase. He looked into the dressing table drawer. The money was still there. Downstairs on the hall table were a pile of his letters, unopened. He went outside again, to look for Gina or Corrado.

Oreste came in, his hair wet and combed down smoothly. He was wearing clean clothes, ready for the dinner. He stood in the doorway stretching and smiling, rolled his head right round a couple of times to loosen the neck muscles.

—That is good. You want shower?

The old woman put her fingers on her lips, and gestured towards the sleeping child. The Englishwoman nodded silently. Got up, moving as little as possible; eased the floppy, topheavy creature down into the crook of her arm. crept stealthily out. As she was about to go through the door, having squeezed her way past the old man's knee, Oreste's mother touched her on the arm. She beckoned. The Englishwoman turned, bent down, presented the child to be admired. Lashes curled along her cheek, lips half open, eyebrows slightly raised, flesh downy and pink.

—*Che bella.*

The old woman stroked her cheek with a gentle finger, and played with the strand of hair behind her ear.

—*Gli occhi azurri.*

—*Si.*

—*Come lei.*

—*Si.* Pause. The Englishwoman added, *adesso. Ma forse più tarde...*

—*Si.*

The old woman shook her head.

—*Stanca.* The two women smiled at each other, and the daughter-in-law took her child back into the bedroom and put her down in the cot. The water of the shower was tepid but refreshing. Louis remained poised on the threshold of the house in his search for Gina and Corrado. Neither of them appeared. Ten days, after all, would not be until next Tuesday, the day after tomorrow. Driving all day she should be there by Monday night, ready to meet him on Tuesday.

After her shower she packed up all her clothes, beautifully ironed and folded and placed on the dressing table by Immacolata. The plastic bag of necessities for the baby was almost empty. Tomorrow she would have to buy nappies, milk, food. She would have to borrow money from Oreste. Give him a taste of his own medicine.

When the Englishwoman emerged, the afternoon was beginning to get cooler. The old man was sitting outside, a fringed parasol attached to the arm of his chair. They were going to eat outside in the hour before sunset. The wooden table was covered with a white cloth, and six places were laid. Were they expecting a guest? The kitchen was empty, peaceful, drained of effort. Several pans stood on the stove with lids over them. The steam of cooking drifted in the air. The shutters were open and light came through the mosquito screen cool and chequered. Outside the shadow of the house stretched for several yards. Immacolata had disappeared like an animal into her burrow. The old woman was in the bathroom. The visitor wondered whether she should go to sit with the old man on the bench in front of the house, offering silent companionship, or trying to entertain him with observations in pidgin Italian.

Oreste appeared from the back of the house.

—Come.

She followed him down the passage, out of the back door, into the yard where she had watched Immacolata doing the washing that morning. Against the back wall of the house was a rough wooden staircase, leading up to a square door. Oreste climbed up, beckoning the woman to follow. She clung tightly to the hand rail. The steps had once been painted white, and were now rotting. The sunshine was hot, bland, beautiful, laid their shadows low on the whitewashed wall. Inside the door was a loft, roofbeams, a rough floor, all once painted white, filled with soft white light from two windows under the roof. Makeshift partitions, old furniture, the junk of many years. Two small rooms that had been partitioned off still had beds in them, but the iron bedsteads had lost castors, mattress, and were veiled with dust and cobwebs.

—When I am a boy I sleep here, and my friend.

They leaned from the windows. Directly below them was the old man's parasol. From this height the lagoons could be seen, glistening a pale robin's egg blue now that the sun had lost its dazzling brightness. The road ran thin and grey beside the mudflats.

—You want really go tomorrow? asked Oreste.

—I have to.

—I come with you.

Panic.

—Oreste, you can't.

—I take the train for Rome.

—Oh. I'm frightened that Louis might be back already.

—If you love me you are not afraid.

They gazed at each other in the clear, warm light, each framed in half of the window embrasure, with golden light from the late afternoon sun touching one side of their faces, and the pale reflected light from inside the room lighting up the shadows on the other. The Englishwoman's face was still pale, oval, expressionless. There is nothing I can say about love. The Italian stared back, his eyes dark and shining, his face given fullness and colour by the light. Women are powerful, gentle, weak. They do not know where their own loyalties lie. He leaned forward and kissed her very gently on the lips. Then took her hand and said,

—We go down now.

On the bench outside the house the old woman had joined her husband. Her blouse was of navy blue chiffon with white polka dots, a bow tied at the neck; but her feet were still in old slippers.

—*Buona sera*, she smiled, she was the hostess. The expanse of sand and dirt, the patches of gravel, the tufts of grass, were transformed into her garden. She conjured another figure out of the evening air. The Englishwoman turned towards the sea. (Why does my heart always contract with hope at the arrival of a stranger? Daddy, Daddy, is it you knocking at the door, walking towards us out of the golden sand?) Approaching along the dirt track from the broken-down house two hundred yards closer to the lagoons, was an old man with a neat Van Dyke beard, wearing a Panama hat, pince-nez, a baggy grey cotton suit and a shirt with a wing collar much too wide for his skinny neck. He carried a walking stick and a bottle of wine.

The hostess smiled and waved at the blurred figure coming into her line of vision.

—*Signor Silvolli*, she said, turning to the visitor. *Professore*. The Englishwoman said to Oreste,

—I thought no one lived in that house?

—For the holidays. He is teacher and scholar. He write a book about the poet Giacomo Leopardi.

He got up and went to meet the teacher and scholar. The two of them stood several yards away, acting out a pantomime of meeting and friendship. The glitter of the sand and sky almost gave the impression that their images were repeated by reflection beneath their feet. Their movements were fractionally slowed down by the twin effects of distance and unusual clarity. The stranger thrust his walking stick with a flourish under the arm that held the bottle of wine, and shook Oreste's hand energetically. They slapped each other on the back, nodded their heads, smiled, shook hands again, walked back to the watching group, arms round each other. The visitor placed his cane neatly on the table, the bottle of wine beside it,

—*Un piccolo dono,* took off his hat, put it on the bench and kissed the hand of Signora Mira with a flourish.

—*Sempre generoso,* she shook her head, smiling, almost blushing, turned to her daughter-in-law, shrugged her shoulders.

Signor Silvolli took up one of his neighbour's hands in both his. He held it gently.

—*Come va, amico? Il figlio è tornato a casa, eh? Voi siete felice.* The old man sat still in his wheel chair. Hospitality, friendship, enmity, irritation, all to be inferred from the strangled sound in his throat, the flicker of one eyelid.

He laid the hand back, carefully, on its fellow, and turned to the foreigner.

—And the beautiful English lady. He kissed her hand with an elegant bow. You see, I speak your language. His speech was very clearly articulated, and each sentence drew to a proper close.

—I learned it many years ago at school, and from reading your great authors Dickens and Shakespeare.

He stood back, hands clasped over his crumpled waistcoat, waiting to see the effect of his words. Oh lovely old man; yes, indeed we have something in common. You used to teach and I have been taught. Perhaps we can pass this dinner in literary conversation? I used to be rather good at flirtatiously discussing Shakespeare with older men. There must be a role, somewhere, in which I can shine. The Englishwoman smiled with pleasure.

—You speak English beautifully. Much better than I speak Italian.

Oreste took the bottle of wine into the house. The hostess gestured towards the bench.

—*Si accomodi.* Signor Sivolli bowed to Miranda,

—After you, Madame.

The Englishwoman sat at the far end of the bench facing the house with Signor Silvolli opposite her, next to the old woman. She thought: as a guest I too should be sitting on the other side of the table to see the view. But then as a member of the family I should be sitting next to the old man and talking to him and perhaps even feeding him. From her seat she could see Signor Silvolli's tortoise head and neck framed by the white wall of the house; a section of brown mudflats, behind them a line of dunes, the distant smoke of the town and the factory, and a section of grey road and greenish landscape leading up to the mountains. No far horizons, no lagoons, not much sky. The sun warmed her left cheek. Soon it would disappear behind the mountains and they would be left in shadow a full three quarters of an hour earlier than the people facing towards the Mediterranean. The shadow crept slowly down the steep side of the mountains. When it reached the flat coastal plain it would race ahead to engulf them.

Oreste came out of the house carrying the opened bottle of wine and a jug of water, and followed by Immacolata *en grande dame*. She was carrying the tray from the dining room with the liqueur glasses on it, and wearing her latest trophy, the mauve dress. The headscarf was tied round her waist like a sash, which did something, but not enough, to disguise the difference in size between the dress and Immacolata, and the blue beads again hung around her skinny brown neck.

Suitable exclamations.

—*Chi è questa bellezza?*
—*Che bel colore!*

Wine bubbled into the tiny glasses, yellow, tinged with green. Toasts were drunk, to the returned prodigal, the English wife, the sleeping grandchild, the host and hostess, the meal. The Englishwoman thought: how strange; I walk in here by chance, off the street, I find a place laid for me at the table, and they raise their glasses to drink to me. She raised her glass in return and looked at them suspiciously.

Every line and fold and change of texture glowed in the golden light, against the white wall. The old woman's cheeks were pinker, with rouge, or excitement, or the light, than they had been on the previous day. In the centre of her cheeks was a patch where there were no wrinkles; soft, melting, fondant pink. By contrast the chiffon of her blouse felt rough to the imagination; grated on the ear; set the teeth on edge. Signor Silvolli, skin and beard the same greyish brown. Skin coarse grained, cheeks and forehead pleated into folds, beard soft, barbered, smooth. Leaning forward, speaking with an accent and intonation forgotten since the turn of the century.

—When I was in England as a young man I have visited Folkestone to pay homage to the house where Dickens himself lived.

Now the long-awaited meal comes steaming to the table. Pasta. In this particular case the long thin version more commonly known in English-speaking countries as spaghetti. Spaghetti? Impossible. Yes, spaghetti, on a large oval platter with tomato sauce on top, and a saucer of powdery grated cheese. The tomato was acid and fresh. For the old man a bowl of minced chicken and rice, spooned between his lips by Immacolata. Another dish of the same mixture was placed by the Englishwoman.

—*Per la bambina.*

The Englishwoman was unable to coax more than a few strands of spaghetti past the cancerous lump in her throat. They will wind down my oesophagus like tapeworms and take possession of me. She crawled under the table, huddling away from legs and feet and gnawed on the grey wood of the table leg until her lips were full of splinters.

Testimony to the existence of a child was heard from within the house. A mother rose to attend her.

The mountain of spaghetti became a hillock, a mere contour map. Oreste ate for several days at a time. So did Immacolata. The old people ate their share, and watched benignly. In the kitchen Immacolata finished the spaghetti left on the Englishwoman's plate.

When the mother came out again carrying her child dressed in a clean pink and green flowered frock, and wearing a bib with a pink lamb in one corner and a yellow duck in the other, new wonders had arrived. Chicken, boiled, then cut in pieces and roasted in the oven with garlic. A dark green cake, empty in the middle, like a large rum baba. Signor Silvolli kissed his fingers.

—This is a great speciality. Not from this region, but from the region where I was born, the Toscana.

The child, pink and white and green, with a touch of yellow, gazing around her with bright eyes and birdlike movements of the head, settled herself down on her mother's red linen lap.

—What is it?

—*Spinaci*. Spinach. *Épinards*. It is like a soufflé, but made with spinach.

It reminded the Englishwoman of something. Oh yes, the shapes of cooking pots piled unused in the kitchen in Volterra. She chewed a mouthful of green cake for some time. The obstruction in her throat was solid and impassible. Can I take it by surprise? Sneak it round the edge? No. She spat into her hand, dropped the spinach, ground it into the sand with her foot, wiped the palm of her hand on the back of her child's bib.

The child, testing the unaccustomed textures of the rice and the chicken with her tongue ate, and was commented on, praised and admired. It was generally agreed that she did not take after Oreste, but had blue eyes, like her mother. Her mother thought: I cannot go through the laborious chore of remaining conscious throughout this dinner, this sunset, this evening, this night. When the child had finished her bowl of food, Signor Silvolli, who had been waiting for this moment, said,

—She is like Oliver Twist, she asks for more! He leaned across the table to grasp the Englishwoman's hand, and burst out laughing.

The edge of the shadow of the mountains reached them before the imminence of sunset had turned the sky orange. The evening became gay. The conversation was in Italian. Signor Silvolli spoke of the dreary provincialism of life in the town, and the romance of living by the lagoons. Comfort was of no interest to him, but he loved to watch the light on the water, to see the changing hours and seasons, to walk among the dunes by moonlight or at dawn, repeating the poems of Leopardi, or on occasion his own humble attempts. Where were you walking last night by moonlight, old man? Oreste, relaxed, smoking, elbows on the table, took over the lead role and began to enlarge on the description he had given his mother about the corruption and venality of the capital city. Ah you poetaster, you cautious man, all your life has been spent in compromise and illusion. Yes, you taught in the university for forty years, yes, you are writing a book on Leopardi (and that for how many years?); yes, you wander the shores of the world at dawn chanting verses, but you were never a true poet. You never hazarded your life on being an artist as I, Oreste, have done. Oreste was transformed into Orpheus, piping with pure notes of artistic ambition and integrity to lure a career from the underworld of Rome. The parents listened, breathless, gasping at his courage, forgiving his neglect. As he spoke the sky over the mountains became orange and then purple and then grey, while the sky over the sea deepened to indigo.

Where have I been? thought the Englishwoman. I have not been here. Her spine was rigid. There was no back to the bench. She shifted her body slightly to see if it was still capable of movement. Buttocks, neck, knees, still present as before; child still cradled in her lap, watching the people talk, moving her mouth in imitation. I don't know where I've been, but I have not been here. You ought to go away more often. Is it not time yet to pack up the last few things, and get into the car and go?

As it grew darker Immacolata brought out two stubs of candle stuck in old glasses, and made some coffee. The old woman held out her arms for her granddaughter, and the child stared up in surprise at this new old face, and pulled and patted at the blue chiffon bow. This is the end. This is the last lap. This is their ration.

The Englishwoman turned to the loving father of the child, who had turned his head away and was staring towards the faint glimmer of the rising moon,

—Have you told your mother we are leaving tomorrow?

—Sh! Not now. Later I tell.

Signor Silvolli gave them a quick, bright look through his pince-nez. The Englishwoman smiled at him.

—We have to be back in Rome tomorrow. Oreste might be offered a part in a film.

—For that, yes, you must go. But the life of this house will be empty indeed without your presence.

A stillness descended on the group of people round the table. The eating, drinking, talking had been done.

—*Scusa!* The Englishwoman got up and went into the house. She sat on the edge of the bed and ground her teeth. Ran round the room yelling,

—I've got to get out, get out, get out. No sound. No movement. She went out again to join the party. Signor Silvolli, about to leave, had shaken every hand but hers. This accomplished (with the flourish of a kiss, his beard brushing her knuckles) and many elegant farewells in Italian and English, he picked up his Panama and walking stick and departed, first his grey suit and then his white hat vanishing into the twilight.

He had escaped. One had escaped. There were still three more to go. They were still a party, even without the local academic. They continued to sit over the coffee. The table was covered with the debris of the meal, open bottle, used plates, crusts of bread, which always look so beautiful in paintings and photographs, as if the essence of life had been tasted at that table. Then, with a sigh, the old woman handed the child back to her mother, and asked Immacolata to clear away. Oreste and the old woman together manoeuvred the father back to his bedroom. The end of the evening was in sight. A wild hope began to blossom in the heart of the Englishwoman. Will I be allowed after all to escape from the monstrous prison of illusion?

She put the child to bed, and packed, again, her suitcase. I have no money to leave for Immacolata (half a crown, or a ten shilling note on the crocheted mat on the dressing table). I have left her dresses, that's enough. She put on her nightdress and lay on the bed. I cannot say goodbye to the old people if he has not told them we are going.

After a couple of hours Oreste came in.

—Did you tell your mother we are going?

—Yes, I tell her. He was sullen, frowning, his lips curved with bitterness and cynicism; turned down at the corners.

—You want very much to go away. To leave me.

—Of course I don't, Oreste, but I can't just not be there when he gets back; he's my husband.

He leaned over her on the bed and stared into her eyes.

—I not want you sleep with that man. You understand? If you sleep with him I kill you.

How the hell will you know? What have you achieved with your male dominance? I'm frightened of you and I'll lie to you, or I'm sorry for you and I'll lie to you.

—All right, Oreste. I won't, I promise.

—Come. He took her wrist.

—Where?

—Outside.

—No, I won't, I can't. That old man is wandering about reciting poetry.

—You must come.

—I can't.

Eventually they made love on the floor, on the opposite side of the bed from the carrycot, with the Englishwoman's legs clasped round Oreste's neck, and her head bumping rhythmically against the bottom of the wardrobe. Back in bed Oreste told her about a girl friend he had once had in England.

—She pick me up in the street. You have notice how the girls all look to me in the street?

It was true. She had noticed. This girl was a nurse, and very passionate, and after they had been having an affair for a week she said to Oreste one evening when they had finished making love: —I've got to tell you something. I'm in love. —I know, he had answered, secure in the knowledge of his body and hers, —with me. —Oh no, I'm engaged to this doctor; he's ever so nice. We're getting married next week.

—That I cannot understand, he said. That is disgusting to me. Oh how well I can understand it, thought Miranda, seeing her lover through the English nurse's eyes. And why does he tell me that story assuming that I am not like her?

—I will get a room in Rome, and write to you when it is ready for you and the child to come.

—It is impossible, muttered the Englishwoman under her breath, hiding her face in his shoulder.

—You must not be sad. We will be together, he answered, holding her close.

In the morning the Englishwoman and the baby were dressed and packed, with the luggage piled high into the car while Oreste was still asleep. Immacolata in her nightgown and wrap made a pot of coffee.

—*Grazie, Immacolata. Arriverderci*, said the Englishwoman.

She was full of confidence and excitement at the prospect of at last seizing her freedom. The sun had just risen, and shed streamers of pale yellow light through the cool grey air. She shook Oreste.

—I'm ready. I'm going now.

He made tender, sleeping noises in his throat, and turned to kiss her arm.

—I'm going. I'm ready.

—What? He sat up, rudely awake.

—I'm ready to go.

He was unshaven, angry.

—You don't have to come if you don't want to.

He seized her wrist and twisted the flesh until she gasped.

—I have said that I will come. Now you wait.

She waited in the kitchen, in front of her cup of coffee, while the day filled with heat and light and her confidence ebbed. I shall never get away from this house.

There was no proper moment of departure. The whole family lined up outside the door, waving, with little gifts for the baby; hand-knitted bootees perhaps, or nightdresses that had been worn by Oreste himself many years ago. No exchanges of photographs, promises of future visits.

Perhaps the parents were never fooled at all. Perhaps they knew all along that I was not his wife, and the child was not his child. Perhaps they know more than he does, that I will never see him again, but will step back into a life in which there is no place for him.

They left as they had arrived, in an atmosphere of sleep and confusion. The old man was not lifted into his chair. His son went into the stinking semi-darkness to say goodbye to him. Very possibly for ever. Possibly this would be his last image of his father. An old man, lying stiffly on his pillows, hair sticking out round his head, flat on his back, no pretence at dignity left. The Englishwoman, embarrassed, hovered outside the door, and said nothing, and was hurt because no one thought of taking the child in for the old man to take a last look at her. Oreste spent longer with his mother, and as he came out of the dining room tucking some money into his jeans, she followed him in her wrap. They are tired, the old people. We have worn them out, shortened their lives, taken their savings, eaten their chicken. The old woman kissed her daughter-in-law goodbye. Touch of flesh. We do not understand each other. And she handed her a small packet, wrapped in tissue paper.

—*Per la casa.*

Inside was a long, embroidered piece of cloth. Table runner? Dressing table cover? And folded inside it in a silver frame, a tiny, circular portrait of Oreste, at the age of twenty.

—Oh! Tears came into the Englishwoman's eyes, flooded down her cheeks. Oh, *bello, bellissimo. Grazie.*

Most cherished portrait of your only son. How beautiful he is. I am truly your daughter-in-law after all. You believe in me. She flung her arms round the old woman's neck, and kissed her again on both soft cheeks. Oh mother, mother, how you love your son. Her stomach felt as if it had been wrung by a giant hand. I shall love him, I shall be true to him, I shall devote my life to him and our child. Noble and lovely old woman. She embraced Immacolata too, and the two Italian women kissed the child.

Oreste led her to the car. She could scarcely see to drive. I want to stay here, to live here forever. The old woman and

Immacolata stood in the doorway and waved as the car jerked and swerved, stalling and starting again, onto the road.

Tears continued to run down the Englishwoman's cheeks. Centuries of my life passed in that house. I wish I could die there.

—Stop. You no can drive like that. Oreste wiped her tears dry, smoothed her hair, kissed her trembling lips. She let him, passive as a child.

—You want so much to leave, and now you cry.

She shook her head and shrugged her shoulders.

—I don't know. I don't know. She felt cleansed and refreshed; somehow purified, in her loyalty and love for Oreste.

For the first time their relationship was close, simple, loving. Every few minutes Miranda would stop the car, and they held hands and looked into each other's eyes.

—I don't want to leave you, Oreste. Your mother is such a lovely woman. It makes me weep to think of your father. Never had emotion flowed more freely, more sweetly, through the Englishwoman's heart. Was it because she was leaving this simple life of love based on family loyalty and physical passion that she found it so attractive? She existed in it, this life, as she drove in the opposite direction. Just that she had the wrong family. Oreste was deeply moved by this tropical flowering of his tall northern plant. He tenderly moulded and caressed the fingers of her right hand as it lay on his knee, she driving with her left. Occasionally the hand took on briefly an efficient and active role of its own, flicked the directional signals, manipulated the gear lever or handbrake, wiped the windscreen. Then it became again hills and valleys of jutting bone and soft flesh, drinking Oreste's kisses as a thirsty landscape absorbs rain.

—I will find a place for us in Rome. One, two rooms. You will come to me. We will be together.

Their love was innocent and tender and loyal as they climbed the mountains, warm and passionate and true. Like teenagers their minds scampered off in visions of tiny rooms overlooking the rooftops of Rome, kindly neighbours, happy children. Oreste's fantasies also included a few useful connections from the haute bourgeoisie, and work. However Miranda's hand was not the only part of her that was leading a double life. More than double. Layer upon layer, or endless reflections, back, front, back, front, in the two mirrors face to face. Her mind decided the route, without too many errors, and allowing occasional diversions in search of scenery. There was plenty of time. Drove the car, remembered to stop and buy food for the child (borrowing money from Oreste). Also planned what she should do when they arrived at the house in Volterra. What to tell Louis if he had already arrived. What to tell him if she still had a few hours or days grace. No problem then. Where should Oreste catch the train for Rome? They had to be together until the last possible moment. She would drive him down to Cecina, thus completing the trip from coast to coast. Oh. He had no money for the train. They would have to go home first, not knowing if Louis were there or not.

—I think I'd better drop you in Volterra, and then go and see if Louis has come back, and if he has I'll make some excuse to creep out again and bring you money for the ticket.

Oreste said nothing, but turned her hand over and caressed the palm, fitting his fingers between hers and folding them over each other.

X

What with their various stops, and the scenic rather than the direct route, it was nearly midnight when they arrived in Volterra. Miranda drove along the tunnel-like sweep of road up to the town and through the Etruscan gateway with a sense of casual familiarity. It was her town, her base. Usually it was quiet and dead at this hour, but tonight there were music and lights in Luna Park, just outside the walls. They were having a dance.

—Is the Feast of the Virgin, said Oreste. She pulled the car in to the side of the road.

—Why don't you wait there? The café in the square will be shut now.

They got out of the car, leaving the child sleeping in the back, and walked down the narrow, cobbled, dark street, out through another old gateway. The moonlight belonged more to the echoing cobbles and greyish shadows of the town than it did in Luna Park, where it was defeated by strings of coloured fairy lights. The ticket sellers had already left the gates so they walked in free, and sat down at a wooden table by the dance floor. Though the band still played energetically only two couples were dancing, gyrating slowly, locked in each other's arms, oblivious of the music, and a few bored young men sat in groups drinking Coca-Cola. Tomorrow was a working day. Oreste and Miranda held hands. Their heads buzzed from the vibrations of the car.

—I'll go and see if he's there, and if he's not I'll come back again and pick you up with some money.

—I no like that you go back alone.

Louis was a mythical figure, an irate husband in a French farce.

The red and yellow and orange fairy lights began to flicker and go out, a string at a time. The band finished *Che sera sera*, and put down their instruments. They were young boys with matching maroon jackets slung over the backs of chairs. The remaining young men at the tables must have been friends of theirs and clapped loudly.

—They finish.

—Do you think they'll close the park?

—I come back with you. I wait outside in the garden.

They could not bear to leave each other.

—What if Louis is back? I'll tell him that I got lonely and miserable without him, went away for a trip by myself, and suddenly remembered that he might be back and drove all night.

—I wait. If you not come in one hour I hitchhike to Rome.

They walked out with their arms round one another, relieved to be free of the vulgarity of Luna Park. I would rather find him sitting under a tree, or against a wall than here.

Back to the car. Roaring and coughing through the narrow streets to the square, a dark hole, the tower with its tiny gable on top of the belfry leaning down towards them like an admonishing black figure. Out through another gate, and weaving down the hill at an angle to the road they had just ascended. Ah yes, here was the turn. Nearly missed it. Miranda swung across the road; up—no, change down, yes—up into the driveway. How far along it dared they go? They crept forward, willing the engine to be silent. For a moment Miranda turned off the lights, but the straight trunks and feathery blue green leaves of the cypresses vanished and they were plunging forward into impenetrable blackness, so she turned them on again. When the iron gates came into sight, closed against them, she stopped the car abruptly, and turned off the lights once more.

—Gina and Corrado might hear the engine and come to see what it is, she muttered under her breath.

The baby still slept. How shall I find out if he's there? What shall I do? Walk up and knock on the front door of my own house? Or do I have the key? Astonishing thought, after so many months and years and lives, that the unwieldy iron key must still be lying at the bottom of her bag. If the door is bolted on the inside that will mean that Louis is back. She felt elated that there was such a simple answer. The car door slammed. Oreste felt his way round to stand beside her. He was trembling.

—I must kiss you again. I cannot bear that you go away from me.

They stood on the rough invisible white stones, surrounded by the scent and faint murmuring of the cypresses, holding each other awkwardly. It was not very warm. It must have rained during the day here. They crept up to the gate, squeezed round the outside (this was a gate to keep out cars and not people). Miranda felt in her bag for the key. Oreste pulled her to a stop and leaned up to press his lips against hers.

—Kiss me.

Mouths opened slowly. Tongues curled round one another. They moved across the circle of gravel, stones crunching against their feet. Any lights leaping on behind the shuttered windows? No. But the dark square of the house listened. Over the terrace into the orchard, and down into the embrace of the rough clumps of grass. Here the chickens were decently abed behind their wooden planks and wire netting. The moon scurried out from behind a cloud, lost and dappled with shadow behind the leaves of the apple trees. An upper window winked and glittered for a moment. Love was soft and tender among the spiky grass. Miranda remembered how Gina had found in the chicken-run a snake, one hot noon, and had run screaming for help, afraid to kill it. Among the bird's soft ruffled feathers the snake had writhed and danced. Let us make love for ever. Let us not stop.

The beautiful sensation faded slowly, and damp, sharpness, cold, forced their way in. They lay for a long time, aware of both together, but unwilling to make the movement that might mean that they had made love together for the last time. But the movement was made, and the woman searched round for her knickers, and pulled down her dress. They clung to each other again, standing under the apple tree.

—I no want you sleep with that man. Oreste caressed her neck with his lips. —Your body is beautiful for our love.

—I won't, I promise I won't, the woman whispered in the same breath. —I'll think of some excuse. Mouths touched. Time passed under the apple tree.

—I wait here, muttered Oreste.

—O.K. I'll wave from the doorway if it's all right. If it isn't I'll . . . I'll throw some money out of the bathroom window. Molière, or perhaps Wycherley; creeping out of the cuckold husband's arms to toss thousand lire notes into the bushes for the lover who was certainly going to turn up in the next act.

The woman crept, no, I must saunter up to my own front door, up to her own front door, and inserted the key in the lock. It turned. The door swung open. No! Not so easily as that. I was expecting a locked door, a farce, a tragedy. Do you mean that . . . everything is all right? She crept—yes, here I can creep, into the hall. Perhaps he forgot to bolt the door. Perhaps he didn't bolt it on purpose in case I came back. Aha! Do the faint sounds I am making sound like the noises made by a burglar? She lit a match. Tiny glow in the cavernous darkness. Gina had moved the table. If I had taken another step forward the noises would have been those of a very careless burglar. On the table were two piles of letters. One, five, seven, eight air-letters in Louis's handwriting addressed to her; on top of the pile a telegram. The other, several letters addressed to Louis, unopened. Oh. Slight disappointment. However, don't give up too soon. The match went out. She lit another, and made her way round the edge of the table towards the stairs. A quick glance into the kitchen, no signs of life here. Upstairs, the wavering light creeping ahead of her as the light of the candles carried by

Oreste had done. First the bathroom. No razor, no toothbrush, no leather washbag. No dressing gown (bathrobe) decorating the door. Easy, casual now, almost relaxed, she opened the bedroom door, turned on the light. The beds were smooth. Empty. It's all right. No need to worry. The house is ours still.

She ran to the upper window over the front door and waved, —It's all right, come. She lit a match, held it in front of her face, —It's all right, come. Blew it out. She didn't turn round. Behind her was the door of the other bedroom. In it stood a figure, dark, still, huge. Slowly, stiffly, she turned her head. No, no, Louis, please. She clutched her knees and buried her head between them, tearing down a curtain to cover herself.

No. The door was shut. A glimmer of white, barely visible in the faint light. If she opened it, inside would be, back towards her, lying on the double bed, a whalelike lump which would rise up to accuse her draped in white, with open mouth and eyes as red as blood.

Oreste's feet padded lightly up the stairs.

—Is all right? He is not here? Tender, boyish, he came towards her, arms outstretched. The woman stood rooted to the ground, hand over her eyes, pointing to the door. On the screen of her lids the two images dissolved and faded into one another, repeating, repeating the dark figure standing in the doorway and the faceless, bodiless white lump rising to accuse her from the bed. The lover stopped in his tracks, his face undergoing a comic transformation, hand extended with spread fingers in an operatic gesture.

—He is there?

The woman shook her head. Pause.

—I don't know.

—You have look?

Pause. The woman shook her head. Oreste came up closer, held her arm roughly, shook her.

—Why you are so afraid? I look.

I could pretend Oreste was a burglar. I heard a noise, came to see what it was. He crept up to the door like a cat, opened it very gently, one hand on the latch, one hand spread flat on the door itself to prevent it shaking or giving too suddenly, ear pressed to the panel, a dancer choreographed with one foot raised to listen in the dark. A long, long pause; the stripe of darkness widened slowly. A cold breath came from it. Noiseless the Greek hero crept into the Minotaur's lair, vanished; the maiden waited, hands clasped to her heart. After many days he reappeared in triumph, the monster slain, flung the door open wide.

—Is empty. Is no one here, he said.

The sound of a normal voice in these halls of fantasy made Miranda shudder.

—Oh. You mean it's all right?

Oreste kissed her, boyish once more, warmed by the sight of these familiar beds, laughing.

—You are silly girl. What you afraid of? He is only a man. Soon you are with me, you have no more need to be afraid.

Poor Louis, I've turned you into a monster. I didn't mean to do that.

—Come, look with me. Is no one here. Oreste took her by the hand and led her through the empty rooms of the house, turning all the lights on. When they reached the hall again Miranda remembered the telegram. She tore it open. EVERYTHING GOES ACCORDING TO PLAN SEE YOU TUESDAY 16TH PISA THREE-THIRTY LOVE LOVE LOUIS. Oh good, he's coming back. Tuesday, that's tomorrow. Today. This afternoon. Oreste can catch the train at Cecina this morning, then I'll drive to Pisa and pick up Louis this afternoon. Everything goes according to plan. She looked at Oreste. The tender familiarity of her love for him began to dissolve. She became efficient again. She showed him the telegram.

—I must get the baby. We can wash and change here, and pick up some money, and then we'll drive down to Cecina and catch the first train. I think there's one at about seven o'clock.

—Why you not come with me?

—I can't. She put the rest of Louis's letters in her bag and went to open the front door.

—Turn out the light. Gina and Corrado might see. Oreste

turned out the light and followed her to the car to help with the carrycot and the suitcase.

The sleeping child was woken, washed, fed, and returned to sleep. The adults washed, flushing the lavatory with caution, in silence. A silence not of intimacy, but of growing distance. The woman picked a fistful of money out of the top left hand drawer of the dressing table, and handed half to her lover. Then added more.

—Here, for your train.

He took it, and thrust it into the pocket of his jeans, carelessly, not taking his eyes from her face.

—Why you go away from me? Because the other man come back? Now you are not afraid any more, you want live with him?

Yes.

—No Oreste, it's not like that at all.

You are disappearing. You have already become almost transparent. When Louis comes back I won't be alone any more so I won't need you. Let's get this departure over as quickly as possible. Now I know that I am undiscovered I want to get back to my old innocent life.

The first glimmer of light appeared in the sky. Miranda smoothed one bed, left the other rumpled.

—Let's get started now, before Gina and Corrado wake up.

Oreste did not know what cards to play. He did not know what cards had any value in this game. He was made impotent by love. Miranda watched him as he helped her carry the child back to the car in the increasing light, eyes, hair, dark stains, blurred at the edges, like Japanese ink on wet paper. Soon I shall be a responsible wife and mother again.

They drove down to Cecina through a magnificent sunrise. Huge banks of charcoal and navy clouds piled up around them, outlined with scarlet, spears of golden light shooting up towards the empty, pale centre of the sky. The beautiful, bare hills through which the road descended, subtly indented, as if they had been formed when the earth was still soft and malleable, by loving caresses of the internal knuckles on the palm of the hand, changed from cool, greyish blue, to amber. The clouds shifted their piles of vapour (which at the moment had more solidity in contour and outline than the hills) and became more transparent as the sun rose, and their colours trumpeted scarlet and purple.

Miranda was possessed of a sense of light-headed glee as nature celebrated Oreste's departure with such glory. She was tempted to sing as she drove, but prevented herself, for fear of hurting his feelings. She saw that he, who had been her lover for a week, was sad to be leaving her, and knew that according to some law or other she too should be sad. But she could only find brisk, nanny-like reactions: he'll get over it in a couple of days; he had his fun, now it's someone else's turn.

As for herself, she had no feelings about it at all, apart from practical ones. Would they catch the train? Did he have enough money? Would she have time to get to Pisa and do some shopping before Louis's plane arrived? (Yes, plenty.) That was all. No, do I love him? Will I miss him? As for his repeated promise that he would get a room in Rome and she would join him later with the child, she agreed with them as one might agree with the fantasies of a child: yes, yes, I'll marry you when you're a big boy like Daddy.

When they arrived at Cecina there was three-quarters of an hour to wait for the train. They found a café that had just opened, and sat outside to drink coffee. They could see the level-crossing, where the railway lines crossed the road, two parallel black and silver lines slicing through the asphalt, and the thin black lines of the telephone wires, and the neat, angular signal box. A dog moved slowly, sideways, across the road, taking plenty of time over each smell. The station building and the houses near it were boxlike, concrete. Across the main road was a row of shops and houses, and beyond that, invisible, the sea. The proprietor of the café, an old man with a bald, domed head and a green apron shuffled out to give them more coffee. He produced a jug of boiled water for the baby's bottle.

Oreste said, slouched low over the table, stirring his coffee,
—I am very sad.
—Why? Because you're going?
He shook his head,
—It is you who make me sad. I love you, but I no understand you. Miranda felt a twinge of uneasiness.
—I'm English, she said. We're all peculiar. It's the way we're brought up.
—What you feel, that you must know.
—Ah, she said brightly, that's just it. We don't.
—When I am in love, said Oreste, then I know it.

The signal snapped down, and the sound of the train whistle slowly expanded as it chugged round the edge of the bay.

—Oh, said Miranda, here's the train. She finished her coffee and got up. The baby's bottle was only half drunk. Oreste went into the café, paid for the coffee, bought some cigarettes. As he came out again, lighting a cigarette and then stuffing the packet into the back pocket of his jeans, he looked very casual, summery, masculine. Miranda put her arm through his as they walked across the road to the station. The train smelled of soot and brine. Oreste bought his ticket. Everything was clean in this fresh morning light, after the sleepless night. An old woman dressed in black with a plastic shopping bag got on the train, also a middle-aged man with highly polished brown shoes and a beige mackintosh over his arm. The station master, in shirt sleeves and hat, walked up and down the platform.

A young couple were saying goodbye. The woman clutched her baby in the crook of her arm, and held up her face to be kissed. Her husband stood in the doorway of the carriage, and leaned down towards her. He put his hand gently on her cheek.

—We will not be apart for long. He stared down at her, with his heavy, dark, masculine look.

—I will write you. Soon we are together again.

She gazed up at him, blank and meek. The station master delayed blowing his whistle for a few seconds, for the sake of the young couple and their farewell. The old-fashioned steam engine chugged slowly, then faster, the wheels engaged, with a clang of iron and puff of steam the train was on its way.

The woman holding the child stood and waved until it was out of sight. Then she returned to the car, still parked outside the café. She sat down at the same table to finish giving the baby her bottle. The proprietor nodded and smiled paternally.
—*Va a Roma, suo marito?*
—*Si.*
The baby gurgled and stretched her legs in the morning sunshine, unperturbed by the night of travel. Miranda breathed deeply the clear, sharp air, the acrid tang of dust and ozone. She was aware of alternate layers of fatigue and keenness of perception. Her eyes focused at a greater distance than usual, which meant that she could see with the utmost clarity the cliff, formed out of crumbling layers of sandstone and quartz, through which the railway had been cut; could see on the far side of the track, between the road and the sea, two summer villas and their gardens perched awkwardly on the sloping ground, and nearer, the grove of umbrella pines which shaded the orange and blue tents of the camping site, and the milky waters of the perfectly curved little bay, milky because of the waste from a nearby cement factory. Her thighs and groin were suddenly leaden with the fatigue of too much sex. To walk the few steps to the car seemed an intolerable effort. She felt weighted by the heaviness of her womanhood, like those Old Testament daughters hiding the household gods in their skirts as they sat immoveable in front of the searching soldiers, proclaiming their menstrual flow. Rooted to the earth by blood.

However, the day progressed. The sun continued to rise, the light grew more golden, the air less sharp. Light and shadow ceased to be two equal constituents of the same image and turned into symbols for describing dimension. Other people came to sit in the sunshine and drink their morning coffee. There were things to be done. The drive to Pisa, shopping, lunch, reading Louis's letters; my God, yes, very important.

Miranda straightened her knees and raised her weighted thighs. Her body still smelled of sex. She wondered how many of the other bleary-eyed, abstracted men and women at the café and in the street had been making love that night. Not the old proprietor, for sure. She waved to him as she got into the car.

It was a pleasant, holiday thing to do, to drive along the coast road from Cecina to Pisa, with the sea sparkling on her left so brilliant with light that it had no colour, windows rolled down to let the scent of pines and sea wash over her, marking down pleasant beaches for sunny, lazy days in the future, smiling at other drivers and pedestrians, a friendly, early morning community, enjoying the best of the day.

Disappointing to arrive at Pisa, to have to park the car, and fix the top of the pram onto its wheels, and shop. It would have been pleasant to drive on for ever in the bright morning. But still, she was keeping up with her schedule. She lunched early, in a quiet, pleasant restaurant not far from the leaning tower and the hoards of tourists, where she had eaten once before with Louis. Between forkfuls of *spaghetti alle vongole* for herself and spoonfuls of *pollo* for the baby she worked her way chronologically through the letters, reading attentively, as if she were preparing for an examination. Affection, jokes, worries about how she was getting on, plans for what they would do when he got back, people they would see, descriptions of the film, the other people on the set (I'll tell you all the details when I see you), messages to the baby, love. A satisfactory family. Mother and child. Food in the shopping bag, money in the purse. All present and correct to meet the husband and father. What luck, what incredible luck that I should have chosen just that moment to come home. The gods are definitely on my side. It was a quarter to three. Several generations of lunchers had come and gone. The baby had eaten, slept, and woken again. Miranda had drunk a carafe of white wine, read the letters several times, and was feeling gay and confident. It's all right. Everything's perfectly all right. Oreste need never have existed. She paid for her meal and set out for the airport.

The young wife parked the small green Fiat, lifted out the child, made her way to the airport lounge. Not much had changed in ten days. The same people worked there.

The friendly official recognised her and smiled, or perhaps he smiled at all women with babies. She sat, unbalanced, in a low black leather chair from which it was impossible to rise without an undignified scramble, in front of a long, glass-topped table. Through the glass doors, or windows (the whole side of the building was glass) she watched a plane from Milan come in. The airport lounge filled with small, rounded Italian women wearing silk-knit jersey dresses, and a group of tall thin English girls wearing Banlon shifts. Miranda thought perhaps if I was Italian I would be able to tell exactly how much those silk dresses had cost. Then she thought, what would those Englishwomen think if they knew what I had been doing for the past week? What would all my fellow schoolgirls say? What would the voice of authority say? Long-limbed, pale, square-jawed, the mirror images of herself vanished to search for their own delights.

And hidden behind their hesitations, and their excitement, and the unloading of their baggage, the London plane had come in. More English people. Families with small children, an Italian businessman, impotent but resigned, bossy air hostesses with glazed eyes and perky caps, skirts too long, saving the sanity of millions. I can't stand it, I'm not ready, I've got to go . . .

XI

Miranda, darling, there you are! Louis, the cuckold, the joke figure from a French farce, the nightmare, the monster, waving from the far side of the passport desk. The cancerous lump that had disappeared, been forgotten since the dinner with Oreste's parents, jumped back into Miranda's throat.

He was showing his passport, being waved through, pushing his way through the crowd, towering over her. How astonishing was the texture of his flesh, the sensation of his lips. Smaller, firmer, more masculine than Oreste's. His flesh rougher, open pores on the nose, hair drier, thicker, curlier, eyebrows sprouting above the bridge of the nose, lashes shorter, eyes smaller, turned up slightly at the outer corners. Strange, strange man. Why is this dry and self-contained flesh touching mine?

—Darling, it's good to see you, I missed you. How've you been? and the baby? He perched on the arm of his wife's chair, and picked his daughter out of her pram. She felt no strangeness, but smiled her toothless smile and stuck out her tongue, and patted the air and her Daddy's face and chest as they approached, with her hands and feet.

—What's new since Daddy left? Haven't you got any teeth yet? On cue the baby gurgled,

—Da . . . da . . .

—Did you hear that? She said Dada. She can say Dada! The mother laughed.

—Yes, she does say that sometimes. I think those are the first syllables most babies can say.

This was the silent witness. This was the one who had seen everything. The mother looked with horror at her daughter, suddenly sprouting syllables. Will she be granted the gift of tongues, suddenly to say: Hey Dad, do you know what Mum's been doing? Louis bounced his daughter on his knee.

—Darling, why didn't you answer any of my letters? I was worried. The wife raised her face, anxious and pathetic.

—I started to, but it made me feel depressed, so I thought I'd just wait until you got back. It was lovely to get yours though.

You're going to need every weapon you've got, so use them all. He put an arm round her shoulders.

—Were you really depressed, my love? You look good. Maybe a little tired. Strange heaviness of that arm; bearlike, young, each finger round and fleshy instead of thin, damp, trembling.

The young couple rise to their feet, embrace once more, the husband cupping his wife's face in his hand as he gently kisses her lips. She pushes the empty pram, weaving in and out of baggage and people, and he carries the baby, sitting up clinging to his shoulder, with one arm, and his suitcase with the other. The friendly official smiles and nods as they pass.

The young couple, in the crowded airport, make their way to the car park. All the new arrivals fanning out on the road to the city or along the coast, south or north. The young man, wearing a moss-green short-sleeved sweat shirt manhandles the baby into her familiar position in the pram in the back seat of the car. He walks round it, the roof chest high, pale green against dark green, smell of tar steaming up from the asphalt, the strangeness of sounds out in the open here, dropped into a desert of space, taking a long time to reach from lips or car door to the ear, longer than in the enclosed airport lounge, or on the tarmac the huge snorts of the aircraft. He holds out his hands for the car keys. The woman hands them over to the wrong side of the car. Laughs.

—I've got used to driving. Her laughter has a touch of slyness. I can tell the truth. I have got used to driving. She sits, smug, passive, wifely, pressing her knees and thighs together, long stretch of damp flesh, curling her hands together in the hollow of her lap. I don't have to speak. Speech is not necessarily required of wives. Louis takes deep breaths of Italian petrol fumes and sun-warmed air.

—I've never been on a movie where things went so well. This was the third film he had worked on.

—There was a great atmosphere. Everyone hit it off beautifully. No fights, no rows. It was like one long party.

—Lots of pretty girls?

—Yes, lots of pretty girls. But I was too busy to chase them, and I've got my own pretty girl. He turned to grin at her, full of vitality, health, success, skilfully overtaking a peasant's blue three-wheeled truck piled high with boxes of tomatoes. He put his hand on her knee, fitting the kneecap into the hollow of his palm. She had an odd, high-angled view of their two arms, huge and muscular, in shadow, at the shoulder, tapering down to long, delicate fingers clearly etched in the sunshine, her own knee, neatly drawn in curves, her green and brown cotton dress, rising and dipping to allow for the existence of her legs, her calves and ankles monstrously foreshortened, and tiny feet in their brown sandals, with carefully defined toenails, like a doll's.

—You're not very brown, said Louis, didn't you do much sunbathing?

—No. I get bored, even if I'm reading.

—What did you do?

—Nothing much. Flicker of the expected guilt. Bowels begin to seethe. If I say I went for drives he'll say: where? and I don't know much more about the surrounding countryside than I did when he left.

—The baby . . . Oh my God, just avoided a hazard there, if I say I took her to the doctor he'll want to know all about the bloody man, might even go to see him, and . . . oh, oh, oh, more hazards than I thought, I must destroy the medicine bottles from Urbino. Or shall I say I went there for a couple of days? Nothing wrong with that.

—The baby?

—Oh, the baby had a bit of a bad tum, I thought I might have to take her to the doctor, but it got better. So we spent most of the time just lounging about in the shade, not doing anything in particular.

—Sounds beautiful. They both had a mental picture of the mother and child lying in the long grass in the shade of an apple tree, with the pale-green hillside tumbling down behind them to the steaming jungle of the gorge, and climbing up the other side to the blue and amber distance. Fields, workmen, cars, roads, town, all tiny and far away. Louis sighed with pleasure and flexed his shoulders.

—Sounds great. That's just what I feel like doing for a few days.

They swung up between the two white houses, bumped along the cypress alley. The iron gate was open. At the sound of the car's approach Gina came from the chicken run, walking slowly, holding the tin bowl in which she carried the corn, with three warm fresh eggs laid in it now, wrapped in a piece of rag; and Corrado, with his straw hat pushed to the back of his head and his spade over his shoulder, came from the potato patch. They came as they had come on the day of that first arrival, nearly three weeks ago. As they had not come before dawn, in the intermittent moonlight, on the previous night. Miranda stared into the eyes of Gina. She became suddenly brittle with fatigue. I haven't slept for two days and a night; I have driven across this entire country. I am too tired, Gina, for you to betray me.

Louis said,

—Ah, *buon giorno*, Gina, Corrado. He got out of the car. Shook them warmly by the hand.

—*Buon viaggio, signor?*

—*Si, si, grazie. Va bene qui?*

—*Si, si.*

Miranda got out of the car too, smiling, silent, the baby in her arms. If she held her tongue Gina would perhaps forget the arrival of the other man, the day of sickness, the morning departure. The lump in her throat had grown larger, but by now she was accustomed to it. She kept her teeth clamped tightly shut to prevent it from escaping, and blessed the tower of Babel.

The heavy door swings open. Sigh of the weary travellers as they enter the hall; cool, fresh, neat. A woman coming into a cool, chintzy drawing room from the heat of a June garden, throwing aside her straw hat decorated with ribbons and faded felt flowers, sinking into the sofa with a sigh of relief, the shining, crisp material cool against her bare legs. Roses in a cut-glass vase. Deckchairs under the elm tree on the lawn. Lunch already forgotten in the cool, empty dining room, a few crumbs still on the polished table, tea brought outside on a tray.

—Here are some letters for you, Louis.

You see? I know there are letters, and I know where they are. Surprised, Gina? Do you imagine that I, too, suddenly left for London with that young Italian, and we joined my husband, and I came back with him on the plane today? Or do you imagine nothing? Louis picked up his letters, looked through them, threw them down again.

—Nothing very important.

I have done my homework. I have read my letters. They are here, in my bag. Miranda sat the child up in her plastic chair, not much used during their travels, and unpacked the food she had bought in Pisa. There was nothing in the fridge except some rancid butter and three rotting tomatoes. She called over her shoulder,

—Take the baby out into the garden, darling, I want her to get as much sun as possible now that she's better, and filled the fridge, half opening various packages as she did so.

Louis carried in his daughter after a few minutes.

—I just want to have a shower and change. I'm all covered in sweat after the plane.

The whalelike lump shifted, about to turn, to rise. What was there upstairs that could give her away? She crouched in the corner of the kitchen like a sick bird in the corner of a cage; vicious, dusty, with bedraggled wings. Louis's voice floated down the stairs,

—Why did you change the beds round?

She called up, —I was lonely in the big bed all by myself.

He laughed. —Well, you won't be lonely tonight, my sweet. Come and help me move them back.

She went upstairs. Set the baby down to watch. Much heaving, straining, effort.

—How the hell did you do this all by yourself?

—I got Corrado to help me.

Why should he deny it, and who's going to understand him if he does? At last they had the beds changed round. They sat down on the double bed in their own room. Louis put both arms round his wife and pressed her against him, leaning his cheek against her hair. He smelled of sweat. The texture of his shirt was as smooth and soft as velvet. He kissed her hair, ruffling a few strands on top, but not the main heaviness of it.

—It's good to be back. Did you miss me?

—Yes, I did. Things weren't at all the same without you.

Now that I remember you I'm beginning to miss you. Now that I remember you I'm beginning to regret the innocent young mother sitting on the terrace, playing with her child. The exploratory drives we might have taken together. We might have gone in the afternoons to the beach, and dipped your little feet into the milky sea under the pines. Your first experience of the foamy waves. She yearned for those lost days of intimacy between mother and child. For whole days, growing slowly to their fulfilment like ripening fruit, and then dropping off the tree. But a sort of wholeness has been preserved in Louis's imagination, she thought, pressing her lips against the soft green security of his sleeve; I mustn't break it.

All her actions were beautiful and graceful, her voice gentle. She changed, and bathed, and fed and dressed the child, the beauty of motherhood expressed in every line and movement. Blue hood, bent head, passive, giving breast.

She cooked spaghetti, and Louis sliced tomatoes and washed lettuce for the salad, and told her about the film.

—Shall we eat outside? I found some candles.

—Sounds great.

I don't see why I shouldn't learn. The lump in her throat was almost a friendly presence now, did not prevent her eating. And the lump in the double bed was only their two bodies, and the heaving of Louis's buttocks under the sheet as he groaned with the pleasure of homecoming and nibbled her neck, sighed and whispered,

—Oh darling, I've missed you so much.

Miranda, very bright and wide awake caressed his hair and kissed his temple and felt herself shaken by a sort of interior hysterics. Between silent screams of laughter she talked to herself in vulgar and sophisticated tones: no one can tell what fish swim in my sea, you could be meeting some of Oreste's sperm coming down, hope they all get along in there. It's too easy. Infidelity and deceit are too easy. People believe what you say. You say something or you don't say something and you've created a fact. The past exists in other people's imagination.

The next morning, over breakfast, she began to be very tempted to tell Louis about Oreste.

They sat on the terrace, late, the sun was already hot, with the luxurious possibilities of the beach, or a town, or nothing, ahead of them. They had both slept, exhausted, ten or eleven hours. The coffee was hot and strong. Louis lounged in his bathing trunks on a red plastic chair, one foot up on the table. Miranda wore her négligé over her bikini. She had not yet bathed, and smelled of bed; shaved hair in her armpits prickled the soft rolls of flesh pushed up under her bra. The baby was being playful, delighted with her own babbling, repeating,

—Da...da...ba...ba... and making a guttural rolling sound in her throat. She sat forward in her chair, straining away from the supporting back, waving her feet and twitching her toes. Louis tickled her face with two acorns on a twig, and she tried to catch them, grimaced with concentration, exposing the empty cavern of her mouth. Miranda said,

—Oh, a friend of yours came by for a drink one evening, about a week ago.

—Yeah? One of the people I knew in Rome?

—Yes. His name was Oreste something or other.

—I remember him.

The baby reached too far, and tipped herself and her chair over. Screams and flailing limbs. Louis picked her up, untied her from the chair, kissed the bumped place, sat her on his knee.

—Nice little guy, but a loser. He wasn't even working on that film, he just hung around the set. He was sleeping with one of the girls.

Miranda went white; abandoned, pathetic, a lump of dried cuttlefish, stained with sand and oil, left behind by the tide.

—I think he was on his way to visit his parents. They live somewhere round here.

—Some of the people I met in Rome were working on this film in London. The designer. Remember I talked about him? A faggot, but a very witty, nice guy. It turns out he's got a house right close to here, used to be a monastery. I think we probably saw it once, on the way to San Gimignano. He's going to come round when he gets back, and take us to see it.

Oreste was a loser and he had lost. It was as simple as that. Some people win and some people lose.

—We'll go to the beach today and relax, and tomorrow we'll go into Florence and look at some museums. O.K.?

—O.K.

On the way to the beach they stopped to get petrol.

—You certainly used up a lot of these petrol coupons.

—I took the baby for a drive almost every day. It makes her sleep.

—Well, we're rich now. We can be as extravagant as we like for a bit.

Then the letters began to come. When the first one arrived, two days after Louis's return, Miranda was alone on the terrace, and the postman, the old one this time, counting the envelopes out from his canvas bag handed them to her. She would have shouted: leave them on the bench, if she had been able to remember the Italian word for bench, and had not felt so lazy, and again sorry for the old man who liked to make his calls into miniature social visits, exchanging comments on the weather, and the progress of her Italian, and the fatness of the child.

This one envelope immediately gave her a presentiment of danger. A threat, six inches by three, white, with writing in black ink, large, square, with many flourishes and underlinings, and an unnecessary number of stamps. She tore it open. Two large, twice folded pieces of paper, written over not only on both sides but on all the spaces left the first time round, so that the end of the letter was in the margin and space at the top of the first page, and she could see, all at once, without even having to turn the page, 'Oh my beloved darling', and the signature, 'your faithful Oreste'. She crumpled it up as small as possible and thrust it into her bag. The postman who had been standing watching, raised his hand in farewell.

—*Buon giorno*, and climbed into his three-wheeled truck.

Miranda picked up her bag and ran into the house, passing Louis on the way. She flashed a smile at him.

—Must go to the loo. Once in security behind a locked door she pulled out the letter again, but could not read it. The two phrases 'my beloved darling' and 'your faithful Oreste' magnetised her eyes, they flashed on and off like neon lights. She felt the heat from them. Her hands were paralysed. She could not tear the letter up and throw it into the lavatory. She had a violent pain in her stomach. With an involuntary movement of horror her hands jerked down and it fell to the floor where it uncurled slowly, cracking like pistol shots.

No, no, no. A Buddhist with a scorpion in his shoe, a repentant traitor confronted by the murdered body of his king; lying there uncurling, spreading, flashing on the floor. With a sharp grunt and exhalation of breath she pounced on it, tore it up—stiff paper, won't tear, don't want to block the plumbing—seized Louis's nail scissors, chopped and hacked at it, threw the pieces into the lavatory bowl, pulled the plug, the upsurge of water flung the words 'our chaste fuck', black ink on white paper, up towards her, she cried out, reached in, but they were whipped away with a roar and a sucking gurgle. And nothing was left. The trembling surface of the water hid nothing (no monsters). More water trickled into the cistern. The morning light was reflected off the white tiles. But oh, the image had been shattered! The normal, happy day, the pretty triangle, wife, husband and child, irreparably destroyed. How can such a faithless woman be a wife? How can such a faithless woman be a mother? Oh, Oreste, I have betrayed you, I have betrayed the trust of your mother and your poor dumb father. I am not worthy to live if I cannot love you as you love me. She lay on the floor, pressing her body against the cold tiles. She banged her head against the cold tiles. Avoid the nose. Not much point in hitting the nose. Penance. I'm a penitent. I'm sorry. I'M JUST SORRY. Put that on my gravestone.

Louis banged at the door.
—Are you having a bad shit? We needn't go into Florence this morning if you don't feel up to it.
—I'll be O.K. in a minute.
She sat up, opened her bag, unzipped an inside pocket, took out the portrait of Oreste given by his mother, which she had wrapped up in tissue paper and forgotten about. She looked at him. He looked back at her. She wrapped the picture in tissue paper again, and put it back in her bag. She looked out of the window. Was there a figure moving down there in the field, beyond the orchard, beyond the terrace? Running lightly up the hill in canvas shoes, jumping from one clump of grass to another, losing himself among the stunted olive trees at the bottom of the orchard? Had he come to fetch her, knowing that she was faithless? I promised not to sleep with Louis. I shouldn't have moved the beds back. He knows Louis called him a loser and I didn't say anything. That isn't loyalty. I don't understand the meaning of the word.

She walked stiffly out of the bathroom, her eyes darting around and behind.

—Are you sure you're all right, darling? You don't look too good.

I deserve to be locked in a dungeon, a hole, no air or light, ankles chained to the floor so that the flesh is rubbed away and the bone shows through, no room to sit or lie, drowning in my own excrement.

—I'm all right.

—O.K. then, come on. Everything's ready. We'll see some beautiful pictures and have a great lunch.

The zombie walked, stiff-kneed, to the car. As they gathered speed down the drive she saw a dark-haired figure in jeans flitting between the trees. He's come to shoot me. He deserves his revenge. There's no one I can turn to for help. She sank low down in her seat, and bent her head, to provide as little target as possible, and he didn't shoot.

The car swung into the open road and Louis started to sing,

—Toot toot tootsie, goodbye . . . Toot toot tootsie don't cry . . . The sun was warm, the day was young, his reputation was growing, and a fantastic wilderness that would be tamed into ordered greenery within twenty miles was scattered richly in front of the car.

The zombie neither moved nor spoke. In the restaurant she didn't eat, and made the answer that required the least effort to any question that was put to her. This technique resulted in a plate of calamaros and a plate of strawberries, both of which were eaten by Louis. She made no effort to feed the baby. Luckily this was a restaurant they had been to before, and the old mother of the owner picked up the child with coos of pleasure and carried her off into the kitchen, where she was petted and fondled and fed by the five other black-clad grandmothers and one skinny pale old chef who formed the kitchen staff. It should have been a charming lunch. Louis began to be annoyed.

—Won't you tell me what's the matter, Miranda?

You can't save me because I deserve it. And anyway I can't tell you because I betrayed you too.

Louis, alternately annoyed and solicitious, jollied his way, alone, through lunch. He didn't wait for coffee.

—Let's go to the Uffizi. I've had enough of sitting here talking to myself.

He paid the bill, joked with the proprietor, took back the baby on one arm, manoeuvred the pram with the other.

The Uffizi was horribly crowded and noisy. The zombie made no pretence of looking at pictures. Louis had a headache and was tired of holding the baby. The pleasure of the day was evaporating rapidly. He could not be bothered to leaf through the Guide Bleu in search of quiet churches with a possible beautiful, hidden altar piece or frescoed cloister.

—Florence in August is hell, he decided. We'd do better to stay in our own garden, or get to know Volterra.

The zombie made no response. Jesus, he thought, I hope she's not going to go on being like this. Is it just because I left her alone for ten days? She seemed O.K. yesterday. They called in at the tourist office to collect some more petrol coupons.

—Might as well, since we're here, and then drove home.

Louis was ruffled and annoyed, but still prepared, given half the chance, to take pleasure in the rest of the day. He really quite enjoyed giving the baby a drink and changing her nappy, which he had done in the men's lavatory at the Uffizi. He didn't think it was beneath his dignity, or woman's work, or anything like that. The small conical hills crowned with cypress trees, the flat green valleys, and orderly rows of vines had soothed him already, before they were twenty minutes out of Florence.

They got back in time for tea. To give the baby her tea. O.K., thought the husband, we'll have a calm domestic evening. Maybe I've been talking too much about what I did on the film. Didn't ask her enough about what she's been doing.

The postman had been again. There was a letter from Rome on the table in the hall. He picked it up, then noticed it was addressed to Miranda.

—Oh, letter for you darling, from Rome. Who's writing to you from Rome?

Thick white envelope, six inches by three, large square writing in black ink, with many flourishes and underlinings. Too many stamps. The sight of it galvanised the zombie into activity.

—Oh, she said brightly, it must be from that funny little man Oreste. I think he developed rather a crush on me. He sent me a postcard the other day.

Remarkable how close to the truth one could go and still be on solid ground. Safe. She took it from Louis's outstretched hand.

—I can't really show it to you; it wouldn't be fair.

—It's damn heavy. I think he's written you a whole cycle of love poems. Louis was more pleased than anything else that his wife had an Italian admirer, adoring her from afar, writing her love poetry.

—There was this little guy in Italy who was crazy about Miranda; used to write her poems. Not too bad, some of them.

Don't suppose Beatrice's husband, if she had a husband, minded too much about Dante flipping over her. After all, he had the girl.

Miranda took the letter upstairs to the bathroom. Locked the door, picked up Louis's scissors, started to cut the envelope carefully into narrow strips, holding it by one corner. Snip, snip, these are my nipples, the lobes of my ears, as she cut and the folded paper spread into fences and trellises she noticed that there was a wad of money in there, and an air ticket, but she went on snipping. Where did he get that money from? She had snipped a neat hara-kiri line round the bottom of her abdomen, and blood was streaming out. He must have loved her very much to get actual money (from another woman?) to send to her. Bourgeois money, and an airplane ticket. She could easily have come by train. But the whole point was that she was not coming. She had never intended to come. She had been leading him up the garden path all along, and his rage and fury when he discovered that would know no bounds, because he was a man to whom his dignity was very important. Not a thing to be taken lightly. Slowly, deliberately, she scattered the pieces of letter and envelope and money and ticket into the lavatory, and pulled the chain. I am throwing away my life. I am delivering myself into his hands for his revenge. The rush of water subsided, but half of the ticket and envelope still floated on the surface. She waited until the trickling of water into the cistern (the tone of the sound mimicking the level of the water, slowly rising) had stopped. Then pulled the plug again. She washed her hands and combed her hair, looking into the mirror. Her face was neither ravaged nor aged. She walked slowly downstairs and out into the garden.

Louis had given the baby her tea, and cleaned her bottom, and dressed her in a sunhat and t-shirt. She looked sporty and dashing like a miniature tennis player. As a nice contrast Louis had fixed the frilly parasol to the pram hood, and when his wife came out was just taking a photograph of his daughter waving and grinning, dappled with light and shade. Crouched, bent over the small black square pressed to his eye. He waved to Miranda.

—Go stand by the pram, I'll take one of both of you. She walked over. What does it matter now? It's too late anyway. She posed, then said,

—I'll take one of you two.

Louis picked the baby out of the pram and held her, her fat little bottom overflowing the palm of his hand.

—You didn't put a nappy on her.

—I thought I'd let her air out a bit.

Thank God she seems to be better now. Maybe she's having her period.

—Was it love poems?

—No, just rambling.

Click. O.K. Immortalised.

—Let's take her for a walk. It's just the right time of day for walking now. Not too hot.

Five o'clock. The afternoon shadows of the cypress trees stretched across the alley, so that they were walking along a striped pattern of light and shade, heat and cool. The baby sat up for a few minutes, looking brightly about her and blinking, like a queen in her carriage. Then she lay down. Her eyelids opened and shut with languorous, rhythmic movements, the unfurling of small waves which spread themselves out at your feet like a fan opening.

Louis was relaxed and cheerful. He forgot the fiasco of the visit to Florence, and began to whistle. He doesn't care. He really could not care less what happens to me. And this is the one person I ought to be able to turn to when I'm in trouble.

She knew where he was going to be. He was going to be behind the last of the trees, where there were a lot of bushes and heavy undergrowth, just before the two white houses, before the drive began to slope down towards the main road. He will probably have got those little girls in their maroon velvet dresses to get him something to eat, and some cigarettes, and has them posted along the side of the road to warn him when we're coming. He didn't bother to shoot me while I was in the car. He might have missed.

There was a rustling in the bushes by the side of the road. Not on the right hand side, but on the left, where there was a thick hedge of hazel, and a field behind. Miranda put her hand over Louis's on the ridged rubber handle of the pram, to make him walk more slowly.

—What's the matter?

—I'm frightened.

Now that she thought about it there was no earthly reason why she shouldn't tell him. He was her husband after all. It was his duty to protect her.

—What on earth are you frightened of? Goddamn it, she's not better at all. I should never have left her alone.

—I'm frightened of Oreste.

They had come in sight of the two white houses and the end of the driveway. Miranda stopped. Louis walked on a few steps and turned round.

—What are you frightened of him for? But foreboding began to flit round the edges of his brain.

—You shouldn't have left me alone. You know what I'm like when I'm alone. She caught up with him. They continued walking slowly, together.

—I saw him this morning. He had a gun. He was hiding in the orchard. He's here now. He's going to shoot me.

Louis's face was grey. A muscle in his jaw twitched. He said between his teeth,

—Why should he want to shoot you? Miranda said,

—I had an affair with him. I spent the whole week with him. He wanted me to go and live in Rome, and I promised I would. That's what that letter was. Money and an air ticket.

Louis stopped and gave a strangled groan. He let go the pram, put his hands over his face, stumbled towards the last of the cypress trees, on the left hand side, banged his head against the trunk just where the branches, still clinging tightly together, started to push their scented way upwards. He bellowed like an animal in a trap, his eyes shut and his head thumping the tree. He seems to be upset. He loves me. Perhaps my husband loves me too. Oh. I've made a mistake.

There was no sign of Oreste, stepping out from behind a tree with the instrument of his revenge. No sign of the little girls in maroon velvet dresses. There was the sound of stones clinking as they were displaced by the wheels of the pram. The pram rolled slowly, then quicker, down the slope to the main road. A lorry trundled up the hill, belching black fumes, the pram gathered speed, Miranda stared at it, not moving, her mouth slightly open. The pram bowled across the road gently swaying, a Viking ship, prow and stern curved upwards. Like a smartly dressed lady in high-heeled shoes it felt its way down into the ditch on the far side, and tipped over. The pram hit the back wheels of the lorry, bounced off, ricocheted across the road, a small white Fiat screaming round the corner hit it again, it spun round, tipped over, out rolled the baby, the parasol lay twisted, spine broken, skull crushed, soft blood vessels torn, delicate organs smeared into the road like a bird's feathers, T-shirt, sunhat. The plastic mattress of the pram had fallen out. Pink lambs and yellow ducks. Miranda started to laugh. A high piercing sound, like a saw cutting through steel. How funny, I was so frightened of hurting the baby, and now I've got my husband to do it for me. Black-clad women rose from the ground like crows, wings flapping, their cries flying up into the still, blue air.

McNally Editions publishes singular, engaging works from off the beaten path. Headquartered at McNally Jackson Books in New York City, our editions are available in the US wherever fine books are sold and by subscription from mcnallyeditions.com.

1. Han Suyin, *Winter Love*
2. Penelope Mortimer, *Daddy's Gone A-Hunting*
3. David Foster Wallace, *Something to Do with Paying Attention*
4. Kay Dick, *They*
5. Margaret Kennedy, *Troy Chimneys*
6. Roy Heath, *The Murderer*
7. Manuel Puig, *Betrayed by Rita Hayworth*
8. Maxine Clair, *Rattlebone*
9. Akhil Sharma, *An Obedient Father*
10. Gavin Lambert, *The Goodby People*
11. Edmund White, *Nocturnes for the King of Naples*
12. Lion Feuchtwanger, *The Oppermanns*
13. Gary Indiana, *Rent Boy*
14. Alston Anderson, *Lover Man*
15. Michael Clune, *White Out*
16. Martha Dickinson Bianchi, *Emily Dickinson Face to Face*
17. Ursula Parrott, *Ex-Wife*
18. Margaret Kennedy, *The Feast*
19. Henry Bean, *The Nenoquich*
20. Mary Gaitskill, *The Devil's Treasure*
21. Elizabeth Mavor, *A Green Equinox*
22. Dinah Brooke, *Lord Jim at Home*
23. Phyllis Paul, *Twice Lost*
24. John Bowen, *The Girls*
25. Henry Van Dyke, *Ladies of the Rachmaninoff Eyes*
26. Duff Cooper, *Operation Heartbreak*
27. Jane Ellen Harrison, *Reminiscences of a Student's Life*
28. Robert Shaplen, *Free Love*
29. Grégoire Bouillier, *The Mystery Guest*

30. Ann Schlee, *Rhine Journey*
31. Caroline Blackwood, *The Stepdaughter*
32. Wilfrid Sheed, *Office Politics*
33. Djuna Barnes, *I Am Alien to Life*
34. Dorothy Parker, *Constant Reader*
35. E. B. White, *New York Sketches*
36. Rebecca West, *Radio Treason*
37. John Broderick, *The Pilgrimage*
38. Brigid Brophy, *The King of a Rainy Country*
39. Ariane Bankes, *The Dazzling Paget Sisters*
40. Vivek Shanbhag, *Sakina's Kiss*
41. John Gregory Dunne, *Vegas*
42. Charles Neider, *The Authentic Death of Hendry Jones*
43. Pamela Hansford Johnson, *The Unspeakable Skipton*
44. Carolivia Herron, *Thereafter Johnnie*
45. Todd Grimson, *Stainless*
46. Dinah Brooke, *Love Life of a Cheltenham Lady*